In Brigand's Woods

By Beau Hays

2017©Beau Hays Books

ISBN-13: 978-1-976-23705-8
ISBN-10: 1-976-23705-X

Cover Design by Ryan North
Cover Photo by Dan Marshall

For Katy, Joey and Vivian

- From the Duluth News Tribune

McLaughlin gets life for Haversham triple homicide

Today Brian McLaughlin received multiple life sentences for the brutal slaying of the Haversham family at their estate west of Two Harbors in early May. Despite losing an appeal, and knowing he would be facing a long prison term, McLaughlin has continued to maintain his innocence in regard to the murder of Richard Devlin in the town of Castle Danger last April. Several of the law enforcement agencies involved have speculated openly on the probability of McLaughlin being the perpetrator in both cases but lacked the evidence to bring charges against him in the Devlin murder. On the morning of May 3rd the Havershams were found slain in their home. McLaughlin was arrested after

Con't on A3

Part 1

Devlin and the Castle Danger Sheriff's Department

1

Oh, to be eighteen again, the fire of freedom in every step. To be young and alive while a life of untapped potential lay unfurled before you. But then circumstance pulls back the happy veil that has shrouded you lo these many years, and you find yourself running for your life through a darkened wood.

After midnight, June 6th
Brigand's woods

Thwack!

The sky and the ground reversed their positions and Jimmy Swansby landed hard on his back. His wind went out with a grunt. He tried to suck it back in but the oxygen had accrued mass and his constricted throat would not allow it to pass. Rolling onto his stomach he tried to catch his breath. His face and hands came up thick with the grime of the forest floor. He was panicking and that wasn't helping him to regain his air any quicker.

Again he attempted to perform the simple function of taking a breath.

Again none came.

Through a sheer force of will he settled himself, and his lungs slowly began to accept the air he was struggling to drag into them. He wheezed and his throat burned, the immediate pain was unbearable but it receded as the air began slowly to flow, and with each labored breath he regained a bit of mental control.

He was breathing.

With that hurtle in his past he moved onto the next, the woods surrounding him and any impending threat that might be lurking therein. His eyes darted across his field of vision absorbing his immediate vicinity, processing every shred of data his overwrought brain could handle.

All was still.

He rubbed lightly at the sore spot on his chest as he stumbled to a knee then regained his feet. Every breath he now managed rattled, too loud in the still night air. Terror began its infiltration. Its appearance, sudden and feverish, preyed upon his instinct and kept him rooted to the spot he stood. Like a spotted deer. It was foolish, for in the moment that's exactly what he was, a deer in headlights; a paralyzed target.

Jimmy Swansby had not found himself in this rotten patch of forest of his own volition, and now he was being chased; hunted. He may not know by whom, but the intentions of those pursuing him could not have been any clearer. The more time he spent standing there thinking, the more the panic crawled all over him.

It was time to move.

Directly in front of him he could see the low hanging branch that had caught him in the chest. He had been running full tilt, and in the darkened gloom it had been all but invisible. He fought down a fresh wave of rising panic and then, heedless of direction, was about to start running again when he realized the forest around him was silent. The distant shouts had dissipated or disappeared.

When he had smacked into the branch he had been running wild, driven solely by instinct. Someone had been chasing him, crashing through the brush somewhere behind him. His ears still echoed with the shouts of angry men prepared to commit violence without thought.

His fear was palpable, a thing of substance. He turned

around himself, his movements awkward and jerky. His head was filled with wisps of sound, remnants of the calls of the men who had given chase. Jimmy had been running blind; terror driving him. But then the sudden pain as he was smacked in his chest, accompanied by more excruciating pain as he landed on his back amid sticks and rocks, followed by a white light eclipsing his vision as he rapped his head on the unyielding forest floor.

But now there was nothing.

Not a single human sound.

He rounded on himself again in a slow circle trying to see everything at once. Between the dense growth of the forest and the darkness around him teetering towards full, looming shapes dominated the landscape.

"Where are they?"

The sound of an audible voice speaking so close to him almost caused him to scream out loud. He realized, just in time to stifle it, that he had actually muttered the words aloud himself. He surveyed his surroundings again, this time with his ears as much as his eyes. Questions began to race through his already dizzy head. *What the hell had happened? Where were the others? Could they have been caught?* By whom they may have been caught was a bigger question than he could possibly consider at the moment.

There was no opportunity to formulate any answers or even reconstruct what had happened since they climbed out of the van. Oh, the van. The van felt like hours ago. In truth it couldn't have been more than fifteen minutes since he had slid the big side door shut and stood in the shadow of the old farmhouse.

A twig snapped.

Somewhere off to his right, too close for comfort. Panic returned, slamming into his heart and chest harder than the errant tree branch had. Without another thought he took off in a dead sprint, running blind into the shadows of gnarled, twisting tree limbs.

11 hours ago –

For the last time ever, Jimmy Swansby pushed through the double glass doors of Castle Danger High School. The sun beat down on him and it felt great. The sky was a bright baby blue, dotted here and there with fat, puffy clouds that looked as if they were painted with watercolors.

Scott was already waiting in the van, an unlit cigarette dangling between his lips.

The van was an old, but loved, nineteen seventy-six Dodge. It was dark green, with an all green, shag interior and it was Scott Patterson's most prized possession. The first section of backseats had been removed leaving a wide open area in the middle, so you either sat shotgun, in the U-shaped bench seat around the pop-up card table in the back, or on the floor in between. It wasn't going to win any races or any awards but for a couple kids in high school with nothing to do and nowhere to do it, it was the perfect place to call home.

Jimmy slid open the side door and sat on the edge taking in the view as the parking lot filled with kids. They were vibrant, filled with the energy of youth, with an exuberance that they would probably never be able to affect again. He watched them drift off into their own separate little cliques. They would all kill time through the afternoon in their own ways, but once the sun went down they would all come together one last time to raise toasts, spill beer on each other and, if they were lucky, play a little grab-ass in the dark.

"Is anyone else comin'?" Jimmy asked closing his eyes and letting the sun warm his face.

"Billy for sure, and Anderson'll probably show up for a bump," Scott Patterson answered from the front seat as he put in a CD. Before Jimmy could reply Alice Cooper began screaming from the van's speakers to the entire Castle Danger school body.

"Schools out for summer, Schools out forever!"
And then Billy was there.
"Come on fellas lets burn one!"

"Right here?" Scott asked. His tone was sarcastic but only slightly veiled his enthusiasm for breaking one last rule on their last day.

"Hell yes, shut that door and let's buffalo this bad boy." Billy Brannigan pulled himself out of the sun, past Jimmy into the warm dark interior of the van. Jimmy slid the door shut and the three climbed to the back taking places, not assigned but always kept, around the pop-up card table. Billy dumped his rolling papers and other accoutrement onto the table. Jimmy watched Billy roll a joint quickly with a level of dexterity that he was sure he could never equal. Not that he necessarily felt this well-honed skill was the most admirable quality a guy could have but you had to give him credit. He was pretty damn fast, and in this here and now that stood for something. It was the little things, after all, that make a life worth living.

He was just about to light the joint when something smacked against the side of the van, hard.

They freaked, each of them scrambling to hide any damning evidence as to what was transpiring within the dark green shell of the van. Papers and lighters and dope were swept from the little table. There was a grace amidst the chaos. The quick, unexpected clean -up was a ballet they had danced a time or two before. They were still on school grounds and while no one was going to give them any real trouble on the last day of their senior year, old habits die hard.

The door slid open fast and Robbie Anderson's large cranium came into view. "What the hell's goin' on in here?" he hollered at them, a big grin eclipsing the rest of his face.

Billy did not seem to find anything funny about the situation. "I almost spilled my entire bag you dumbass!"

"Sorry, dude." Anderson laughed him off as he climbed in and pulled the door shut behind him "Well come on, can ya spare an old buddy a hit?"

Alice Cooper finished doing his thing and the Smashing Pumpkin's took over. The intro of the tune paralleled the ride of their buzz. The rhythm section was thrumming, and then the guitars came in shrieking and dancing all around the bass line.

The boys passed a joint and had a laugh. It was a perfect start to what should have been a perfect summer. The sun was hot, later the beer would flow and kids would be kids for just a little while longer.

It should have been perfect. Would've been maybe, if things hadn't gone so wrong. As it turned out, that moment was to be cherished for it was one of their last together. By dawn the next day, half of them would be dead.

Now –

Small, invisible branches clawed at his face as he ran. He could feel blood trickling down his cheek. Determining which direction he was running was impossible.

Were they still back there?

Jimmy couldn't hear anything, yet he didn't dare stop and look. That he couldn't hear them was not enough to convince him that they weren't out there somewhere, and the sounds of his labored breathing continued to obscure all other sounds anyway. He tried to clear his head and focus on what he was doing, where he might be heading, but he couldn't form thoughts. He could only concentrate on the sound of his shoes pounding through the rough brush. The rhythm helped him focus a little and was keeping the panic at bay. Then his foot came down at an awkward angle, pain shot up from his ankle and he was rolling.

He tumbled down a short hill. He hadn't seen it coming and the change in elevation had caused him to come down on his foot wrong. He thudded into a fallen tree at the bottom of the hill. Pain exploded, searing through his body, and he knew he wouldn't be running anymore. He hauled himself back onto his feet but his ankle gave out again the instant pressure was applied. He collapsed in a heap of gangly arms and legs. It was time to face the music. Somewhere in the woods the nameless bandits were coming for him but whatever happened next would be out of his control.

He laid half-conscious in the shadow of the fallen tree.

3 hours ago –

Jimmy Swansby had arrived at a place the kids called 'the rocks' just as dusk was falling across the North Shore. A huge extrusive igneous rock formation standing on the bank of the Knife River was where the apropos, if not very clever, name derived from. It was an out of the way place, a hidden place, a place that was difficult to find and nearly impossible to stumble upon. These were attributes that the youth of Castle Danger and the surrounding area took great advantage of.

Jimmy had found his way to the keg a couple of times but having enjoyed being stoned with his buddies for the better part of the afternoon, he had taken it easy on the beer so far. He didn't know it at the time but his moderation would be paying dividends a few hours later when he would need all of his wits about him.

He'd been wandering in and out of conversations taking advantage of the anonymity provided by the darkness. A girl he recognized vaguely from his biology class, a sophomore he thought, grabbed him and gave him a big slobbery smooch on the cheek. She pulled back. They looked at each other and laughed. Then she was off down the darkened path. He saw her stumble into another group further down the trail and pass along that same kiss to some junior girl. He smiled as the hooting and hollering from the group began and laughter broke out all around.

He moved on.

She had smelled good, like something familiar that he just couldn't place. It would come to him later, lying in the shadow of a fallen tree.

Up ahead on his left was the keg and next to it Robbie Anderson. Jimmy drained the last of his beer and notched the lip of his plastic cup with his teeth. So far it was only the second notch, only two beers. He found it funny that they all did this to keep a tally of their efforts for the evening but the more they drank the less they remembered to notch the cup and the whole thing became an exercise in futility. It was silly, but he enjoyed all the silliness he could get his hands on while the getting was still good. He went to see Robbie Anderson and refresh his libation.

"Swansby!!"

"What's up, Anderson?"

"Nada, just chillin' here, babysitting the keg."

"And I see you're doing a fine job of it."

"A man should know his strengths."

Jimmy chuckled and grabbed the tap, ever dutiful, Anderson pumped. The frosty beer hit the side of the cup and careened to the bottom. Jimmy watched it swirl and fill.

And then Billy was there, a sudden apparition in the night.

"Come on let's roll." He said. Scott was right behind him.

"What do you mean let's roll?" Jimmy asked.

"You know what I mean, let's go."

"Now? You're seriously gonna leave in the middle of a party to go chasing some bullshit urban legend?"

"Nobody's forcing you to come along Swansby."

"We're never gonna find anything out there in those stupid woods because there's nothing to find. There's a better chance that I'll be named the next pope then there is that we'll find some fictional farmhouse out in the middle of nowhere."

Billy just shrugged and turned. He struck off up the trail and Scott Patterson followed.

Jimmy cocked an eyebrow in Anderson's direction. "You going out there with them?"

"Not tonight, I've been hangin' with Tanya Jeffers. I think I might see how that pans out."

"Tanya Jeffers, really?"

Robbie said nothing. He shot Jimmy an awkward half sly, half stupid smile and turned back to the keg. Jimmy watched Scott and Billy heading off into the darkness. He took a long pull on his nice, cold, beer and chucked it into the garbage. "Assholes." He muttered under his breath then followed them up the trail.

Robbie Anderson was unable to consummate anything with anyone that night, but hanging back just in case turned out to be the smartest thing he ever did.

Now –

He felt groggy. He wasn't sure if he had passed out or not. He checked his watch. At first he couldn't make sense of his naked wrist staring back at him. Then it dawned on him that he must have lost it. The watch had been a gift from his folks. A bad night continued to get worse. He was laid out flat on his back, again. Before he dared to sit up, he took a moment to listen.

Nothing.

Strike that, not nothing, there was a plethora of sounds. The creatures of the night were going about their natural business. There was nothing abnormal about it though, no crunching of brush as dark tormentors pounded through the woods, nothing to indicate the presence of Scott or Billy either.

How the fuck did I end up here?!!

The rage behind that thought came unbidden but with unbridled force. He bit back an intense urge to start crying. He was lying on a muddy patch of unforgiving earth, no one knew he was out here, he didn't even know why the hell he was out here, and that smell wasn't helping either. *What is that?*

Lilac.

The girl that had kissed him earlier had smelled like lilac.

His mother loved lilac.

She used to steal little bunches off of the neighbor's bushes. She'd sneak out to the fence in secret, only after dark, then reach over and snip a little off with her scissors. As if anyone that saw her would give a damn, but it was her little secret and that was part of the fun. Then she would put her little treasure in a small vase on the table in the kitchen and like clockwork, it cheered her up. His silly mom, he sure did love her. He sure hoped he'd see her again.

He lifted himself up off the ground, being careful not to rustle any of the foliage he had been lying in. He listened, intent, attempting to hone in on any incongruity.

Nature's song, the music of the night, was the only sound in the impenetrable dark of the forest.

Would that prove a positive omen, or just the opposite? And how long was he planning on standing here waiting to find out? Taking that first step was like trying to wade through drying concrete, his tender ankle continued to make excuses for staying put. His brain was sending instructions to move, his muscles tried to execute orders, yet nothing happened. He tested his lame ankle and found it would hold his weight. Finally he managed a step.

The sound of his foot hitting dead, dry twigs rang through the woods like a gunshot.

He waited.

Nothing.

He took another step.

Again, the sound thundered out through the trees and echoed back to him but still he registered no movement. He took in his bearings.

He was so lost.

A light cloud cover had obscured the small sliver of the waning moon. After about two minutes of standing stock-still he decided that he had started out running in an easterly direction, then drifted to the north a bit, and that would put the highway somewhere on his left. There was not a shred of fact to corroborate such a theory but nothing that would disprove it either. At this point he figured having any plan, even a terrible plan, was better than no plan at all. He started off at a slow deliberate pace in that direction.

A scream rang out.

It came from far behind him and off to the right. No question about it, it was Billy. In an instant the panic was back and this time it owned him.

Jimmy Swansby had no prior knowledge as to what the

screams of a dying man might sound like. He knew it for what it was though, when he heard it rippling across a darkened wood from the throat of his best friend.

2

After midnight, June 6th
Township of Castle Danger

Sheriff Bob Gurley sat on his porch gazing at the stars and letting the heavy, humid air ease his achy bones and achy soul. On the other side of the highway the trees edging the forest rustled and sighed in a light, warm breeze. From right to left Highway 20 stretched out across his field of vision. He watched with an absent, partial interest, as the few cars that could constitute traffic at this hour, occasionally drifted by. He drained off the end of his beer, his third of the evening. That was more than the usual but probably not the end tonight.

A warm, late spring night was growing more humid as the hours grew wee yet a chill and a deepening sense of unease had settled in over the Sheriff of Castle County. He looked across the small wicker table on his right, to the rocking chair on the other side. The rocker abandoned only moments ago by his wife. She had kissed his forehead and taken herself off to bed, not interested in hanging around for any extended drinking Bob might get up to this evening. She didn't care if he got a little shnockered, her word for it, but she'd heard all of his stories a time or two before. She decided to leave him alone with them tonight, and as far as he was concerned that was just fine.

Tonight Bob had some thinking to do. A conversation he'd had over lunch was lingering and the more he gave it thought the more it gave him pause. Some men look for trouble, some are searched out by it, and some men just happen along and find it in their road.

Regardless of how it came to be there, there was

trouble in his road.

For Sheriff Gurley it had begun, as so many unfortunate things do, with the ringing of a telephone.

Yesterday –

Bob Gurley sat at his desk preparing to shuffle some paper. He'd just finalized the rotation of his deputies for the weekend. This coming Saturday his cozy little burg would kickoff 'Superior Days'. Two days of turtle races, watermelon eating contests, and good old fashioned, small town, drunken frivolity. It would be the busiest couple days of the year for Bob and the deputies of Castle County.

The department was in charge of the dunk tank ('as well as the drunk tank' they would joke with each other) and he had just worked out the shifts in the tank, the former not the latter, for any deputy not on duty at any given moment. He kicked his feet up on his desk and turned his gaze to the other side of his window where the warm, late morning sun was peppering the parking lot through the trees.

He had fifteen minutes until he'd have to meet with Rich Halverson from the Rotary and listen to him bitch about how the bowling alley was screwing him on his rate to rent their party room for meetings. They'd been having the same conversation for years and would probably continue to have it for as long as he held office. So go the woes of the Castle County Sheriff. He and Norma had already discussed the fact that he probably wouldn't run again in the next election. He would leave the job, and the likes of Rich Halverson, to a younger, more eager soul. In all likelihood that soul being Ryan Tomlinson, his best deputy and on most days, his best friend.

But right now he had fifteen minutes of no one bugging him and he did not intend to waste those precious moments on Rich or anyone else. He stared out the window at sunlight and glory.

And the phone began to ring.

Bob gave it a long look and in the interim it rang a

second time. He was accessible as Sheriff yet there were a very few people Gale would put right through to him in the office without buzzing first. He looked through the glass wall of his office into the pit and saw Gale Sebathany giving him a big dopey grin. It could be nothing. Or it might be his wife poring over the bank statements wondering about the extra hundred bucks he had taken out the night he and Deputy Tomlinson had been out to the casino. Or maybe it was something else entirely. He scooped the phone off of its cradle, and barked "Sheriff here."

And then things changed, and old ghosts came to call.

One thirty rolled around.

Bob had cancelled with Rich, without many regrets, to meet an old friend for lunch. He stepped into Mike's Diner and was consumed by the sweet smell of burgers frying on the grill. The namesake no longer owned the place. Mike had moved on and now a darling little old lady by the name of Glenda Jenks ran the joint. To meet her on the street Glenda was about the nicest, sweetest thing you could ever meet. When she was in her kitchen it was a different story, it was like she swapped personalities with a sailor. Bob grabbed a booth in the back and listened to Glenda let some poor sap have it back in the kitchen.

Just like Mike before her, Glenda's grill and her burgers bore the benefit of a long standing residual flavor. It had been a long while since Bob had enjoyed a burger here on account of the doc telling him to take it easy on the red meat but he thought maybe he'd give one a shot today. Mitch Kollman's daughter made her way over to take his order.

"Can I get you something to drink, Sheriff?"

"Has Glenda put fresh coffee on lately?"

"About fifteen minutes ago."

"Good enough, I'll take a cup."

"Are you waiting on someone else?"

"Yeah, there's one more coming."

"Should I make it another coffee then?"

"My guess is he'll take a tea."

"Then a tea it will be." She smiled, left to fetch his coffee, and Kirk Hanlon walked through the door. He was a short, little, rail of a man with an affable smile. He was thinning a little on top but did not show a strand of gray yet. His shirt was starched and pressed. His glasses seemed to always be readying themselves to slide down his nose. He looked every inch the middle-aged librarian that he was.

Kirk Hanlon ran the show at the Castle Danger Public Library. Kirk was a man who loved books. He loved reading them, caring for them, and sharing them with others. Kirk also loved history, which was what had brought him to the shores of Superior in the first place.

The library sat kitty-corner to the municipal building that housed the sheriff's department. Kirk and Bob had been friends since Kirk had moved to the North Shore from out east some fifteen years ago. They were not as close as he and Ryan Tomlinson were, but they were close just the same.

Close enough to share lunch, a drink, and maybe even a secret.

Kirk slid into the booth across from him and the two men exchanged pleasantries. The first thing that struck Bob was that his usually mild mannered friend was anything but. He was scared. He was composed for the most part, but he was fidgeting, throwing glances here and there. Nothing too outrageous, but the real truth was in his eyes. Fear can be covered in a lot of ways but it's tricky to keep it out of the eyes.

"No Ryan?" Kirk asked.

"He's off today. Everyone in the department is trying to rest up for the big weekend," Bob replied, his eyes holding steady even if Kirk's were not.

The Kollman girl, Bob could never remember her name, returned with his coffee and a tea then took both of their orders. Bob opted for the burger in spite of, or perhaps with the intention *to* spite, better judgment. They shot the breeze for another second or two. Kirk looked over one shoulder then the other.

Bob was not a man to work himself into a state of agitation. He was more a man who might become uneasy.

Kirk's demeanor was beginning to cause him some unease.

"Alright Kirk, spill it. You're jumping at shadows over there."

"I'm sorry, I didn't know... I just..." He stammered, paused, looked at the Sheriff then down at his tea. He picked it up and sipped cautiously. Bob was patient. "I'm sorry," he said again, composing himself. "It's just I've had an odd couple of days. Do you remember that I was recently hired on as a research assistant for that publishing company in the cities?"

"Yep, a book about Superior shipwrecks or something along those lines, right?"

"That's right." He paused. Too long, and now he was fidgeting again, fussing with his napkin.

"I guess I'm failin' to catch the problem."

"Sorry Bob, this... it's all just a little strange." He paused again. "This publishing company, on the phone when they first contacted me, they asked me general questions about some local wrecks. Nothing like the Edmund Fitzgerald or anything, they were more interested in smaller, more obscure wrecks. They mentioned the Benjamin Noble, the Criss Grover, stuff like that."

Again, he paused. Again, Bob waited.

"So I'd started some research, sent them a few things, they seemed generally happy with my work. Then they called me the other day and asked me to come down there to the cities for a meeting at their corporate offices downtown Minneapolis. I met them there early this morning." More hesitation. "During the meeting it became clear that their interest in those ships I just mentioned had waned." He let out a slight, humorless chuckle. "Forget waned, they couldn't have cared less. All they seemed to care about was a boat called the Angelina. Ever heard of it?"

Bob shook his head.

"They pushed really hard, for info on this Angelina."

The food arrived. Hot steam rose from the plates as Mitch Kollman's daughter placed them before the two men. Neither of them acknowledged her. Neither was really aware of her presence at all.

"I guess I'm still not sure what the issue is." Bob said biting into and chewing a mouthful of delicious greasy ground beef, but his stomach was starting to become disagreeable and any attempt to lay fault at the foot of the perfectly grilled burger fell short. Kirk was out of sorts, his behavior out of the ordinary for an ordinarily, ordinary man. In Bob's book that was cause for unease.

"The Angelina has connections to what happened in Brigand's Woods."

Bob stopped chewing.

He swallowed hard and the under-chewed beef tried to lodge itself in his throat. He worked it through but it burned on the way down.

Brigand's Woods was a name old timers, most of whom passed their days passing fiction for fact out in front of the general store, had given to a particular stretch of forest just out of town on County Road 7. Brigand's Woods was also the site of the least pleasant experience of Bob's professional career.

"How do you mean?" Bob's speech was slow and deliberate.

"The Angelina has a direct correlation to Richard Devlin."

He paused.

Bob eyed him for a long moment but said nothing. Eventually Kirk realized he would receive no response and so he went on.

"If Devlin really was who we believed him to be, that is."

Kirk had lowered his voice to an almost inaudible level but to Bob it still sounded too loud. Brigand's Woods and the name Richard Devlin dredged up some memories perhaps better left forgotten.

"What if we were right, Bob?" Kirk's eyes had lost the

nervous edge and a reserved excitement was creeping in. "What if Devlin's murder wasn't random and Brian McLaughlin was nothing more than scapegoat. What if Devlin was really killed by someone else entirely, because of who he was?"

Pots and pans clanked, the grill sizzled and in one booth the air grew thin. Bob let his eyes slowly rove over the other patrons, assessing whether or not anyone was paying them any mind. No one was, but he still felt as though he looked suspicious. He hated that feeling.

"Okay, let me get this straight. After all these years spent trying to forget, based on the inquiries of some publishing company that hired you to help write a coffee table book about shipwrecks, you want to rehash all of this old Devlin nonsense?"

"It wasn't right, Bob, this meeting. They were pushing me hard about the Angelina, to the point that it started to freak me out."

"So now you think this publishing company could somehow be interested in the Devlin story?"

"I'm not saying that. I don't know. I'm just saying, look, it was weird, their specific interest in that ship. And it's not that I want to rehash the Devlin business but we both know that McLaughlin didn't kill him, official story or not."

Bob chose his words carefully.

"We discovered some exciting leads in the Devlin case, things that pointed away from McLaughlin as the perpetrator, but it's important we recall that we could not prove any of them."

"That doesn't mean that they weren't true."

"If we can't prove it then there is hardly a damn difference!" Bob had raised his voice. Not much, but more than he had intended. No one had seemed to notice and he checked himself and his emotions.

Two old friends eyed each other from across a stained, Formica café table. The space between them had never seemed so vast. Kirk broke the silence but not before it had stretched out towards awkward.

"It's not my intention to open old wounds here, Bob, but there was a reason you came to me about the Devlin thing in the first place. What about that scarring pattern that was on his forearm? That's a direct connection to his lineage."

"Alleged lineage."

"Bob, we both know…"

"The Devlin case is officially cold."

"But…"

"No buts about it. Those markings on his arm, his family history, it's fascinating. Fascinating, but without proof, it's also fiction, at least as far as I'm concerned." Having made his position clear, Bob bit off another hunk of burger indicating the end of the conversation.

They finished, paid the bill, and stepped back out into the late spring sun. They made light chatter as they walked back to their respective places of employment. Mostly about the Twins and whether or not they would be able to retain the services of their gold-glove centerfielder.

Typical chatter for a typical day, but there was no heart behind it. Unspoken concerns hung heavy on both men. The world fell to shadow as a single cloud drifted before the sun.

Now –

Sitting out on his porch in the early morning hours, Bob was thinking about making a trip for another beer and he was sorting through so many divergent thoughts. Sorting, sorting, sorting.

He was thinking about many things, about old friends, about his job, about the interesting way the world spins on it axis and still the past can deny all natural law and hunt a man down. Most of all, in spite of monumental efforts to push it away, Bob Gurley was thinking about Brigand's Woods.

Thoughts of that particular spot were dark, unhappy thoughts, for they were thoughts of death.

People die all the time.

Cancer kills people. Car accidents kill people. Old age

kills people. And every now and then, people kill people. Although in a place like Castle Danger you're more likely to die in one of Kirk Hanlon's shipwrecks than you are to be murdered. That being said, from time to time it did still happen.

In this part of the world wrongful death was almost never premeditated and conversely, almost exclusively, it came as a crime of passion. Sometimes it was kids who haven't grown up enough yet to see life in the big picture and instead live trapped in the magnified drama that is the microcosm of small town life. Sometimes it's a drunk who can't get over a certain way a guy looks at his girl, or the certain way they got fleeced at the pool table. And sometimes, more often than not, it's domestic abuse.

In their many years together as Sheriff and Deputy here in Castle County both Bob Gurley and Ryan Tomlinson have had the distinct, unpleasant privilege of dealing with a domestic abuse turned homicide four times. In seventeen years on the job; four times.

And this was the most common form of murder in their county.

Things like grisly, storybook, premeditated murders just didn't happen in precious little burgs like their own.

And so they both believed until six years ago when they took a little walk into Brigand's Woods and a man named Richard Devlin first entered their lives.

Devlin had been found tied to a tree with a thick rope. The official reports said he had been beaten to death. With what had never been determined and 'beaten' was a pretty hefty understatement. At the time of the murder, Ryan and Bob had both just recently been promoted into their current positions. They now carried higher ranks, better titles, and more weight, both literally and figuratively. They were excited about their new jobs, but then Richard Devlin went and got himself killed and the excitement wore off quickly.

Devlin's body had been beaten, that much had been widely reported, but he had also been quite specifically marked on his right forearm. Some might have gone so far as to say he was branded but not Ryan Tomlinson or Bob Gurley. No, they kept that little tidbit to themselves. Only later did they share it and only with one person, that person being none other than their local librarian, Kirk Hanlon.

Leads were scarce and lacking any motive or a suspect, the investigation stalled, until a man named Brian McLaughlin murdered a family in Two Harbors County. The M.O. was similar. McLaughlin was definitely guilty of killing the Havershams and amongst law enforcement agencies it was commonly assumed that he was also the culprit in the Devlin case. Assumptions were not proof though. The case was never closed but it was moved from the top of the stack to the bottom. It was a solution that a somewhat terrified community could buy, even if the two men in charge of the case were not so sure.

And indeed, they were not.

With the help of Kirk Hanlon they had discovered that there were many dark, dank, nooks and crannies to the tale of Richard Devlin. But none of their theories could be backed by proof and in time, left well enough alone, those nooks and crannies had developed substantial and not entirely unwelcome dust.

Bob stepped back out onto the porch with a fresh beer in hand.

Castle Danger had secrets, secrets that had been buried. Much to the chagrin of the good Sheriff of Castle County, they weren't going to be staying that way very long.

Headlights crested the hill just to the east of Bob's property. The car slowed as it got closer.

It rolled by out on the road at a moderate, careful, speed. It was Chuck Anderson's kid on his way home. It was the last day of school today and he probably just didn't want to go burning by the Sheriff's house with maybe one more beer in him than he should've had.

Bob watched the taillights disappear around the bend in the road. When the deafening quiet had resumed he reached into his breast pocket and grabbed the pack of Camels he'd picked up on the way home. Norma would kill him if she knew, but he was pretty sure she was asleep, and pretty sure he'd earned a smoke today. He lit the little bugger and pulled hard. His throat burned and it was the best he'd felt all day, make that all week. He exhaled a large plume of blue smoke.

Trouble was in his road, he could feel it. Tomorrow it would become all too clear. He was three hours from a phone call that would change his life forever. Tomorrow, Chuck Anderson's kid, who had just driven by, would lie right to Ryan Tomlinson's face about Jimmy Swansby and his friends. Tomorrow was not going to be pleasant.

But that was all still unknown. Right now he smoked, and while he smoked it didn't seem so bad.

Bob looked out at the country road that passed his home, his home where he had lived for twenty-seven years with his wife. He watched the trees sway gently on the other side of the highway. Come autumn, the leaves would change and eventually fall, just as they had since time out of mind.

But autumn was still a long way off.

3

Before dawn, June 6ᵗʰ
Castle Danger

The Sheriff was guiding his cruiser down a dusty gravel road. The low hanging branches made horrible, shrieking sounds as they slid by, tearing at the roof and sides of the car. To Bob it was reminiscent of the sound little talons would make, clawing for purchase on the passing metal and not quite succeeding. The road was vaguely familiar but he couldn't quite place why, or from where, he might know it.

His headlights bounced as he hit a rough patch of road. He slowed to a crawl as to not bottom out the cruiser. Was there something in the trees there, a second ago when his headlights jostled around? He clicked on the spotlight and played it across the forest. Anything he might have seen would be behind him by now. He rotated the spot back as far as he could, but for some reason he couldn't slow down. His foot wouldn't respond to the command to brake and instead stood pat on the gas. Deciding it was nothing, he allowed the cruiser to take him forward into the gloomy darkness.

Shaded, mysterious memories came on hard but like the thing in the trees, and everything else in this moment, they were shrouded, hidden.

Or hiding.

Bob could recall this spot, this moment even, and yet he could not. The feeling was as inexplicable as déjà vu, and not entirely different either. It was like trying to look at an old photograph through a century's worth of dust.

The road turned to the right and in the glow of his headlights he saw an old iron bridge. Bob was so consumed by the sight of the ratty old monstrosity that he didn't even notice that his body was now receiving the messages his brain had been failing to relay just moments before. He had hit the brake and the cruiser came to rest just shy of the bridge. His knuckles had gone white on the steering wheel.

Terror gripped him.

He knew where he was now and it had his testicles hiding somewhere up around his lungs. He'd been here before, when he was just a kid. Somehow he had forgotten this place and all the mystery it harbored. But it was back now. Oh yes, it was back. His pulse was pounding all the way up behind his ears. His eyes stayed focused on the peeling paint of the bridge in front of him, his memory recalled every detail of this particular spot.

There was the short slope leading down to the creek bed, then the bridge jutting out over its breadth, stabbing into the darkness. He remembered the way the car would buck on the grating of the bridge. Sudden, total recall left him awash in nostalgic panic.

He slammed the cruiser into reverse and hit the gas but

instead of the expected and anticipated feel of taking off backward, the car shot forward out onto the bridge. It jerked on the grated decking just like he knew it would. He stomped on the brakes. The tires locked up and he screeched to a halt in the middle of the bridge. He looked to his right, not wanting to, but not being able to stop himself either.

The side guardrail of the bridge was bowed out, like a pregnant belly. Just like he knew it would be, just like he remembered it. He remembered all sorts of things in those couple of seconds. A combination of old forgotten terror and realization poured over him, dowsing him. He opened his mouth to scream and…

He shot up in bed.

He was soaked in sweat, totally disoriented. He looked around unable to make any sense of his surroundings at first. Then he saw Norma next to him. She was covered in a massive jumble of sheets and comforter that he must have kicked off onto her. Had he been dreaming? Yes, yes, he had been, of that much he was sure. And it had been a corker, but everything about it was dissipating.

Maybe he would have been able to bring the dream back into focus if he had really tried right then, before it drifted back into that mysterious abyss where dreams get lost. And perhaps he could've held onto it, but the chill that started in his gut and spread all the way up to the little hairs on the back of his neck told him it was one of those bad dreams that it's best to send on its merry way.

He sat up and swung his feet out of bed. Gravity, ever the enemy of the aging, pulled them to the floor hard jostling his old bones. He was exhausted. He ran his hand through his hair, of which he still had a lot, albeit much more on the silver side these days. He decided a glass of milk would settle his nerves and his aching bones, but he wasn't entirely sure his legs would hold him if he tried to stand. It had been a long time since he'd been shaken like this by a nightmare much less one he couldn't even remember thirty seconds after coming out of it.

He looked at Norma on her side of the bed. She slept soundly despite the fact that it looked a bit like the aftermath of a small tornado over there. A small smile rose to his lips. It was a smile he'd worn millions of times and never known it. It was his smile that he wore for her. She was a good strong woman who had helped to see him through many trials and tribulations in his years as a deputy and then as Sheriff. He decided if she was strong enough to put up with a crotchety old man such as himself for all these years, he ought to be strong enough to get a glass of milk after a bad dream.

He hauled himself up and headed for the stairs, being careful not to let them creak any more than necessary. A glass of milk was sounding more like a miracle cure with each cautious step he took. He hoped it would help on a couple of fronts as his head was still ringing a bit from the extra porch beers he had indulged in earlier that evening.

Thinking about sitting out there, on the porch, allowed some of his former unease to creep back in. Coupled with the residue of the dream, it seemed oddities were working themselves into omens and he didn't care for the feeling at all. Far off in the back of his brain the dream tried to resurface but it fell away, receding like a tide.

Shadows hung lazy in the dark corners of the kitchen. With more effort than he would have been pleased to admit, he managed to keep himself from jumping at them. He crossed the cool linoleum and grabbed the handle of his old Frigidaire.

The phone began to ring.

He stood there for a long moment with his hand on the fridge, listening to the silence between rings. He let his head droop. He looked at the now dormant, old-fashioned cuckoo clock on the wall of the kitchen.

3:47a.m.

No good ever came of a phone call at four in the morning.

Bob walked back into his bedroom in a daze. He sat down hard on the side of the bed and exhaled. He didn't turn to look at Norma but he could feel her climbing back from the depths of her slumber.

"Was that the phone, Bobby?" she asked, her voice was thick with residual sleep.

"Sure was, Sugar."

"What time is it?"

"Too early for good news, that's for sure."

"Was it the station?" She was awake now, her voice lucid and nervous all at once.

He didn't reply.

"What's wrong?"

Well that was a whopper of a question. And what should he say to his wife? How should he go about telling her that two kids had just turned up dead. No, not just dead but murdered. There was no question about that little fact either. Someone had made an example of those kids.

"There's just some bad stuff happening out in the world, Norma." His voice was flat.

"What is it, Bobby?"

"Nothing. Go back to bed. I'm gonna have to go in for a bit." Norma Gurley, formerly Norma Janski, had never been fooled by Bob Gurley. Not when they were young and he was telling pretty lies trying to get her to do things that proper girls didn't do, and most certainly not now after all these years of marriage. It was rare that he was called into work in the middle of the night. When he was, it was almost always for one reason and one reason only. Too many youngsters from Duluth or Two Harbors had found their way up to the River Garden, a local watering hole, and then took offense to some of the locals and their particular idiosyncrasies. Whatever the cause it was always similar, and the effect was always identical. The River Garden Saloon was no stranger to a bar brawl. Late night calls to the Sheriff happened, but not enough to call it often.

Any potential trouble at the Garden had nothing to do with the situation this morning though, and she didn't need to hear a word from Bob to know it. "Bobby?" She said to his back as she put her hand on his shoulder, he still hadn't looked at her since he'd sat down on the bed. He didn't speak but he put his hand over hers.

There would be a storm coming, you could practically taste it the way the humidity had been starting to build over the last couple of days. Their bedroom was a converted attic space and Bob hadn't given in and put in the window air conditioner yet. Her bedclothes were sticking to her skin, and yet her husband's hand, laid so delicately upon her own, was as cold as ice.

"I'll put on a pot of coffee." She said, and hugged him tight.

4

The small hours, June 6th
Castle County Sheriff's Department

The call had lasted for mere minutes but it would change lives in their little town, and not for the better.

At three twenty-eight in the a.m. the phone rang in the Castle County Sheriff's Department, a relatively rare occurrence in the dead of night. Deputy Jessy Tremely answered the phone and a man, sounding out of breath had said six words and hung up.

"Kids are dead... Split Rock Lighthouse."

Click.

The call was terminated. Jessy sat for a moment, the phone still in hand, not knowing quite what to do. Working the overnight in a sleepy lake town he was pretty good at sorting out calls that were serious and calls that were not. This one seemed like the latter but there was something off about it. There was something strange about the caller too. Something... That was a pretty vague word, and vague was a perfect description of the feeling that had begun to gnaw at him. It was nothing specific, just a wisp of an idea. It was probably just a prank, probably.

Jessy made the routine dispatch to the State Troopers, apologizing in advance for what was most likely going to turn into a wild goose chase.

Fourteen minutes later his phone rang again and a gruff voice belonging to a Minnesota State Trooper had told him he'd better wake the Sheriff and get somebody out to Split Rock. They had two boys, roughly between the ages of fifteen and nineteen, displayed at the foot of the lighthouse. There was no question as to their condition. They were dead, and someone had helped them get that way.

"What was the cause of death?" Bob had nearly shouted into the phone, regretting his tone before he'd even finished speaking. Deputy Tremely was built like a rock and could be quite intimidating when it came to rowdy late night drunks but he'd had a rough upbringing. His dad had been an asshole of the highest order. In a lot of ways Bob was like a father to Jessy but emulating the biological jerk never went over well. After a long moment he responded, and Bob could tell by his voice Jessy was just barely controlling his anger.

"They couldn't tell me, Sheriff."

Bob did his best to control his own flaring emotions. This young man who had been through so much in his short life was handling himself like a pro through his first murder call, the least he could do was the same.

"What do you mean they couldn't tell ya, Jess?" Bob's voice was steady. He sounded like a man in charge again, despite the fact that he felt about as far from in charge as you could get.

Silence.

Not motivated by anger this time.

Standing in his kitchen in his skivvies with a carton of milk still in hand, Bob could feel the fear radiating off his young colleague through the phone. They had started this conversation angry, and that was alright. Anger was a natural and comfortable conduit for fear.

In silence fear could bare its fangs. In silence people become defenseless.

"They couldn't tell me what the cause of death was without a report from the M.E. because there were too many options to choose from."

The bruised, misshapen face of Richard Devlin swam in front of Bob's face and he dropped the milk carton. It exploded on the floor, he was oblivious to it running over his feet and pooling between his toes.

"Sheriff?"

"I'm here, Jessy. Get Tomlinson up. I want him on the scene ASAP. Tell him I'm on my way."

"Got it."

Deputy Ryan Tomlinson was the first man from the Castle County Sheriff's Department on the scene at Split Rock Lighthouse.

With the help of what seemed like a small army of State Troopers, he saw to the final stages of barricading the crime scene. Preservation of the scene would be of the utmost importance. The county medical examiner was on her way but the forensic investigators from the Bureau of Criminal Apprehension, commonly referred to as the BCA, would have to drive up from Duluth. That would take time, and time was not conducive to keeping evidence intact at a murder scene.

Everything seemed in order so Ryan wandered back to his cruiser to check in at the station. He hoped Bob would get there quick. They needed to discuss a couple of things. He had played it cool with the other Troopers but those dead boys were sounding all manner of warning bells in his head. He glanced back over his shoulder. Everything was locked down. They were working on generators to get lights going. So far all the action was from fellow law enforcement, but that wouldn't last. The media would catch wind soon enough and he had a feeling that they might be around for a while. Small town life as they had known it was going on an indefinite hiatus.

Before he reached his cruiser, his phone began to ring. He checked the caller ID and answered it.

"Hey, Boss. What's your E.T.A.?"

"About ten." Bob replied. "What do we got?"

"Two boys dead. Neither of em' a day over twenty." He hesitated, after a long pause Bob took the bait.

"Any leads?"

"The state boys have everything locked down and so far nothing's popping." Again he hesitated.

"No holding out now, what's eating you, Ryan?"

Still Deputy Tomlinson held his silence, choosing his words with care. "I might have caught something but I'm hesitant to say anything until you have a look."

Out on a dark highway that was illuminated only by the throw of his headlights, Bob maintained his calm but goosed the accelerator just a bit.

"What is it, Ryan?"

"I noticed a peculiar sequence of lacerations on the forearm of one of the boys. Maybe it's nothing, but maybe it's not."

Not one to put much stock in coincidence, Bob's skin began to crawl. "Like Devlin?" he asked fearing the response before it came.

"I'm afraid so, boss."

"I'll be there in three."

Bob terminated the call, fired up the light bar on the roof of his cruiser, and pushed the pedal to the floor.

The clock in the station moved slowly. It was an old model, the kind that could often be found in an elementary school. The minute hand, instead of always being in motion, would lurch forward with a sudden clacking sound every time the second hand completed a revolution.

Jessy watched the clock, wincing each time the minute hand slammed forward, the sound echoing around the deserted station. He could feel the old anticipation welling up and tried to keep it in check. He couldn't stand being stuck in dispatch while Bob and Ryan were out on the biggest call he'd ever been a part of thus far in his short career. He was antsy. He had a debt to repay to his Sheriff and now could only hope he'd be given the opportunity to do so. Bob was more than a mentor to Jessy, he was the closest thing to a father Jessy had. At least since the stinking, drunken, biological one took a swan dive off the top of the stairs at the Tremely home and broke his neck. Bob had kept him and his mother safe during those dark days. Bob had showed him a path to follow, not just in choosing a career, but also in becoming a man.

He wanted nothing more than to be by that man's side right now and instead he was stuck here listening to the clock sound off the passing minutes.

Jessy Tremely could recall the exact moment that he had decided he wanted to be a cop. He was seven years old, cowering in the corner of the two-bedroom, split-level house his father had slaved to buy for them. 'Slaved to buy', was a phrase Derek Tremely used with his young son and his once beautiful wife every time the opportunity arose. Jessy would never have said it aloud but even at his young age he knew his dad could've afforded a lot more house for their little family if he hadn't spent so much time at the River Garden, drinking away what little extra income he had. But those were the sorts of things one never brought up around Derek Tremely.

So little Jessy, age seven, sat cowering in the corner, bruises just starting to bloom all purple and scarlet on his arms and chest. The Spaghetti-O's he had been enjoying now strewn across the kitchen floor. Noodles clinging to the old wooden cabinets as desperately as the cabinet doors hung to the cupboards, little Jessy, crying so hard that his sobbing was making it hard to breath. Not crying because his arms hurt so badly that by morning he wouldn't be able to lift them over his head. Not crying because his dad had foregone the belt for his fist tonight.

Crying because he could do nothing for his mother in the next room, she was getting it worse than he had. Right then Jessy decided he would someday do something to stop assholes like his father. He would not sit idle.

And yet now he was again sitting, waiting, idle. His fingers drummed the desktop as the minute hand on the clock continued to bang its way around the face. He would have to listen to that thwacking sound eighty-three more times before Gale Sebathany was due in to relieve him.

Clack.

Clack.

It would make him crazy if he let it. He didn't even know for sure that Bob would bring him in once Gale and the others came on duty. He could only cling to hope.

Clack.

Infuriating.

Clack.

As Jessy waited in the station for his turn to shine, there were a few things to which he was not yet privy. He didn't know about nor would he have realized the implications of the markings on the arms of the young boys. He knew nothing about Richard Devlin other than that which was already public knowledge.

He was unaware that his call to action was indeed coming and shortly.

He was also unaware that the clacks emanating from the station clock, droning and monotonous, would not go on forever. They were running out on him, on his time as a Deputy of Castle County.

5

Just before day break, June 6th
Split Rock Lighthouse

The Sheriff got a better look at the two boys than he ever would've liked. They were situated at the foot of the lighthouse and had been covered in white sheets while they awaited the medical examiner.

He pulled back the sheet covering the head of the boy closest to him.

Despite Deputy Tomlinson's attempts to prepare him

for the situation, Bob was still shocked. The systematic abuse that had been perpetrated on this kid was abhorrent.

He gingerly grabbed the boy's wrist and turned it to get a look at the forearm. After six years spent actively forgetting, it was hard to recall exactly how the markings on Devlin's arm had looked. The pattern on this kid was not well defined, he probably wouldn't know what it was if he hadn't been looking for it; but much to his dismay Bob Gurley was.

The boy had been carved, branded in the same fashion that Devlin had been all those years ago. He didn't know yet what the hell that might mean, but the implications continued him well along on his path of unease.

He moved over to the other boy. He pulled back the second sheet to be greeted by a similar barrage of atrocities. He knew before he even flipped this kid's arm that he would find a matching set and sure enough it was there. It looked like an X stabbed through the middle by the base of a cross that stood out above it. Two thoughts ran simultaneously through his head. '*What the hell is going on around here* and *we need to talk to Kirk.*'

He had seen enough and was about to cover the body when his hand froze dangling the sheet above the dead kid's head.

He hadn't caught it at first.

The trauma to the face and skull had left the boy virtually unrecognizable, but not completely.

"Hell's bells." The words came out of Bob's mouth flat lined, but Ryan had spent enough time with the man over the years to sense the nuance in his inflection.

"What'd ya see?" Tomlinson asked coming over.

"I know this boy, Ryan."

"What?"

"He pals around with Robbie Anderson, Chuck's boy."

"Are you sure?"

"Yeah, just last winter they were out snowmobiling and one of their sleds ran out of gas a quarter mile or so from my place. Robbie and this boy here showed up on my front porch looking to borrow some gas."

Deputy Tomlinson and Sheriff Gurley took a long moment to look at each other. Both could read the other's eyes as easily as if everything they had to say was written on their foreheads.

"Trooper Larson," Ryan hollered. His eyes never broke from Bob's. "Neither of these boys had any ID on them right?"

"That's right," the Trooper called back.

"Looks like we best have ourselves a little chat with Robbie Anderson, huh Sheriff?"

"Yeah, I think we better." Bob replied. "I suspect that I'm going to be handcuffed here for a bit, I'm gonna have to file a report for the BCA once they show. You know Chuck Anderson a bit don't you?

"A bit."

"Why don't you head over to his place. Better to hear from one of us than to have a Trooper pull up their driveway and scare the hell outta him and his wife. I'm going to get some of the fella's up and back on duty then send Jessy out to pick up Kirk Hanlon. I had lunch and a conversation with him yesterday that is providing more coincidence than is to my liking." Ryan looked at him sideways, but Bob denied him. "It's too much story for right now. We'll hash it out together, the three of us, back at the station. Right now you go see if you can't put some names to these boys."

"You gonna mention Devlin?" Ryan asked. Bob looked off into space. It could've been that he hadn't heard the question but Ryan knew better. Probably knew better than to have asked but he had to. Bob had taken a lot of heat for pressing the Devlin case after the powers that be had decided that McLaughlin was the perpetrator. The markings on Devlin's arms had led him to Kirk. Kirk had led him to some wild and wildly unpopular theories, which in turn led to a fair amount of embarrassment for the Sheriff of Castle County.

"Not til' we talk with Kirk and the sooner the better. Go talk to the Anderson boy."

Ryan nodded, stood, and walked back to his cruiser.

***

Bob found Lieutenant Stan Witkowski overseeing the final stages of securing the scene. He was the commanding officer of the State Troopers and charged with maintaining the integrity of the crime scene until a team from the Bureau of Criminal Apprehension, or the BCA, could arrive from Duluth. Bob knew the man reasonably well and liked him well enough. He found himself coordinating with Stan and his Troopers with some frequency. A fond familiarity was not the same as a friendship though.

After the Devlin mess Stan had never looked at him like so many of his other colleagues had, with a mixture of condescension and pity. He would always appreciate that, but he wouldn't be taking any chances. Until he had something concrete, the words 'Richard Devlin' wouldn't pass his lips.

He informed Stan that Ryan was attempting to obtain IDs on the boys and that they should have something soon. Everything on site was in a holding pattern until forensics showed up so Bob made his way back to his cruiser and called in to base.

The phone rang in the quiet of the station and Deputy Tremely answered it. "Castle County Sheriff's Department."

"Jess, is Gale in yet?" Bob asked.

"Yeah, he and Brad Withers just rolled in."

"Good, as soon as Gale is settled in dispatch, I need a favor of you."

"Anything Boss."

"I need you to get out to Kirk Hanlon's place."

"Hanlon?"

"That's right, I want you to personally pick him up and then personally deposit his hindquarters in a chair in my office. I should be back in an hour and I want him present and accounted for the second I walk through that door. Clear?"

"Five-by, boss." Jessy responded and signed off.

Escorting Kirk Hanlon was not precisely the duty Jessy had hoped for but he knew better than to question it. As soon as Gale was set and logged in Jessy headed out. The streets were deserted as he guided his cruiser into the softening darkness. Back in the station the clock went right on clacking, and another minute slipped away.

As Deputy Tomlinson headed south back towards town, the sky began to lighten. It appeared that dawn was going to break after all. There had been a stretch of time there when he hadn't been so sure. The whole night had taken on the foreboding feeling of a horror movie where day might never come, but now the light was beginning to stalk the horizon and the lake started to turn from a black void into a blue sea.

It was June 6th and the daylight was breaking.

Tomlinson rolled by the Sheriff's place on Highway 20. The house looked still and lifeless. Ryan hoped Norma was getting some sleep but in his heart he knew better. It was hard to imagine the life of a cop's wife, all those long nights, never really being allowed to be in the know. Sleep being plagued by nightmares containing monsters of half fact and an over active imagination. He pushed these thoughts to the back of his mind. He was distracting himself from the task at hand, and he could ill afford to be distracted right now.

The sun was technically up by the time he arrived but still the Anderson residence loomed in the soft, first light of day. Loomed might not have been quite the right word, at least it wouldn't have had it been any other morning, and had Tomlinson been on any other errand.

But this morning it loomed.

As he got closer to the house he saw that Chuck and Mindy Anderson were already sitting out on the front porch. They were enjoying the morning; having coffee, reading the paper. They had no reason to expect anything out of the norm to transpire.

Tomlinson swallowed hard. He'd been in a few rough spots over his career, some uncomfortable spots. He hoped uncomfortable would be as bad as this little errand would become. Chuck looked up as he pulled into the driveway.

"Ryan Tomlinson, I'll be damned. You're the last fella I expected to see this morning." Chuck hollered down to him as Ryan got out of his car and strode towards the porch.

"Well Chuck, this is about the last place I expected to find myself."

"What can I do ya for?" Chuck asked with a welcoming smile.

"I'm afraid I've got a bit of bad news."

Chuck's smile faltered and drew in upon itself. Mindy's cordial expression slipped and she halted the soft rocking of her chair. Let the discomfort begin, Ryan thought. He took in a deep breath.

"I need to see Robbie."

Chuck stiffened, the whole set of his body changed. Mindy stood and walked up behind her husband putting her hand in his. The last strains of any congeniality drifted from her face at the mention of her son.

"What for, is he in some kinda trouble?" Chuck asked. He was squeezing Mindy's hand tight, displacing blood and whitening his knuckles. Her face registered no pain though. The entirety of her being was focused on the extent of Ryan's interest in her only son.

"No, no, it's nothing like that." Ryan said, trying to alleviate the sudden tension in the air. It seemed to work, at least for the moment. They both relaxed a bit.

"Then what in hell is this about, Ryan?" Chuck asked.

Ryan looked at them both, from one to the other. The uncomfortable teetered towards rough, he took another deep breath.

"Two boys that Robbie pals around with were found dead up at Split Rock about an hour and a half ago."

"Dead?" Shock colored the tone of Chuck's voice.

"Murdered as a matter of fact."

Ryan heard the audible exhalation of air as Chuck Anderson lost his breath. Mindy said nothing, but gripped Chuck's hand even tighter.

"Who... who was it?" Chuck managed. His voice was

little more than a small rasp. It was a lot to put upon a man before he'd even worked all the way through his first cup of coffee. From his vantage point Ryan could see the morning paper, sitting on the little end-table, folded back to the crossword, half done. He had never thought of his position or his job as ugly but it seemed ugly now.

"That's part of the problem, Chuck. We haven't put an ID to either of them yet. It just so happened that the Sheriff recognized one of them as a friend of Robbie's."

"So you need him to identify the bodies?"

"I'm afraid that's a decent possibility."

"Shit, Ryan."

"I know, I know."

"How do you know they were murdered?"

Nasty images flashed through Deputy Tomlinson's head. He saw every tiny laceration as if it had been imprinted on the back of his eyelids. His gorge threatened to rise.

"There wasn't really any question about it." He replied.

"That bad, huh?" Chuck asked.

"It's the worst thing I've ever seen, Chuck," Ryan answered. The truth behind his words was evident.

For a moment they all just stood there staring at each other, soaking up the horrendous turn of events in their own way. Then Chuck nodded, patted his wife's hand and with a gentle tug removed his own from her grip. He reached back and opened the door to his home for the deputy.

Ryan stepped into the Anderson's house and gave an involuntary shudder. Chuck and Mindy were doing battle with the stifling humidity that had been descending on the town for a day or so. Their air conditioner was already working hard.

Chuck led him up the stairs to the second level of their nice, comfortable, little farmhouse. The stairs creaked just the way you would expect them too. Ryan had a passing thought about Robbie trying to keep the stairs from creaking when he got home last night. Last night, when he was lucky to be home and safe while his friends were… He opted not to finish that particular thought.

He followed Chuck down the short hallway to Robbie's door. Ryan was provided a bit of an insight into how the Anderson household was run when Chuck knocked once and waited only a moment before opening the door to Robbie's room. Robbie sat up in his bed, eyes wide with surprise.

"Hey buddy, sorry to barge in but we need to talk to you for a second."

Ryan took in the room as he entered. Posters adorned the walls and dirty clothes the floor. It was a typical teenager's bedroom. Tomlinson inventoried the room in a glance without appearing to snoop. There was nothing out of the ordinary but a feeling descended on him, it was so minute it couldn't even really be classified as feeling. It was more like the intangible sensation one might get walking over graves in a graveyard, an oddity. And an oddity was best marked and remembered.

It was silent for a moment then Chuck spoke.

"Robbie, you remember Deputy Tomlinson?"

"Sure. Morning Deputy." Robbie's voice was dry and cracked.

"Listen, buddy. He's got some news for ya and it ain't good."

Ryan took in Robbie's reaction, it was slight. He bit his lower lip and twisted the bed covers in his hands. It was a nervous reaction but normal, there was after all a cop standing in his bedroom first thing in the morning. He was probably a little hung-over too, poor kid.

"Robbie, before I get into too many details, I need your help with a few things."

"Alright." Robbie answered. Doing his very best to sound sure of himself.

"Do you remember last winter being out snowmobiling with a pal and running out of gas? I believe you stopped by the Sheriff's place for help."

Robbie's face lost a bit of color. Ryan didn't know just what to attribute it to, but he could see that something was tripping triggers in the boy's head.

"Yeah, I remember that." His speech came slow and

deliberate. "Me and Scott Patterson stopped by his place for some gas. The Sheriff helped us out."

Just like that Ryan had his first ID. One of the dead boys they had found that morning was named Scott Patterson. He took out his notebook and wrote down the name. Ryan tried to determine the best strategy for moving forward. The best way to present the devastating news he had arrived with.

"I don't know how to tell you this." The two looked at each other for a moment that felt longer than it was. "Scott was found dead this morning."

Ryan waited for a reaction.

He didn't know quite what he was expecting but realized it was not what he got. Robbie's registration of his last statement seemed to be minimal. He added some blinking of his eyes to the repertoire of twisting his sheets and biting his lip. The silence was stretching. Ryan knew he should say something but didn't know quite how to drive the conversation forward. There was after all still much to say, but how to say it was the question. He opened his mouth, still unsure as to what words he might be formulating but was then delivered a momentary reprieve.

A strong breeze kicked up, blowing through Robbie's open window, and slammed the closet door shut. The closet was right behind where Ryan was standing and he hadn't even noticed that the door had been ajar.

It gave everyone in the room a slight jolt, not least of all the calm, cool, and collected deputy of Castle County. Instinct caused him shoot a look to the closet door as it slammed shut. He couldn't help but notice the grime built up on the handle. The muddy sneakers kicked off to the side. It made him think about boys, and the carefree carelessness of youth. The kid in the bed before him probably still needed to be reminded to floss at night and to wash his hands before supper, not to mention closing the window when the air conditioner was running.

He was here to strip a healthy chunk of that youth away.

Before Ryan had the time to return his gaze to the bed, the significance of the situation seemed to have caught up to Robbie and his former lack of reaction was replaced by an effusive expulsion.

"Oh my God Scott's dead! He can't be dead! What the hell happened? He can't be...Oh my..." Then he sputtered out. "I'm sorry." He managed to say, but nothing more.

Chuck went over and put a hand on his son's head. Robbie winced before relaxing under the comforting feel of his father's touch.

"I don't really have much information at this point Robbie. In fact we wouldn't even have known who he was if the Sheriff hadn't recognized him."

The silence again spun out across the room.

Deputy Tomlinson, feeling less sure of himself by the minute, went on.

"There's more, there was another boy."

Robbie again gave no real reaction, but his lips were quivering, just a bit and he had the look of a man who could be sick at any second. He got himself under control and spoke.

"I think I can help you sir, but would you mind terribly if I put some pants on first?"

Ryan felt horrible enough about this errand as it was and he hadn't even given any thought to the fact that this poor kid was taking all of this trapped in bed in his underwear. Ryan gave a look to Chuck and he nodded.

"We'll go downstairs." Chuck said. "I'll get Deputy Tomlinson here a cup of coffee and you can meet us down there, alright?" Robbie nodded and the adults made their exit.

In the kitchen Chuck handed Ryan a steaming mug. Mindy went about cleaning and straightening the kitchen. She hadn't said a word but from the glances he was getting Ryan could tell that she was unsure of which side he stood on the line that separated friend and foe. Who could blame her, he thought, as he sipped at the coffee and tried not to burn his tongue. They could hear drawers slamming upstairs and moments later Robbie came down the steps and into the kitchen, wearing beat up jeans and a t-shirt. Ryan flipped open his notebook.

"Now again, I can't tell you how sorry I am to be putting you through this Robbie but I need to try and figure out who the other boy might…"

"Billy Brannigan." Robbie said cutting him off.

"Excuse me?" Ryan asked, pen now at the ready.

"I'd be sure it was Billy Brannigan. Scott and Billy did everything together."

"Do you have any idea what they might have been doing out at Split Rock?"

"No, Sir."

It was a definitive answer. The most definitive Robbie had been since Tomlinson arrived. He made a mental note to go along with the physical one.

"When was the last time you saw them?"

"We hung out a bit after school let out yesterday, it being our last day and all. They dropped me off here about five thirty. There was a party at 'the rocks' last night. I saw them there but they left around eleven."

"You're sure about that, that they left at eleven?"

"I'm not exactly sure about the time, I didn't check but it was around then. I saw them right before they left."

"And they were alone, just the two of them?"

Robbie gave him a slow nod. "Yep, as far as I know it was just the two of them."

For all intents and purposes the interview ended right there.

Ryan asked a few more questions then flipped his notebook shut. He thanked them all for their time, again relayed his condolences, and took his leave. Chuck saw him out and as he stepped onto the porch he was tickled again by that feeling of walking over graves. He looked back one time.

Robbie Anderson was looking right at him.

Not looking to his parents for comfort after the breaking of such horrible news, not crying, not acting out in any typical teenage fashion. He was just watching the departing deputy with eyes that didn't seem to focus.

Ryan nodded to him. Robbie returned the nod but without conviction. Tomlinson walked down the porch steps and made his way across the yard to his cruiser fighting back an aggressive case of the heebie-jeebies. He said his goodbyes to Chuck and told him they'd be in touch as soon as they had any information on the Brannigan boy. Then he was on his way.

Still he couldn't shake that odd feeling. It was like he missed something that was right in front of his face. There were just too many unknowns at this point, so many facts to which he was so far unaware.

One of which being, at that point, he didn't know that Robbie Anderson was a better than average liar.

6

Just after daybreak, June 6th
Kirk Hanlon's residence

The shotgun effect of knuckles rapping hard on solid wood echoed through the crisp open air. A slight morning fog was creeping back from the house into the stand of trees around the front yard. Deputy Tremely could just make out the neighbor's house down the slope of the yard, through the trees and soft mist.

He knocked again, and again nothing.

The air hung still around him. The singsong call of morning birds was present but distant. As if they knew better than to be hanging around Kirk Hanlon's dooryard this morning. Jessy did not care for the feeling he was getting that those birds might just be onto something. The silence that was emanating from the house between knocks was disheartening.

The house felt empty.

"Empty".

Jessy said the word out loud and it sounded right. He hoped it was right anyway. Standing on the front stoop with the night still clinging feebly to the western horizon, the only other word for how the house felt was dead.

Empty was definitely better than dead.

He knocked on the door again, hard this time, harder than he had intended. The big oak door shook a bit in its jamb. Jessy took a deep breath and focused himself. He didn't know much about what was unfolding this morning but if he had read the Sheriff's tone of voice accurately, speaking to Hanlon was important to Bob. The library didn't open until eight but that alone shouldn't be enough to cause concern over Kirk's absence. He could have been out for a jog or on any number of other errands. In general the simple answer tended to be the most accurate but this morning simple wasn't sitting well. Something was amiss and instinct put his blood up.

Jessy reached for the doorknob.

A slight sheen of sweat had greased his palm. He lowered his other hand to his gun belt. It was probably an overreaction. Fact and logic had provided no inspiration for such a move, but 'better safe than sorry' seemed to him more than just a quaint turn of phrase at the moment.

The knob turned easily in his hand.

No big deal, nobody locked up out here.

Although that particular little idiosyncrasy of small town living may have just changed as of about seven minutes ago when the morning news had started airing stories about two boys lying dead at the foot of a significant North Shore point of interest.

Jessy took a deep breath and swung the door inward. The door opened onto the living room. He entered, cautious, calling out as he crossed the threshold. There was still no response.

The living room was a reflection of Kirk in a snapshot. There was no T.V. but every shelf and end-table was piled with neatly stacked books. The room was clean but not pristine. Comfortable, lived in.

And then he stumbled upon the cup of tea.

It had been spilled between the coffee table and the

sofa, and just left there, a small but thick dark stain spreading from the lip of the cup into the rug. It was incongruous. In person, and in practice by the look of the house, Kirk did not seem like the kind of man that would leave tea soaking into his rug.

Jessy's adrenaline kicked up a notch and now he did remove his weapon from the holster. The settling sounds of the house echoed, amplified, in giant contrast to the silent spaces in between that had drawn so tight that they were almost ringing. He moved toward the back of the house, through the kitchen where again, everything was in its place. Off the kitchen was a small mudroom with a door that almost certainly led to the garage. With three quick steps he crossed the kitchen into the mudroom and grasped the handle of the door.

He stopped.

He had become acutely aware of how alone he was. No one but Bob knew he was here. There could be three guys on the other side of that door, guns trained, just waiting for the handle to turn. No back up on the way, just him, all alone. He put his ear close to the door. Nothing came through. He counted to three. He threw the door open and hopped back out of the line of any fire with the speed of a surprised snowshoe hare.

The clamor arose from the right and without a thought Jessy fired. The report of the gunshot was enormous in the enclosed garage.

There was no volley of return fire and the silence descended once more, broken only by the high pitched whine that had taken up residence in his ears. He flipped on the light switch and discovered what he already knew, that which he had realized the minute he pulled the trigger on his firearm for the first time, other than on the range, in his career.

In swinging the door open with such force, he had knocked over a shovel and a few other gardening tools that had been leaning against the wall just inside the door. He cursed himself for the lack of restraint, and praised God that he hadn't just made one of those mistakes that put your name on the front page and effectively extinguish careers.

Kirk's car was parked in the garage. The presence of the vehicle didn't prove anything in regards to his whereabouts, but still, Jessy didn't like it.

He returned to the house and found nothing else that would qualify as odd until he reached the study. The room was dark, and from it emanated a slight smell of furniture oil. Using a pen from his pocket he flipped the light switch. The study looked like what Jessy imagined an English Prof at some hoity-toity college's office would look like. It was all dark wood and a shining hardwood floor that peeked out from beneath a thick rug that was covering it. Floor to ceiling shelves packed with books dominated three of the four walls. On the fourth wall was a large wooden desk with maps and papers and open books strewn across it. On one corner of the desk was one of the few bastions of technology Jessy had seen in the whole house, a home computer. It looked old, utilitarian. The internet was a necessary evil but Kirk seemed a man who still preferred researching with books whenever possible.

Jessy examined the papers and maps on the desk. Most of the literature involved shipwrecks and other random Superior lore. He looked at the maps spread across the desk. They were all complex aquatic maps, most were of the north shoreline of Lake Superior. Here and there were a few notations in Kirk's easy scrawl, as well as a bunch of roman numerals, none of which made much sense to Jessy. He lifted the maps and found a book beneath.

It was titled 'Mysterious Waters: Tales of the Great Lakes'. He thumbed through it. It was a pretty standard looking tourist book. It was full of short chapters about mysterious happenings on Superior and the other Great Lakes. There was nothing particularly special about the book, although somehow Jessy got the sense that it had been placed beneath all those maps with some purpose, to hide it perhaps? Or perhaps he was just jumping to conclusions.

He was about to move on, leaving the room and his search, when he caught something out of the corner of his eye.

The computer was on. The monitor had been shut off but the little indicator light on the tower under the desk was glowing green. He stepped back to the desk and, again with his pen, pressed the button on the monitor. The indicator light on the monitor blinked on and deep in its ancient guts a tired fan whirred. The screen remained dark. It took what felt like an eternity for the thing to warm up, but he was rewarded for his patience, or at least for the moment, placated.

One line of incoherent text appeared on an otherwise blank screen. The cursor was blinking at the end of the line, a testament to the fact that there had been more to say, but Kirk hadn't had the time, or been allowed the time, to say it.

6u4 r4g9pe o466p4 630 –k i8j4 e4gj6u

Jessy stared at the nonsensical grouping of characters for a long moment.

Two kids had been found murdered this morning and the first thing that the Sheriff wanted was to talk to Kirk Hanlon. And now, Kirk Hanlon was nowhere to be found.

He had disappeared. Vanished.

But he hadn't gone without a trace, he had left a clue.

A code.

While Jessy had been on his way to Kirk's house, Sheriff Gurley was on his way back to the station. The Bureau of Criminal Apprehension had arrived at the Split Rock Lighthouse and had begun the tedious sequence of processing the crime scene. A young lady by the name of Barlow was the lead investigator. To Bob she looked a little too fresh faced to be the lead on an investigation but he had to remind himself that pretty much anyone under the age of thirty did these days.

Agent Barlow had informed him that the autopsies would be handled at about two o'clock that afternoon and Bob agreed to keep her apprised of the situation in regard to any identification on either of the boys. And at that, Bob had left the crime scene in the capable hands of the BCA.

On the drive back to the station he put in a call to Ryan Tomlinson who brought him up to speed on his interview with Robbie Anderson and the potential ID of both boys.

Twenty minutes later, Ryan rolled into the parking lot and saw the Sheriff's cruiser already in its stall. He walked into the station to the sound of phones ringing off the hook and Gale Sebathany doing his best to keep up with them.

"Sheriff's in his office, wanted me to send you in right away." Gale hollered between rings. He got back to the phones and Ryan headed for Bob's office.

Bob was seated behind his desk. His hands were laced behind his head but not in relaxation. More as if he had run them both through his hair anxiously and they had found each other by little more than luck. The two men didn't say anything at first. In a long look, the weight of their current situation settled around them as best as it was going to. Ryan broke the silence.

"So we know those two boys were at 'the rocks' last night. They left there about eleven, but that's about it."

"Someone's gonna have to talk to all those other kids."

"What about Jessy?" Ryan asked.

Bob shook his head. "He's out picking up Kirk and I think I might want to bring him in on this." He grabbed a toothpick from the jar on his desk and bit down on it.

"Have we heard from Brad yet?" Ryan asked referring to Brad Withers one of the other Castle County Deputy's.

"Yeah he's here. Why don't you get him on compiling a list and taking statements from all the kids that were at 'the rocks'. Give him Reese and Michaels."

"He's not gonna like that detail." Ryan said, a small smile curling the ends of his lips.

"Tell him I know it's a shit job but we all have to take our turn in the crapper." They both chuckled but it was an uneasy sound. The laughter petered out.

Then silence.

Words were warranted but never more unwanted. The

men who helmed the Castle County Sheriff's Department had some skeletons to pull out of long forgotten closets. Brigand's Woods and Devlin and everything else from that treacherous piece of past aside, Bob had still not expounded on his lunch date of the previous afternoon.

The time had come.

"I had lunch with Kirk Hanlon yesterday." Bob said.

"That so?"

"Yep."

Bob was chewing the toothpick raw in the corner of his mouth. He'd kept the toothpicks on his desk since the days when he used them while trying to quit smoking. He hadn't started chewing on them again until just lately. Thinking about the toothpicks was just a distraction though, a sidebar to keep the real topic at bay. He tossed the now ratty sliver of wood into the garbage can beside his desk and looked Ryan square in the eye.

"I didn't think much of it at the time but the second he walked in I could tell something was off."

"Where'd ya go?"

"Glenda's joint."

"Did you get a burger?"

Bob nodded but didn't elaborate. It seemed Ryan was attempting his own little distraction dance. As much as Bob would've liked to acquiesce he fought it and stayed on topic.

"He wanted to talk about this publishing company out of the cities that he's been doing some side work for." Ryan nodded confirming he was familiar with Kirk's new-found employment but he didn't interrupt or interject. "He seemed concerned about their sudden interest in a boat called the Angelina. You ever heard of it?" Ryan shook his head and maintained his silence. "Apparently he saw it as cause for concern as it has some connection to Devlin, or at least to his alleged lineage."

"Alleged?" Ryan asked, raising an eyebrow.

"I stuck my neck out on a hunch with all that Devlin bull-crap and nearly had it cut off. Until a theory can be corroborated by fact it will remain just that."

Ryan could hear the agitation mingling with frustration creeping into the Sheriff's voice. While their assertions regarding Devlin's murder had seemed plausible, after being unanimously and unceremoniously shot down, he could understand Bob's reluctance to hoe that particular row again. He zipped his lip and let Bob take it at his own pace. Bob grabbed another toothpick and popped it into his mouth. Ryan had the distinct feeling he hadn't even realized he'd done it. Bob worked it around a bit then went on.

"So after six years, out of nowhere Kirk gets me out to lunch and brings up Devlin, then not twenty-four hours later, we have a couple dead kids with that same..." Bob trailed off. At a loss for words or maybe not wanting to say it out loud, somewhere in the middle most likely. "With that same crap carved into their arms."

Ryan noted the pause as well as all of its extraneous implications. He tried a different tact.

"What about this company Kirk's working for? Have we looked into them?

"I checked them out a bit yesterday after our lunch. They're a small publishing house owned by a company called Hawking Inc. Hawking is huge, a giant conglomerate. They've got their fingers in a little bit everything, one of those things being, apparently, the publishing business. It all seems to be on the up and up but how do you tell, really, with a company that size?"

"Okay," Ryan said. "So for the sake of argument let's say Kirk was right and they really did have some ulterior motive for seeking information on this ship, this Angelina. What potential interest could they have in Richard Devlin, or his family history?"

"Alleged history."

"Right, alleged."

Bob shook his head, any reasonable response eluding him. Silence seeped in and filled the empty spaces. Both men drifted into thought, rearranging the pieces of the puzzle and trying to make them fit.

Six years Bob had spent trying to put the Devlin murder in his past, and now it was haunting him once more. Ryan returned from his musings first and broke the silence.

"Did Kirk give you any indication about what he thought the connection between Devlin and the Angelina might be?"

"Nope, and at the time I wasn't exactly interested in hearing about it. I practically ran him right out of the diner. I guess we can ask him ourselves soon enough though, once he and Jessy get back here."

"I guess we can." Ryan replied and then drifted off into thought again. "The thing that gets me," he said after a long moment, "is the publishing company." To this, Bob had no response. "What would be their angle? Wait a second…" The gears in Ryan's head were in motion. "You said they were owned by some big corporation, right? What was the name?"

"Hawking Inc."

"If this Hawking is such a big company, you don't suppose their interest could have something to do with the lawyer do you?"

With that question, as innocent as it sounded, the air went out of the room. "The lawyer…" Bob repeated. He wasn't asking for clarification though. He knew exactly who Ryan was talking about.

"Yeah, what was the lawyer's name?" Ryan asked.

"Leland, Victor Leland," Bob said slowly.

"Could there be a connection there?"

Bob paused for a very long time. When he did speak he did not seem excited to be doing so. "If any of the theories we had in the Devlin case actually had any truth to them, then yes, I suppose the lawyer would be as good a place to start as any."

"Tell me again what we know about him," Ryan said, ignoring the Sheriff's hesitation.

Bob exhaled, releasing a long, slow breath. "Victor Leland was the family's lawyer and he disappeared on the very same day that Devlin's parents were murdered."

"Disappeared and took a then young Richard with him, right?"

"Allegedly." Bob let the word sit there for moment.

He chewed on the toothpick in his mouth. "Victor Leland and the kid disappeared. He changed the boy's name to Richard Devlin and they started fresh in hopes that the kid might dodge the fate of his father. But he didn't. He wound up just as dead himself. Right out there in Brigand's Woods."

6 years ago –

The call had come in on a chilly, overcast, early April morning.

One of the boys from the Jansen brood that lived out southwest of Beaver Bay had found a body in the forest. The boy's father had called it in and told the Sheriff he'd meet him out near the spot at the edge of Brigand's Woods.

Jansen had told them that his son had been out four wheeling so Bob and Ryan hooked up the trailer with the sheriff's department ATVs and made their way out to the potential crime scene.

When they arrived, Jansen was there waiting with his son. It was one of the middle boys. He was probably about fifteen and he looked scared half to death.

Bob would never forget that next moment, standing on the shoulder of County Road 45. There was a stiff breeze blowing out of the north and the gray sky washed the world in melancholy. It was the kind of moment that might inspire another man to write a poem about it. To Bob Gurley it was life, and it was feeling about as far from poetic as a moment could possibly get.

Bob and Ryan revved the engines on their respective four wheelers and headed off into Brigand's Woods. They followed the elder Jansen's directions as best they could knowing all along that he had received those directions himself from a terrified young man who had yet to put his adolescence behind him. They did their best to compensate for any natural inconsistencies there might be. The directions weren't half bad, and Bob saw the body before they had been off the road for no more than ten minutes.

He pulled up a few feet from the tree. The body was hanging at an awkward angle, tethered to the monstrous trunk of an ancient oak tree. He tossed up a hand to indicate that Ryan should stop and then heard the other engine slow and drop into an idle.

Bob had stared death in the face in the past. Sometimes it was sad. Sometimes gut-wrenching. This was wholly different and horrible was the only word that seemed appropriate.

Ryan sidled up next to him. Bob looked to him hoping their mutual camaraderie would steel him for the task ahead, but Ryan had turned away and was looking everywhere except at Bob or the body. Bob killed his engine and Ryan did the same. Neither said a word as they dismounted and made their way towards the lifeless hulk attached to the tree.

They got close and the smell was overpowering. Bob heard Ryan turn away and make a short, ugly, wet, retching sound. To this day Bob was pretty sure that the only thing that kept him from doing the same was the fact that the body was beaten so badly that it almost didn't look real. The smell was real, visceral, but the body looked almost fake.

He looked closer, enthralled, half believing that he was actually appreciating some makeup artist's work for a haunted house. But it wasn't October, it was April and someone had made a serious mess of this young man.

That was when Bob noticed the guy's arm.

He could have missed it. The pattern of laceration on the forearm was far from distinct. It could have blended in with the countless other atrocities that had been perpetrated upon this man. The symbol it was meant to be was somehow familiar, but at that moment he couldn't place where he might have seen it before. If he had realized sooner, if he had made the connection before Brian McLaughlin had murdered the Havershams maybe his case would have held more water.

But he didn't make the connection and by the time he

did, all parties involved were so convinced that McLaughlin had killed Devlin that Sheriff Gurley was the odd man out.

Now –

Back in his office, Bob stood and walked to his window. Ryan remained silent behind him. He looked out across the parking lot and marveled at the beautiful day outside.

The morning sun was glinting off of chrome and mirrors from the cars in the lot. It was the kind of day that was supposed to be spent at leisure, with a line in the water and a cold beer in hand. It was not supposed to be spent like this, rehashing the dealings of death.

Staring into the warmth of a perfect day and feeling cold, he turned to his number one, to Deputy Ryan Tomlinson. Jessy would return with Kirk soon. The prudent thing to do would be just wait until they could all discuss this mess together. But thinking back to that initial moment with Devlin, and his inability to put the pieces together fast enough, he felt his hand being forced. For better or worse, action was inevitable and Bob turned down an avenue perhaps better left alone.

"Ryan, I need you to do something for me."

"Anything boss."

And here Bob paused. Just long enough to cause Ryan a moment of hesitation, allowing the slightest regret to seep in at the magnitude of what he may have acquiesced to.

"I assume you still have the key."

Ryan blinked and the ability to speak vacated.

The key.

He'd almost forgotten all about it. Or had put it so far out of mind as to be more likely to forget it, was perhaps closer to the truth. And perhaps it was better left forgotten. The key carried...implications

Ryan was taken aback and Bob took his expression as if it were an affirmation.

"I want you to go get it."

"So we're going after this again?" Ryan asked, finding his voice. Bob made no response but he didn't need to. Ryan could read it in his eyes. "But we didn't mention any of this to the gal from the BCA?"

"I want you to get that key. When Jessy and Kirk get back here, we're going to have a nice long chat. We're going to go over every thought, every detail, every theory we ever had on the Devlin case. See if there is any way we can connect it to what happened up at Split Rock this morning. If, and only if, we can find some way to prove they are related I'll march right into Agent Barlow's office and tell her how I just remembered something about those markings on those boys' arms and we'll open this whole can of worms. But first we need to talk to Kirk and I need you to go get that key."

Ryan said nothing. The ends of his mouth curled into what may have been a smile, but just as easily could have been a scowl. He stood and left Bob's office.

The first domino wobbled, began to tip; behind it stood the many.

7

Now Sheriff Bob Gurley alone bore the burden of the station house clock. It clacked and smacked its way around the face, counting the minutes as they drew long and began to feel like hours. Jessy had not yet returned with Kirk. If they didn't show up soon Bob might have to add that to his list of worries, and he had already done more worrying today than was to his liking.

He had sent Ryan for the key.

While the simple act of sending Ryan for the key was not strictly an admission that he was ready to revisit the Devlin case, they had known each other a very long time. He wasn't fooling anyone, not between the two of them. He popped another toothpick into his mouth, put his elbows on the desk, and rested his head in his hands.

The déjà vu was fierce and immediate.

He had been sitting in this very spot, in this very same manner when he had originally realized why those marks on Richard Devlin's arm had looked familiar. From the first moment that he saw the markings they had struck a chord with him, and he knew it went beyond the absolute and natural disgust at the atrocities perpetrated upon the young man. The markings had been familiar. Not just unique but familiar, and at that moment, head in hands, he had known why. He'd seen it before. Or rather he had seen a picture of what the crude representation was intended to be. Once upon a time he had noticed the original symbol in a charcoal rendering on the desk of an old friend.

An old friend that should have been occupying the chair across from him, but as of now, was not.

He would never forget the awkward moment discussing that symbol with Kirk Hanlon, not entirely sure himself if he was inquiring or questioning. But Kirk had withheld nothing; in fact he had been quite forthcoming. Unfortunately for Bob, the information he provided only muddled the situation further.

Kirk was familiar not only with the symbol but with its significance in relation to Devlin as well. That symbol was Bob's introduction to Richard Devlin and his family. A family shrouded for generations in mystery and murder. The story of Devlin's ancestry spilled from Kirk like a folktale and should've been treated as such. But the man was convincing, every item he gave up for consideration so plausible.

Still, Bob should've known better.

6 years ago –

"I need to know everything you can tell me about these markings." Bob said as he slid an evidence photo of Devlin's mutilated arm across his desk. Kirk pulled his glasses from his breast pocket and eyed the photo. Just as it had for Bob initially, the significance seemed to elude him. Bob looked out the window of his office, patient, certain Kirk would realize. The evening was stretching as they have a tendency to do in the spring, as the days begin to lengthen. He heard the small, sharp intake of breath from across the desk as the moment of discovery descended.

"My god, that's the Plundering Pike."

"It's what?" Bob asked.

"The symbol that it's supposed to be, it's called the Plundering Pike."

"So you're familiar with it?"

"Absolutely, but it's so," he struggled for the right words, "crude. How did you know to ask me about it?"

"Dumb luck really. I happened to remember seeing its likeness in a rendering out on your desk one day."

"Unbelievable." Kirk muttered.

"What can you tell me about it?"

"It was a symbol used by the man of the same name. He put it on his flags and banners. It was his version of the Jolly Roger." Kirk was shaking his head absently as he spoke, as if he couldn't quite believe what he was seeing.

"The Jolly Roger?" Bob asked.

"You know, skull and crossbones, pirate flags, that sort of thing. Pike just had his own symbol, a dagger stabbed down through the top of an X, The Plundering Pike."

"Whoa, hang on a second. You're talking about an actual pirate?"

"Yeah, I'm kind of surprised you've never heard of him. He was a Lake Superior legend."

"A pirate? On Lake Superior?"

"Maybe not the swashbuckling buccaneer that your mind would like to conjure, but yes, a pirate just the same."

The Pike legend had enthralled Kirk for years. While he loved all Superior lore it was not adored equally. Pike was the masterpiece, to be studied and dissected endlessly. The excitement that had begun to infect him was blunted as the reality of the situation began to worm its way in. "Wait, what is this?" He indicated the photo.

"That's the forearm of the young man we found out in Brigand's Woods last month. We've been working it day and night but the case has been nothing but dead ends, and now it looks like it will be put to bed. Unofficially, and without ever being solved, because the BCA believes it was committed by the same fella that killed that Haversham family out by Two Harbors. They can't prove that it was him. It makes some sense I guess, but it just wasn't sitting right with me. Then I remembered the rendering of the…what did you call it?"

"The Plundering Pike." Kirk had responded without hesitation but he looked lost in thought.

"Right. Well, after seeing that rendering I thought it was worth my piece of mind to at least have a chat with you and see what you could tell me about it before a murder case was just left to go cold."

"Who was he, the victim?" Kirk asked indicating the massacred forearm in the photo.

"His name was Richard Devlin."

"Devlin?"

The blood drain from Kirk's face was immediate, leaving him ashen and pale.

Bob leaned forward, "Does the name mean something to you?" That it did was in little doubt based on the sudden change in his pallor.

"I've heard the name Devlin before." Kirk said after a pause, but that much was obvious.

"Yeah?"

Kirk nodded. "And I believe there may be a direct correlation between Pike and the Devlin name."

Bob's eyes were riveted to his friend seated across the desk from him. "Tell me." He said.

Kirk remained quiet for a long moment presumably collecting his thoughts then spoke. "Ok, stay with me here, I think a bit of back story on Pike is necessary." Bob's focus was locked onto him. He was fully engaged with whatever it was that Kirk was about to say.

"I've followed the Pike legend for a long time, hoping to write a book about it someday. Through my research I've developed some sources, one particularly good one, and I've discovered some things that may not be public knowledge."

Bob said nothing. He did not want to derail Kirk's train of thought but there was no need to worry. Kirk was on his favorite subject and he was on a roll.

"Pike had a son who grew up and married. Both are well known facts and are not disputed. The fact that Pike may have had a grandson however, was disputed and often. There is no record of the child but in many of the stories there are rumblings that the son and his wife also had a baby. I believe this to be true even with no facts to back it up."

"Why's that?" Bob couldn't help but interject.

Kirk smiled. "You see, the further into the Pike legend you dig the more you'll find information, which in normal cases would be relatively easy to corroborate, has somehow become fuzzy or has disappeared altogether."

"Hang on a sec," Bob said as he pulled his notebook out and opened it to a fresh page. He jotted the name 'Pike' across the top. He drew an arrow down and wrote 'son/wife' and circled it, below that he added 'grandson' and after a moment of hesitation he punctuated it with a question mark. Kirk went on.

"The Pike family also had a lawyer, a guy by the name of Victor Leland. He handled all of the family's legal affairs and probably quite a few that were not legal at all. Pike eventually passed away but Leland continued in service to the family until a summer night over twenty-five years ago when Pike's son and his wife were murdered. That very same night Leland's office was attacked and everyone there was killed."

That last tidbit raised Bob's eyes from his notes but Kirk's story never broke stride.

"But Leland wasn't there. He had disappeared. Most accounts say that Leland was never heard from again but I think that I tracked him down once, or a trace of him anyway. I followed the paper trail of a man that I now believe was Leland. Shortly after all of those murders, this guy purchased a bus ticket to a small, rural town in western North Dakota. While he was there he spent time with a young couple named Myron and Willa Devlin. After leaving that little town I lost any trace of him but a short time later the couple he had visited adopted a young boy. I think Leland rescued Pike's grandson from whatever it was that happened the night his parents were killed and hid him away… with a family named Devlin."

Bob set his notes aside and rubbed his eyes before meeting Kirk's gaze. He held it for a long moment then settled back in his chair and exhaled a heavy sigh. "So, it sounds like you are actually trying to tell me that it's a possibility my victim could be the grandson of this Plundering Pike?"

Kirk chose his response with a careful precision. "Devlin is nothing more than a name, not that common but not uncommon either, but combined with the symbol of the Plundering Pike being carved into his arm, I guess I would call it intriguing at the very least."

And with that last statement Kirk could no longer suppress the eager smile that stole across his face.

Now –

And so they had pursued.

They had attempted to connect the Devlin case to some old pirate legend. But their theory was wild, out of the box, and in a business based solely on facts it proved out to have found no purchase. Up the chain of command the whole idea was considered ridiculous and even comical. The repercussions of having put forth such a theory, Bob did not care to linger long on. He gave a slight shudder, even now, just thinking about it.

It had been an embarrassment.

And then there was the key.

It had been a week or so after being told in no uncertain terms that he was to leave the Devlin case alone that the key had surfaced. The elder Jansen had showed up in the

Sheriff's office. As it turned out his boy had found a skeleton key hanging from a tree branch at some point shortly before coming upon Devlin. The kid had just thought it was kind of cool, so he pocketed it. It was understandable that the young man had forgotten about the little hunk of metal in his pocket in the aftermath of stumbling upon the body. But when it came out in the wash, quite literally, his mother had asked him about it. He had explained how he came to have such a trinket and his parents decided it should be given to the authorities.

The key itself was elongated. It had an odd phrase engraved down the length of the shaft and back up the other side of it, but it was otherwise unremarkable. The engraving seemed nonsensical.

But one look at it back then, sitting in the very chair where he sat now, had turned Bob's stomach. He had kept his reaction measured and thanked Jansen for bringing it in. But after Jansen was gone he had stared at that little hunk of metal for a very long time. He had known two things about that key right from the get go.

It had been Devlin's, and it would never see the light of day. Devlin had turned into an embarrassment.

Brad Withers rapped on the door, startling Bob from his reverie.

"Gale got the names of some of the kids at that party from one of the parents. I'm gonna take Reese and go follow up." Brad said sticking his head into the office.

"Thanks, Brad." Bob managed. Brad looked at him sideways for a second then closed the door. Bob noted the look and reminded himself that he needed to keep his focus in the moment. He checked his watch. He checked the station clock.

No doubt about it, Deputy Tremely should have been back by now. He picked up his phone and placed the call, leaving the key and its implications to Ryan for the moment.

The sunlight shone bright in Ryan Tomlinson's face. The sky was blue, the air was warm, but he had goose-bumps standing out on his arms and neck. He was cold despite the humidity and the warmth of the sun magnified through the windshield of his cruiser. The road to hell is paved with good intentions, his father liked to say. That phrase had never seemed more appropriate than it did right now.

He had still been a relatively young man when he had laid those first stones on the proverbial path to damnation. If they could prove now what they could not six years ago, perhaps vindication could still be in the cards. Before leaving Castle Danger, Ryan had stopped by his house and grabbed a piece of paper that had, for so long, been lost amongst the rubble of his study. It was a hand drawn map. It looked a bit like a kid's treasure map. The day he made it, Ryan never would've believed it necessary. To his mind he would never have forgotten where he put that key. Now he was awfully glad he had taken the time to jot down some coordinates. Memory had a funny way of running out on you, especially when it came to things better left forgotten.

Ryan's in-laws owned some land just northwest of Gooseberry. A nice piece of land, ten acres, partially wooded. A tidy little farmhouse lay at the dead center of the property. Just off the southeast corner of the house was a shed. This shed was the only building on Ryan's map. It was the jumping off point. Like kids playing treasure hunt, he had just scribbled off the map the day he hid the key. Twenty paces this way, forty that way, turn right at the elm tree, etc. And with an accuracy that is characteristic only of the games of children, the map he had made six long years ago, led him directly to the spot he had buried the key.

He had put it in an old tobacco tin that his father had given him when he was nine. He had kept his baseball cards in there once upon a time. Now it housed a key. Soil crumbled from the sides of the container as he removed it from the earth. Memories of his favorite sluggers immortalized, washed over him at the sight of the old tin. Then he opened it.

It seemed so empty.

Occupied only by that single skeleton key.

That little tin had always held such fond memories,

baseball and the smell of summertime. It reminded him of everything that was good about being a kid. Crouched in the dirt behind his father in-law's house he removed the key from the tin and held it in the palm of his hand.

Happy memories faded quickly, the only memory the key recalled was death.

8

The cryptic message stared him down from the soft glow of the monitor and Jessy Tremely couldn't tear his eyes away. The line of mismatched letters and numbers was taunting him. Bob would want answers and the only thing he was certain of at this point was that something was seriously amiss.

Jessy shook his head, a physical manifestation of his mental attempts to shake off his insecurities. As a child, he had been a member of the junior detectives club and he loved his Encyclopedia Brown books. But no matter how much he loved the books and decoder rings and playing the part, the answer was rarely as simple as lightly running your pencil over a pad of paper to create a reverse picture of what had been written on the previous sheet.

He pushed himself back from the desk, his eyes moving with a slow, cautious, determination around the room. Every couple of seconds though, he would cut his gaze back to the monitor.

Jessy was awash in overwhelming, unwarranted, and unwelcome emotion. Adrenaline had gotten him out to the house and through the front door. Now his resolve was starting to slip. He pulled out his casebook and jotted down the single line of code. He was in the field now, possibly sitting amidst a crime scene at that very moment. He tried to keep his head together and make sense of what was happening.

If, and it was still a big *if*, Kirk was missing and not just out picking up a gallon of milk or something as simple as that, although in his heart of hearts he already knew that would prove out not to be the case, what possible connection could the town librarian have to what happened up at Split Rock?

He shut the monitor off and looked around the room, he was satisfied that it was just as he had found it. He was struck by the 'lived in' feel of this room compared to the rest of the house. Kirk had spent a lot of time in here chasing his passions.

The house made a settling sound and Jessy jumped. It was time to call in the cavalry. He was about to punch the speed dial for the station when the phone rang in his hand.

"Tremley." He said answering the call.

"Jess, where are you?" Bob asked.

"I'm still out to Hanlon's place." He paused. "Kirk's not here."

Sheriff Gurley was silent for a moment as he processed this piece of news. "Is anything out of place?" Bob's tone was cautious and reserved.

"Not really." Jessy paused again, not quite sure how to proceed. "But there are a few... incongruities."

Bob did not care at all for the sound of that word. "Tell me." He said. Jessy explained the oddity of the spilled cup of tea as well as the mumbo-jumbo that had been left on the computer screen and his belief that it was some sort of code. When he finished Bob was silent again. Silence, it could be almost hateful sometimes. Finally Bob responded.

"Stay put, I'm coming to you." The line went dead.

Jessy sighed and let his weight settle heavy back into the chair. It would be a long ten or so minutes waiting for Bob to arrive. He let his eyes drift to the gigantic, aged bookcase lining the wall on his left.

Strange.

A single book in the bookcase was turned backward, with the pages, instead of the binding, facing out.

He pulled it off the shelf noticing as it came down, that although cracked and old, it was not at all dusty. It was on a shelf full of tomes that carried a thin layer of dust. This particular book had been off that shelf and somewhat recently. He sat down at the desk sliding the maps and papers and the tourist book about the Great Lakes, 'Mysterious Waters', out of his way. He set the book he'd taken from the bookcase down.

It was a heavy hard cover. Jessy flipped it open and looked at the contents page still not sure what, if anything, he had just found. He fanned through the pages and one caught his eye.

It had been marked, the corner dog-eared.

This made Jessy stop and take note. Kirk Hanlon did not seem the type to dog-ear a page to hold his place. As if to accentuate this point he had but to glance across the desk, on top of which, there were no less than seven bookmarks just lying in wait. Kirk was the kind of man that appreciated everything about his books, all the way down to the paper they were printed on. So why mangle this precious page, what could be so important as to deface this perfect specimen of pressed pulp.

Jessy flipped to the page and found a story about an old painting of the Superior shore line entitled 'Angel at the Rock'. The story indicated that a photo of the painting would be found on the opposite page.

But the page had been torn out.

2

Bob pushed his chair out from behind his desk and stood in a fog. He stepped to the window and again took in the bright, beautiful day coming full on the reverse side. Yesterday Kirk had come to him and at the mere mention of Devlin, Bob had nearly run him out of Mike's Diner. Now he was nowhere to be found. If this ended badly, that was going to be an awful lot to live with.

He called Ryan and caught him before he had left his in-laws and told him to meet him out at Hanlon's place. Ryan informed him that he had the key in his possession. It was all beginning to feel so inevitable. Turning away from the window and the day outside, he left his office.

Gale Sebathany was still fighting the phones but their incessant ringing had died off a bit.

"No calls from Barlow or anyone at the BCA?" Bob asked.

"Nothing yet," Gale hollered back. "Although, I think they're the only people in this half of the state that haven't tried to get through to you today."

"I gotta go meet up with Ryan and Jessy. You raise me on the radio right away if they call, Roger?"

"10-4, boss." Gale called back but the Sheriff was already gone, back into his office to grab his keys.

It was time to go meet Jessy and see if there wasn't any kind of sanity to be redeemed from this morning. He was about to walk out of his office when the phone on his desk started to ring.

It wasn't the standard ring. It had a quicker rhythm. It was a specialized ring to let him know the call was coming in from one of the cruiser's radios. After a moment's hesitation he scooped the handset off the cradle. It was Brad Withers.

"Sheriff I might have some good news."

"Christ, Brad, that was sure quick."

"Yeah, I know. One of the first kids I talked to was a relatively regular acquaintance of Billy Brannigan. He said that he thought Scott and Billy had left the party early, shortly after eleven. The kicker is the kid said it wasn't just the two of them. There was another kid that went with them." Bob could hear Brad shuffling through his notebook. "The name of the other kid is Swansby, Jimmy Swansby."

The name was familiar to the sheriff. No one he could

picture off the top of his head but a family name he had heard with some regularity.

"A third kid, huh? Well where is he now?"

Brad hesitated for just a moment.

"That's where the first bit of bad news may start."

"Well, I didn't think I'd heard all the bad news that I was going to today," Bob said as he sat back down behind his desk. "Give it to me."

"I called the kid's folks, hoping to talk to him since he was probably the last person to see either of the other boys." Again Brad paused.

"Go on, Brad."

"Swansby never came home last night. His parents hadn't really worried what with it being the last day of school and all, but now they seem to be in a bit of a huff. I can't say that I blame them."

"And we don't have any idea where this kid is?"

"Not as of right now, no. We just found out about him though, we'll find him, Sheriff."

Brad was trying to be optimistic yet the little thing in Bob's stomach, which would probably be the start of an ulcer, grew another notch.

"Alright, Brad," Bob managed. "Are you on your way over to talk to the parents?"

"Affirmative. I'll get full statements and see what else I can unearth."

"Sounds good, and that's good work you've done this morning."

"Thanks, Bob." He paused. "There is one other thing."

Bob got the distinct feeling that whatever Brad had to say, it was something that he did not want to hear.

"What is it Brad?"

"This kid I talked to said that Billy and Scott and this Swansby kid had been obsessing over some old legend. Some story that was supposedly associated with the woods out beyond Castle Danger.

The saliva in Bob's mouth made itself scarce.

"You still there, Sheriff?"

"I'm here, Brad, go ahead."

"Well I don't know much more than that. This kid said he had heard the three of them talking about it a lot lately. Apparently they had been out hunting around for evidence that the story was more than a myth and that may have been where they were off to last night. He couldn't give me much more, just that they referred to it as 'Old Farmer's Road'."

Clack.

The minute hand slapped forward, and it was almost as if it knocked loose some sort of mental log jam in Bob's head. Not enough to allow it to run freely but enough to let the water start to slip past. Old Farmer's Road was a name he knew, had known in the past anyway.

The phone slipped and Bob juggled it for a moment before catching it, he said goodbye to Brad and replaced it in the cradle.

His hand defied him by the slightest tremor.

On the drive out to Hanlon's place Bob tried to turn his thoughts to the development that was Jimmy Swansby. What might he know? The kid had just become a central player in this little drama. He was with those boys last night. What happened to them could possibly shed light on what had happened to Devlin and that just might rip this kerfuffle wide open. But of course, if Swansby were to help in the mystery surrounding what happened to Devlin, or Billy or Scott, Bob would first have to find out what it was that may have happened to the young man.

He turned left on County Road 51. The cruiser was kicking up a rooster tail of dirt and gravel. Moments later in his rearview mirror he saw Ryan turn onto the road behind him.

He thought of the key.

He thought about Old Farmer's Road.

Fragmented snippets of memories were stealing their way into his mind, gnawing but not able to take hold. The wisps of recollection bore little comfort. For Bob, they seemed more cause for more unease.

He saw Jessy's squad car parked on the shoulder in front of Kirk's house and with very little reluctance, allowed his brain to shift gears. He pulled into the driveway, got out of the car and waited for Ryan to catch up. He looked at Jessy's cruiser and at Ryan's pulling in. He glanced up and down the road and hoped that no casual passerby would see this festival of police cars and start rubbernecking before they even had a chance to find out what the hell was going on. Ryan pulled up and killed the engine. He got out and stood next to his boss.

Standing side by side they looked up at Kirk Hanlon's house. It was quiet and dark.

A painting?

Jessy was bewildered.

He had put the book back on the shelf just as he had found it, but couldn't put it out of his head. He turned back to the desk. He was drumming his fingers on the edge trying to make sense of why Kirk may have marked that page, when he was interrupted.

He heard them a second before they were there.

He had just enough time to spin the chair around and face the door. He tried to stand, but didn't make it.

He had enough time to see the fist before it smashed into his upper cheekbone, but not enough time to avoid it.

The impact was hard and it rocked him backwards tipping the chair and spilling him onto the floor. He rolled into the fall and tried to stand. He counted three of them, all wearing generic utility company uniforms and black facemasks. That was all he could register before another punch landed on the bridge of his nose. Blood sprayed from his crushed septum and the pain exploded behind his eyes. His vision had blurred but there was nothing wrong with his pain receptors.

He felt the kick that blew out his knee just fine.

Standing was no longer an option. He slumped to the side of his damaged knee and his hand shot out to support himself. It came down mashing the keyboard of the computer.

An image of the blinking cursor shot through his head and he realized the code would be wasted now, mixed in amidst true gibberish. At least he had written it down. Then his strength ran out and he slid to the floor. His vision was still blurry but he saw the eyes, angry, hateful eyes, sunk in the facemask that appeared before him. The man grabbed him by the collar.

The mask before him spoke, its breath hot and rank on Jessy's face.

"Dumb-dumb deputy, what are you doing here?"

Jessy took a long look into those ugly eyes, mustered all the strength that he could find and spit squarely into them. He saw the spittle dangling from the cotton blend of the facemask. He watched it with a hard focus.

And then his head exploded.

Ryan and Bob approached the house with slow, cautious strides. Bob's skin was crawling. The way it sometimes would as the leading edge of an electrical storm passed over, but the sky above them was as blue as blue could be. Bob looked to Ryan. Ryan glanced back at him at the same time. Bob could see that he was nervous too.

A sound, not dissimilar to a loud firecracker split the silence emanating from the house. Neither man mistook it for a firecracker.

A look barely passed between the two of them before their cautious strides turned into a sprint to the heavy oak door. Bob tried to get a visual through the window but the shades were drawn. Bob dropped his right hand leaving it hovering just above the holster. They were both at the door. They nodded to each other that they were ready. Ryan grasped the handle, turned, and pushed the door open.

Bob lifted his firearm out of his holster.

Ryan followed suit.

On Bob's lead they stepped into Kirk Hanlon's home.

The door opened onto the living room. There was nothing wrong with the room and yet everything was wrong with the room. The feeling was indescribable and yet it was there. The quality of the silence was off. Bob entered the house with Ryan right behind him.

A loud smacking sound rang out from the back of the house.

It was a sound Bob knew. The sound of a heavy glass patio door sliding shut, hard.

"Patio!" He barked.

Both men sprinted to the back of the house.

They saw two men dressed in utility company uniforms disappearing into the dense trees at the back end of the yard. Bob was a man who could organize and compartmentalize. It was a large part of his attraction to the voters of their fine county, his attention to detail. He had seen the spilled cup of tea as they ran through the living room. In the kitchen he noted the open door to the garage. Jessy had not mentioned his mishap in the garage, so to Bob this was a new wrinkle to be put in a new folder, filed for later use. All of this ran through his head in matter of seconds.

Ryan on the other hand fed on instinct. It only took a second for Bob to make a mental picture and start working scenarios, but it was more than it took for Ryan to whip the door open and go chasing across the yard.

"Ryan." Bob snapped, but he was already halfway across the backyard. Bob whirled at a sound from behind him, deeper in the house. It was a small sound but in Bob's adrenaline heightened state, it echoed through the corridors of Kirk's home. Gun trained, Bob crossed back through the kitchen and into the hallway.

Jessy had not been with the men dashing across the backyard, that was certain. Bob moved down the hall. He came to the study door on his right. It was closed most of the way but he could see a jumble of books through the small crack that was provided.

He waited and listened a moment at the door.

Nothing.

He pushed the door. The rug in the study was thick and it pushed up against the bottom of the door keeping it from swinging open easily. Bob gave it another shove, harder this time and it swung open. What it revealed caused Bobs knees to grow weak. He wavered for a moment in the doorway before steadying himself.

Deputy Tremely lay in the middle of the floor in a pool of his own blood.

Jessy was on his back and he wasn't moving. His right arm was outstretched, his service pistol resting on the palm of his hand but his fingers were lax on the grip of the weapon. The upper left hand quadrant of his head was not quite gone, but above the eye it was reduced to a mush of pulp and blood and gristle. His eyes were open and glazed but not lifeless, at least not yet. His lips moved but they weren't doing much but pushing a small amount of the blood in his throat, up and over his lips to dribble down his chin.

Bob dropped to his knees, assessing the situation and how best to go about CPR. There didn't seem to be any good place to start.

Jessy Tremely was dying right in front of him.

Bob watched as his deputy belched up a thick wad of blood and managed an awful groaning sound. Bob realized that he was trying to say something. His first instinct was to tell him not to talk but there was little question as to whether Jessy was leaving this room alive or not. He leaned close while pulling his cell off of his belt to radio for an ambulance.

The smell of blood on Jessy's breath made Bob's stomach turn but he refused to wretch or show any discomfort while this brave young man's life force was pouring out into the rug around them. Jessy's eyes were glazed but urgent, his lips moved without pause but he was barely making sounds much less words. He was trying to speak, desperate to form words but Bob was afraid he would never be heard, not on this side of the great beyond anyway.

Bob leaned in a little closer to him, not with any hope of comprehension but more as an act of comfort. As he did, Jessy's eyes went wide and his labored breathing gained pace. He was looking past Bob and at first he thought it was that the poor kid wasn't focusing, but then his ears tuned in and Bob realized what Jessy must have been trying to say.

He and Ryan had arrived at the house and saw two men running into the woods behind the house. Ryan had chased them. Bob had come in here and found Jessy, dying on the floor.

He had never secured the house.

He knew there had been at least two men, but there could have been more. He was suddenly very sure that the latter was true and that in his rush to tend to Jessy he'd been flanked.

And so, the deafening roar of the gunshot came as no surprise.

10

Morning, June 6th
Kirk Hanlon's Residence

Ryan crossed Hanlon's backyard and into the woods in a matter of seconds, his heart pounding hard in his chest. He tried to look everywhere at once, but in his haste he was seeing nothing. He pulled up and stopped running, listening for any audible trace of the men retreating through the brush but there was nothing.

Weapon in hand, he moved in the general direction he guessed they would've been heading based on where they entered the woods.

The forest sounds were being amplified. He moved ahead, slow. Concentration was causing a light sweat to break on his forehead. He noticed some matted down grass and foliage heading off to the east and his breath came a little easier. They'd been through here and had broken off towards the highway. That was logical, and the presence of logic this morning was a rare, but welcome sign.

He was about to resume a trot in that direction when

another gunshot rang out from the direction of the house.

All thought drained without resistance. The Sheriff, his best friend, was still back there. Ryan reversed course and retreated in a dead sprint toward Hanlon's house. Again he made the dash through the clearing between the tree line and the deck in a matter of seconds, feeling the extreme lack of cover as he crossed Kirk's backyard. He reached the sliding door without incident. He leveled his gun and peered inside.

There was no sign of movement.

He stepped through the open patio door and into the kitchen.

He could feel his heartbeat in his temples and it was pulsing so hard that it hurt. The kitchen floorboards let out a ratcheting squeak as he took a step and Ryan froze, waiting for a response to the noise. When none came, fear of what might have happened to Bob overcame him and he was on the move. He walked into the hallway, gun raised and ready to fire.

Sprawled on the floor was a man dressed in an identical uniform to those that he chased into the woods.

The ski mask looked similar as well except that it was now a mess of blood and gore.

Ryan heard a soft whimpering sound from the room adjacent to the dead man. It was Bob, still alive, so far anyway. Ryan took five quick steps to the open door, stepping over the body in the hall. He looked into the room and found himself in a deluge of relief and confusion.

Bob was fine.

That much registered immediately, right behind it though followed the realization that Jessy was not.

Bob was kneeling on the floor of the study holding Jessy's lifeless head in his lap and making soft, sobbing sounds. Jessy's arms were stretched back above his head, wrapped around Bob in some sort of macabre embrace. The sight turned Ryan's innards, wrapping them around themselves. He wanted to look away, as if somehow that would allow him to believe that the scene before him wasn't real. He forced himself to keep his eyes steady, steady and strong.

Jessy was dead.

He had given his life in the line of duty. That was a phrase that they never would have thought could ever apply to their quiet little department. Now and forever it would.

Bob looked up at Ryan, tears standing in his eyes. Ryan waited, expecting Bob to begin to lay a litany of blame upon himself. He tried to steel himself against the idea that Jessy's blood could possibly be on their hands. In truth, of course, it wasn't. Jessy had stood and taken the oath, been sworn in as a Deputy of Castle County. Something like this, the inherent dangers the job possessed had always been a possibility, but Ryan knew Bob would never see it that way. Jessy was in his charge, to Bob that made him his responsibility.

"He wasn't dead yet." Bob said. "That sonuvabitch came in behind me. I had no idea he was even there. Jessy tried to tell me but I didn't understand." Bob dried his eyes and cheeks. "I don't know how he managed it but he lifted his weapon and took the shot. I couldn't tell what he was saying... If he hadn't been able to fire, I'd be dead."

He looked up and Ryan was surprised by the fiery intensity he saw. Bob's eyes were red and cracked but he looked angry. Ryan preferred that to a messy puddle on the floor any day. He did not feel in control, the fact that Bob was managing some level of authority was a relief.

"Call it in." Bob said. "I can't leave him alone just yet."

Ryan was still having trouble wrapping his head around the fact that the mass of dead flesh in Bob's lap had, until recently, been Jessy Tremely. Spider-webs appeared and tangled at the edge of his vision and he fought them back. He would not faint, not now.

He nodded. It was slow in coming but he made himself do it. He stepped out of the room, pulled his phone off his belt, connected to the station, and in a voice steadier than he would've believed himself capable of, he reported to Gale Sebathany that an officer was down.

From where Bob was sitting with Jessy's head in his lap he could see what was left of the jackass in the hallway. He still couldn't fathom how Jessy had been able to lift that heavy iron that had been resting on his hand and take that shot.

His mind was reeling. He realized that it was partially from shock, but not totally. He could already hear his conversation with Agent Barlow of the BCA. With Kirk's disappearance and then Jessy being killed in Kirk's home, it wouldn't be so difficult to impress upon her the connection between the kids at Split Rock and Richard Devlin. The problem was, with everything happening so quickly he couldn't see the plodding, methodical tactics of the BCA locating Kirk before it was too late. Officially, he would file his report and tell Barlow everything he knew.

Unofficially, he was going to do whatever it would take to find Kirk Hanlon.

He knew it was possible that it could cost him his job. In fact he would be lucky if that was all it cost him. He hoped Ryan could be spared, but he also knew Ryan would inevitably be loyal to him, even above his loyalty to the job. He was sorry and thankful for that at the same time.

Ryan stepped back into the room. "They're on their way."

"I held him, Ryan." The tears again began their descent, running tracks down his cheek. "I held him, and he tried to hold me. He was trying so hard to wrap his arms around me as he went. It was so…desperate."

Then he slipped into a heavy silence.

Ryan, unable to fight the urge any longer turned away to collect his thoughts. As he glanced away he noticed something odd on Kirk's desk. There was a box of tissues to his left and resting on top of it was a broken key from the keyboard.

It was the letter X.

Ryan noticed it, but at that point made no connection to its significance. Seconds later he had already forgotten the most important discovery made during their time at the home of Kirk Hanlon.

Part two

Eddie

1

The road just rolled and rolled and rolled on by.

It was so familiar and yet so foreign, a conduit from here to there, wherever 'there' might be. Towns came and went, changing from crumbling, tired, old 'Main Streets' into prairies and then forests in the blink of an eye. This cycle seemed to repeat itself over and over again.

Eddie Watson watched the landscape change and zip by, his head resting heavy on the passenger side window. He would occasionally lift it and look at Jacobs, but Jacobs stayed singularly focused on the road ahead of them.

It had been exactly two hours and seven minutes since Eddie's life had changed utterly and completely, utterly and completely for the second time in the last month.

So far Eddie had been unable to make any real, coherent, sense of what had happened at the formerly comfortable confines of Itasca State Park.

Park Rangers had arrived.

He was clear on that at least. Jacobs had provided some manner of ID. The department, or level of authority that said

Identification provided remained a mystery to Eddie. Whatever it was, though, seemed to supersede the Park Rangers who were first on the scene. They seemed more than happy to defer to a higher authority in the matter of the bloodbath that had ensued upon their property. While Jacobs had dealt with the Rangers, Eddie had sat hunkered down looking at the man wearing the crazy fishing hat, mesmerized by how different an eyeball looked when it was devoid of life.

Off in the background, like radio static, Jacobs had delegated to the Rangers. Eddie still couldn't quite fathom how their position had been usurped by him yet he knew better than to be surprised. Jacobs was a man of means.

Eddie had tried to stand but wavered and reached down to steady himself.

His hand came up sticky.

He had looked down and saw the dead man's blood running into the creases on his palm. At that, time slipped and Eddie lost track of things for a piece.

And now they were on the move, again. Just as they had been three weeks ago when Jacobs had pulled him from the depths of hell and had delivered him to this little idyllic escape. But Itasca had gone bad now too, and so the cycle repeats and now they were rolling by another rundown town on a road to nowhere.

But that wasn't precisely true either. All roads run to somewhere, and Eddie was now beginning to acquire an uncomfortable intuition about where this particular road might run its course.

They were heading east. While there were many potential destinations lying in that direction, one shone like a beacon in the night.

The place where Eddie's part in this little drama had begun, the place he was born thirty years ago, almost to the day.

What lay ahead was unappealing. He could only hope that what was in the past was worse. If it was not, he was unsure how equipped he might be for such dark days ahead.

Trapped in the now, he allowed himself a bit of reflection on what was then.

Beneath the floorboard, beneath his feet, the pavement peeled away.

2

Early morning hours, June 6th
Itasca State Park

Eddie Watson lay prone in his bunk focusing every ounce of his being on not making a noise. He had heard something move right outside the cabin window. He prayed he wouldn't hear it again. Eddie didn't know any real prayers but he had watched a lot of TV so he improvised. Sweat broke on his forehead and ran off the side of his face. His eyes shot from the soft, off-white curtain covering the window to the front door of his stark, one room cabin. In between his stumbling attempts at piety he tried to convince himself that the sounds he had heard were natural. It was probably a raccoon. It wasn't inconceivable. He was currently a ward of the Minnesota State Parks System. A foraging raccoon would not be considered an anomaly.

Unfortunately for Eddie it was neither an anomaly nor inconceivable, that it also might be someone who wanted to kill him.

More rustling.

It was right outside his window, there was no question about it.

As far as Eddie knew there were very few people in this world that actually wanted him dead. That anyone would want to kill him in the first place should have been laughable, the odds that one of them was standing outside his window right now were ridiculous.

Eddie had very little interest in odds at the moment.

All he cared about was the 9mm that Jacobs had given him, the 9mm that was inches from his head on the night stand, the 9mm that he was too scared to reach for. If only he'd had another day or two with Jacobs, if he'd had a little more training.

A day, a week, a month. It wouldn't have mattered. The truth was he hadn't believed it could come to this. He'd never fired a gun before he met Jacobs and now he was sleeping with one on his bedside table. In spite of the fact that over a matter of weeks he had gone from selling used cars to sleeping with a loaded gun beside him, he never believed he would have to use it. And yet here he was.

Steeling his resolve he snaked his hand out and laid it on the cold steel. He lifted the weapon slowly with a more pronounced case of the shakes than he would have liked. He checked the safety just like Jacobs had taught him. Then he said another of his pseudo prayers, this time it entailed never finding himself in such a spot where it would become necessary to turn the safety off.

The wind rustled and a shadow appeared on the curtain in the window.

Eddie launched himself out of bed, clenching his teeth to hold back the yelp that was trying to fight its way out. He went flat against the wall to the right of the window, just like he'd seen in a million movies.

The wind picked up again and the shadow moved.

He clicked the safety off.

His heart was trip-hammering in his chest.

Silently he counted to ten to try and calm himself. He was on seven when he heard scratching on the window.

His heart doubled its pace. A moment ago he wouldn't have believed that possible. If someone tries to run faster than they're physically able, their legs tangle and they fall ass over tea kettle. Eddie squeezed his eyes shut against the image of how that might translate to his heart.

The wind kicked up, the shadow repositioned again, and the window creaked as if it were being pushed up. It was now or never, do or die. Phrases that had never been a part of Eddie's life before tumbled through his head. He had reduced himself to clichés. Not sure exactly when that had happened, he made his move.

He whirled in front of the window yanking the curtain down as he spun. The rod pulled free of the brackets and came clanging to the floor beside him. He brought the gun up, his index finger tensing on the trigger.

He stopped just short of destroying his window and pouring round after round into the large red pine outside. The pine tree with the branches that were swaying in front of the window creating shadows. Those same branches that would brush the window pane as the wind picked up making a soft scraping sound.

Eddie let out a long sigh realizing only just then that he'd been holding his breath. His heart was still pounding but with the action over it was at least slowing a bit.

Thwack!

Something smacked against the front door, behind him. Eddie whirled and dropped into a shooters crouch, apparently a few of the tips and techniques Jacobs had showed him had sunk in after all. He managed some self-control again just before unloading the clip, this time into the front door.

Was it possible to overload on fear? Eddie thought that perhaps it was and maybe he just had. He was still frightened, but he had been so petrified at the window that he was just too exhausted to get all worked up again. Before he could come back to his senses and work his way back up to being scared to death, he stood and walked straight to the door. He moved to the right as he grabbed the handle and swung the door open hard to the left, pressing himself against the wall. When nothing happened he dropped quickly into his shooters crouch again, this time in front of the open door. He brought the weapon up and smacked his gun hand into the palm of the other to steady the shot, quite possibly ready to actually kill something this time.

While he had pushed his fear aside and strode across the cabin he had been running on instinct and adrenaline. He hadn't really given any thought to what might be waiting for him on the other side of the door. Whatever thoughts flitted through his mind as to who or what he may discover there, it was most certainly not what he actually found.

At first his overwrought brain couldn't make sense of the orange and yellow flames. Then it clicked and despite the harrowing ups and downs of the last ten minutes he couldn't quite suppress a smile.

Sitting on his stoop was a flaming bag of shit.

Literally, a flaming bag of shit.

Goddamn kids.

The man sat in the dark and he watched, and he waited.

He was patient.

Always patient.

It had given him a start when Eddie appeared at the window wielding the gun, but only for a moment. He was far enough back, deep enough in the brush that there was no way Eddie could see him.

He turned the knife over in his hands, the knife was beautiful, a gift from the man who had taught him to use it. For now he was to watch, to remain stalwart and patient but when the time came, if the opportunity was his, he would use the knife. He liked to work close.

At that moment he heard movement on the road out in front of the cabin. It was time to move on for now. The man drifted deeper into the darkness, then was gone.

3

Jacobs was late.

Eddie sat on the front stoop of his rented cabin, the cabin that had been his home now for about three and half weeks. It had been a full four weeks since he had first been torn away from his life and this horror began, and three and half since a stranger named Jacobs had come to the rescue. Oh, what a month it had been.

Itasca was beautiful.

It was also, for all intents and purposes, a prison. This was the second such prison in which Eddie had found himself since his life had been altered irrevocably four weeks ago. The first had been more literal, whereas Itasca was certainly more metaphoric. He would take the latter over the former any day of the week and twice on Sunday. He watched the morning sunlight dance playfully through the boughs of the giant red wood pines and breathed the clean fresh air.

He sat and did his best to enjoy this picturesque morning in his new, far more pleasant, prison. The only thing that subdued his enjoyment of the tranquil morning was the absence of his would be jailer.

Over the couple of weeks they had spent together Jacobs had become many things to Eddie: mentor, savior, and not least of all, a large pain in the ass.

One thing he had never been was tardy.

A couple teenage boys walked by on the path in front of the cabin. They had been staying with the mother of one of the boys in the cabin next to his for a few days now. He waited for them to make eye contact so he could bid them a good morning. Neither of them looked his way. Their avoidance of him seemed a bit too intentional and he passed his judgment right then and there that they were the most probable candidates to be the culprits in the case of the flaming bag of crap.

One mystery solved.

The bigger mystery still loomed.

Where was Jacobs, and more to the point what would he do with himself if Jacobs didn't turn up? He hadn't given this scenario much thought. After all, panic was still premature. At least he hoped it was.

Eddie pulled out the phone Jacobs had given him. He checked the time then the call log. There were no missed calls. Jacobs had told him never to call him unless it was an absolute emergency; the phone was for Jacobs to contact Eddie. This didn't constitute an emergency yet, but 'yet' was the key word.

Every morning Jacobs would arrive at the cabin at the same time. He would update Eddie on any news coming out of the real world. At first Eddie had waited, anxious for exciting reports from Jacobs about his disappearance, about the wild searches for the missing Duluth man. After the first few days he began to come to terms with the fact that he was not being missed. He was just another guy, kind of a loner, acquaintances would say, that had picked up stakes and pushed on. It was odd, maybe, but not necessarily mysterious.

Jacobs had pulled the messages off of his voicemail. There were three calls from the car dealership where he worked. The first two were wondering why he wasn't showing up for his shifts. The last was a simple, don't bother coming back, we'll mail your check. Just like that he had been cut away from the only thing tethering him to the world anymore. He was 'in the wind' as they say and the only thing he could count on was Jacobs.

Every time his mind would drift toward those hellish three days, the three days before Jacobs had come for him, he would run his hands over his still tender ribs, and thank his lucky stars.

Jacobs had saved him. Jacobs had brought him here. He had given him the gun and showed him how to use it.

And now he was late.

Eddie hauled himself back from his reverie as a big white GMC Yukon rolled slowly around the bend in the road. There was nothing out of the ordinary about it but something set off a little warning bell in the back of Eddie's head. His new sixth sense, that was all suspicion, was another thing he could thank Jacobs for.

He watched it roll by.

The driver seemed oblivious to him but an unsettled feeling began to slowly creep up on Eddie. The guy behind the wheel was maybe mid-forties, looked to be heavyset. He didn't seem familiar to Eddie at all. The back windows were pretty heavily tinted. If there was anyone in there he couldn't see them. If there *was* anyone in the back it was probably kids, not gun-toting maniacs but still, one could never be too sure in this bold, new world in which Eddie found himself living.

He tried not to stare.

It was just some guy looking for his campsite, probably.

But as soon as the truck rounded the bend out of sight Eddie stood up. He tried not to move too quickly or betray any alarm, just in case. Nice easy strides for the two steps to the door. Once in the cabin however, he slammed the door and sprinted to the bed, and the 9mm in the end-table drawer.

It felt good in his hand.

It never really had before. The events of the previous night may have jumpstarted something in him that so far Jacobs had been unable to tap. Sometimes a man has just got to get his feet wet. He checked the window by the bed, the one that had given him such a fright last night. There was nothing to see but leaves, trees, and brush. He checked the east window.

His breath caught in his throat.

A fisherman, carrying his rod and reel and wearing a crazy fishing hat, was walking up the path across the little road.

He'd seen the guy before.

The guy with the plaid shirt on at the bar?

Something was seriously amiss. Where the hell was Jacobs?

Late.

4 weeks ago –

The cemetery was at the top of a hill. The day was gray and the wind was bearing a chill Eddie couldn't shake out of his bones as it blew across the wide open land. It was a crappy day, in every sense, on the day he laid his uncle, the only family he had ever known, to rest. Being the only family member, Eddie stood alone at the head of the casket that was waiting to be lowered into the ground.

He hadn't been home to North Dakota in years. His relationship with his uncle, who was also the only parent he had ever known, had been somewhat strained ever since he had decided to spend his college years at the University of Minnesota - Duluth.

In retrospect, standing at the edge of the grave, it all seemed so petty. He could never explain how, after visiting the school once, he had been so drawn to that locale. No more could he explain his uncle's vehement opposition to him going there.

He loved him very much.

The man in the coffin was Dean Watson. He wasn't technically Eddie's uncle but had always preferred to be referred to as such. He and his wife had taken Eddie in as a baby. His biological parents had been little more than babies themselves when Eddie was born and were unable to raise a child on their own. Through the church they had found a couple to raise him, that being Dean and his late wife. She had died long ago, further than Eddie's memory could stretch. Eddie had never met his parents, but that's how his uncle had always wanted him to think of them, and so he did. But for as long as he could remember it had always just been the two of them. It was anyway until he left. Since then they had both been on their own.

In almost any other instance he would've heeded his uncle's advice to stay close for college, but something about that school and the North Shore had seeped into him. He thought constantly about how to get back there after that initial visit. And so he had gone, against the adamant wishes of the man who had raised him.

Once the decision had been made that he was going come hell or high water, his uncle had softened his position but Eddie knew he was never happy about it. He visited Eddie often, being forever concerned about his safety, about him being so far from home. Yet since the first year or two of school, Eddie had never made it back, not until the funeral.

The wind kicked up again and Eddie pulled his coat

around him tight. The pastor was saying some words but Eddie heard little of it. The funeral was attended by a nice smattering of friends and parishioners of the local congregation. He felt as though he had somewhat abandoned his uncle but was comforted by the show of support from the people that had surrounded him.

Eddie started to cry.

The house had burned down in the middle of the night. What started the fire was unable to be determined. In fact the only real information that Eddie was able to glean remained of no comfort at all. His uncle had not died in his sleep. At some point he had awakened and got out bed but had been unable to escape the inferno that the house had become.

Through his tears Eddie looked around at the faces of his fellow mourners but he looked without seeing. He was lost. The only family he had ever known was gone.

At that point, had Eddie had any cause for caution, he may have paid closer attention to the cast of characters present to mourn the passing of his uncle. He would have perhaps noted the man hanging at the back of the small gathering at the side of the grave.

And maybe he would have been more wary when he saw him at a bar back in Duluth donning a plaid shirt just a few days later.

Eddie left after the funeral and headed for home. He had some time off coming to him, so his return trip was made leisurely. He stopped in Bemidji and spent the night, utterly unaware of the fact that he would be back in this neck of the woods just a week later. He returned home and three days after laying his uncle to rest, he was back at work.

It was Wednesday and Wednesday was dwindling away.

Time was doing its thing and the clock was fighting it. Eddie was sitting at his desk, his thoughts mostly focused on what he might fix for dinner when he got home. Frozen pizza or pasta? He was back to his routine, and back to the daily decisions that plagued him.

Selling cars had fallen far from his mind. Selling had not been at the forefront of his brain for some time now. Not today, not yesterday, not for weeks. It had only fallen further since returning from the funeral. His mind, lately, was otherwise occupied. He would probably need to do something about that before long or both his job and his bank account could be in danger, but he was not quite ready yet to find the cause to care and it was almost quitting time. Anyway, if he were going to sell a car today he would have already sold it. Now it was all about due diligence. And if the big hand on the clock would ever find its way to twelve, and if the little hand could fumble its way to the six, Eddie would be on his way.

The wide-open spaces of the Duluth Ford Dealership echoed with the quiet. Through the big plate glass of the window, the falling sun sparkled in the mirrors of the floor models displayed in the middle of the showroom. Eddie kept one eye on the clock and was becoming mesmerized by the hum of the air exchange unit. The temperature inside was not that different from the actual temperature outside but here in wonderland the climate must remain constant and controlled. Nothing was left to chance or Mother Nature. The sound of high heels clicking on tile rang through the building as someone made their way across the large showroom. It was probably someone that worked there but it could have been a potential sale. Eddie didn't even bother to check, he was busy.

He was just beginning to entertain the exciting idea of foregoing the frozen pizza and stopping off at Pizza Luce on the way home to pick up a hot, fresh pie. It was then that he heard the beep of the overhead intercom popping into service.

A woman's voice said. "Eddie Watson to reception please, Eddie Watson, sales, to reception."

Eddie groaned. The owner of the voice was a woman named Sandra Jackson. Once upon a time, when people sometimes went out for drinks after work there had been a short period when they almost dated. Eddie had liked her but for some reason found the idea of letting someone into his life difficult. It was more than just a commitment issue. Eddie was a solitary man. Over time most of the people he socialized with had found partners and moved on from after work Happy Hours with co-workers. After an extended period of flakiness from Eddie, Sandra was no exception. She found a boyfriend and moved on as well. Eventually Eddie found himself doing things like going for pizza alone, just like he would probably do tonight. He and Sandra were still friendly enough but she wasn't calling him over to reception for a chat. Someone was going to make him work.

He hauled himself out of his chair and shambled his way over to the desk.

"What's up?"

"There's a guy in the west lot, wants you to show him some cars."

"I'm almost done, why don't you give it to Brooke, she's here for a couple hours still."

"He asked for you personally, Eddie."

"What?" Eddie asked, but Sandra just shrugged. He shook his head, turned away and headed for the lot.

Eddie saw the man immediately. He was short, portly and balding. The late afternoon sun was shining off the dome of his forehead. Perspiration was standing, slight, on his brow. Eddie didn't need him to lift his arms to know he would have pitted out his short-sleeve dress shirt. It was warm in the sun, but not that warm.

Eddie moved gracefully from his shamble into a confident erect stride. He didn't want to be there, he wanted to be on his way home, but this guy looked like he was just waiting to be talked into more vehicle then he could possibly need. Eddie was a good man, a quiet man, respectful and kind. He never quite understood the moral ambiguity that came over him when it was time to make a sale.

"Eddie Watson." He said, extending his hand to the little man. They shook and the man's hand was sweaty, just like Eddie knew it would be, but the guy was giving him a funny look.

"I know your name, Eddie," the guy said, the odd look

still in place on his round face.

"I guess you do, somebody referred me to you?"

"I suppose you could say that." The guy just let the words hang there.

The sun beat, the pavement warmed, and time droned on in silence. Eddie exhaled and gave a slight shake of his head, giving in. He was not so interested in a sale to start playing games with some knucklehead, not this late in the day.

"What can I do for you, sir?" Eddie asked through a smile that was patently false. For a second the guy just stared at him, smiling a dopey half-smile. Then just as sudden as this strange moment had come on in the first place, it passed and 'Baldy' launched into his story.

They all have their story.

It was a variation Eddie had heard a hundred times. He was looking for a new vehicle for work, construction of some nature. He must have filled some sort of executive role for the company because he looked as though he might cause great bodily harm to himself if he tried to swing a hammer. He went on and on about how he'd been using the same truck for twelve years now and 'boy howdy, if it weren't going to be difficult to put his baby to bed'. Over his years at this job Eddie had seen more than his fair share of men who loved their trucks above all, more than their wives, more than their kids, hell, even more than their own mothers. In general Eddie had never really felt like he fit in, and the whole truck lovin' demographic only added to those feelings but it was one count on which he didn't mind being the odd man out.

As he could tell the tale was wrapping up, Eddie began to lead him slowly back past the Explorers to the Expeditions. Eddie stopped before a sleek, jet-black, lease return. The low sun was gleaming off the metallic paint acting as a constant reminder that the day was getting long in the tooth quick.

If he had wanted to work harder, this would have been the point where he launched into his own shtick. He didn't really care though so he just let the truck do the talking.

Baldy let out a low whistle. "This baby might just be the

one that gets me over the old girl. She doesn't have black interior does she, that's just too damn hot in the summer."

"Naw, not black, cream and it's all leather." Eddie had to force the smile even more than usual. There was something about this guy that Eddie was pretty sure he didn't like. He couldn't quite decipher why, but when he had these sorts of feelings about clients it usually turned out to be something along the lines of bad credit and no financing, a lot of work and at the end of the day, no sale to show for it. He wasn't sure if that was what was happening here, but whatever it was it wasn't sitting well.

"All leather? Whoo-ee! Ain't that just the cat's ass, Eddie?" He leaned in and smacked Eddie on the back. Eddie almost drowned in the sudden overpowering odor of the man's cologne. It took everything he had not to gag. This deal was tiring and quick.

"Well would you like to see some other models?" Eddie sputtered through the cologne haze, just barely managing his gag reflex.

"No thankin' you Eddie, I do believe I'll take this bad boy for a ride."

"Great." Eddie said, false smile on the outside, dripping with sarcasm on the inside. "I'll just run in and grab the key." He turned back toward the building.

"You go on and do that Eddie *Watson*."

Eddie felt a strange sensation prickle at the bottom of his neck. "Will do," he said, but before he turned away from the man he asked one more thing. "Can I ask who referred you to me?"

"It was a friend of a friend. Go get the key, Eddie. We've got business to attend to."

With an unpleasant taste in his mouth left by the exchange, Eddie turned and walked back toward the building.

He crossed the threshold walking back into his own comfortable, controlled environment and shrugged off his little bout of unease. He'd be damned if he was going to let this little twerp ruin his day any more than he already had. Eddie thought about ditching on the whole thing while the guy was out on the test drive and letting Marty McIntyre mop it up. The thought brought a smile to his lips.

Eddie went to retrieve the keys from none other than Sandra Jackson. He walked up to the desk and waited for her to finish a call. Standing there in the cool conditioned air he gave an involuntary shudder. At least he told himself it was from the A/C, he wasn't about to admit that his little interaction with the weasel outside was getting to him. Sandra hung up the phone and then found the keys for him. As he was about to turn away he stopped.

"When that guy came in and asked for me, did he say anything else?"

"Nope, just asked if you were working and then pointed over to the lot where he'd meet you. Why?"

Eddie sat for a long moment wondering how he might answer that question. "No reason, just curious." He forced a smile and headed for the door.

The forced smile was still in place as he pushed open the door and stepped back into the orange light of the setting sun.

The smile faltered as he surveyed the lot around him. The guy was gone. Eddie walked to the Expedition they had been looking at, nothing. He walked all the way around it. Standing behind the car he looked up and down the lot, no sign of him. He walked down to the edge of the building and looked into the next lot, squinting into the low hanging sun.

The guy was gone.

It was all for the better probably, now he could get on to more pressing matters like his pizza. Still as he walked back into the dealership, dropped the keys and collected his personal stuff, he couldn't shake the odd feeling brought on by the short encounter.

Something wasn't sitting right.

To hell with it, it was nothing a little pizza couldn't fix.

He walked into Pizza Luce and it was hopping. He

spotted a free table towards the back by the stage. He made his way to the back squeezing between the tables and the backs of the folks bellied up to the bar. As he was squeaking by, he bumped a guy in a plaid shirt sitting at the bar and nearly spilled his drink.

"Sorry, man."

"Don't worry about it." The guy replied without even looking at him.

Eddie never gave the guy another moment of thought.

Not until much later anyway.

While he worked his way through his Luce Deluxe, a trio that called themselves 'The Planet of the Sheeps' were working their way through a few numbers on the little stage in the back. They weren't bad; they had a catchy little pop sound and a funny name that he liked. He saw that they would be playing again next week and thought about maybe trying to get a few of the guys to come out after work. A fleeting thought slipped by in which he considered asking the new girl that had moved in across the hall to come out. She had moved in a few weeks ago and he'd talked to her a couple of times, the likelihood of actually asking her to join him at a bar seemed slim though. He'd probably stick to his work friends. But could he really call them friends anymore? It made him think about the way life had gone for him. Had they all really gone their own ways over time, or had he just gone his? Why did he always have such a hard time keeping people in his life?

He let it go and then let himself go with the music, losing himself in it. For Eddie it was a welcomed reprieve from his life just lately. While a little escape may have been just what the doctor ordered in the short term, it would prove ill-advised in the long term. While he was lost in the moment, the guy in the plaid shirt left the bar unnoticed.

When he stepped out of the pizza place back onto the street an hour later, the sun had gone down and the wind off the lake had turned the air chilly. He pulled his windbreaker tight around him and set a brisk pace back to the apartment. In the lobby he checked his mail, all junk. No surprise there. He dumped the whole wad in the trash by the stairwell and made his way up to the second floor.

He dawdled for just a second outside his door looking across the hall at the apartment opposite his. The new girl lived there, Shannon was her name. She lived by herself and the few conversations they'd had while standing in the hallway was the closest thing to a friendship that Eddie had managed to kindle outside of work for quite some time. Again the thought of asking her on a date crossed his mind but he knew he was a ways off from working up that kind of confidence. He listened intently for any sign of her on the other side of her door, the babble of the TV, anything. He resisted the urge to cross the hall and stand by her door. That sort of move had a creepiness factor involved with it that he wasn't quite ready to ascend to. He heard nothing and turned back to his own door.

He slid his key home in the lock of the door marked 2C and opened the portal to his lonesome existence. The darkness was complete, but it was strange because he almost always left a lamp on in the living room. Stepping inside he flipped the light switch in the little entry hall.

Nothing happened.

This is weird. He thought.

Then the door was ripped out of his hand and slammed shut behind him. Something crashed into his jaw with what felt like the force of a locomotive. As Eddie slumped against the wall of his entryway his nostrils were assaulted by a familiar, overpowering stench of cologne.

"Hello, Eddie *Watson.*" The darkness muttered.

Eddie's eyelids cracked but the darkness did not. He was sure his eyes were open but the world around him was in a blackout. His head ached at a constant dull roar but spiked in intensity with every thud of his heartbeat. He accepted the pain though, satisfied that his heart was indeed still beating and therefore he could still count himself as a member of the living.

For a moment disorientation and confusion enveloped him, then he remembered opening his apartment door, being smothered by that awful cologne, and taking a fist to the jaw. The time in between then and now had been lost in a stupefied haze.

His eyes were adjusting a bit, but only dull shadows presented themselves. Wherever he was, the absence of light was almost total. He was lying on some sort of cot. He moved first his arms and then his legs and they moved freely. He sat up and swung his feet to the floor then attempted, successfully, to stand. He took a step but his equilibrium hadn't quite caught up to him and he fell hard to the floor. The pain in his head had been receding slowly but returned now with a vengeance. Lying on the floor waiting for the pain to abate at least a little, he realized that perhaps his equilibrium wasn't so far off after all. He just didn't have his sea legs. The whole world rocked in lazy time as he made the astute judgment that he was on a boat.

He managed to get his feet back under him, this time compensating for the gentle sway. Moving slowly, with his hand pressed out before him, he felt out the walls of this makeshift cell. He found a handle for the door but couldn't make it budge. He stumbled back to the general vicinity of the cot, located it, and collapsed back onto it, confusion for the moment still displacing most of the fear that was certain to be coming.

He lay there for an indiscernible period of time, attempting to collect his thoughts, but had a difficult time locking onto anything that could be translated into something resembling coherence. At some point later he heard the lock being thrown and the door slid open. The dim light thrown from the hallway was still enough to blind him. Through squinted eyes he saw a shadow enter the doorway. He recognized the man by his short, squat silhouette even before the cologne reached his nose.

"Get up, Eddie."

Eddie did as he was told.

The man moved out of the way, gunmetal glimmering in the low light as he invited Eddie toward the door. Eddie passed him then received a hard shove in the back that sent him reeling through the door. He was hustled up a small flight of steel stairs and emerged into a pale perfect moonlight on the deck of a small ship. The ship was moored at a pier. Eddie was directed down to the dock then put into a vehicle and driven away.

Time remained beyond his grasp and an indeterminable amount of time later, deep in a wooded labyrinth, they pulled to the end of a long driveway. The vehicle he was in stopped and Eddie was unceremoniously yanked from the car. As he came out into the night, Eddie caught his first glimpse of the house and his confusion deepened.

Whoever owned this place was loaded. The house left no question in that regard, yet it had a quaint feel about it. Eddie was no stranger to the fact that people with money sometimes enjoyed having a secret hideaway home way up in the northern reaches of the state, where they felt isolated from the world. A place where they could go about whatever business it is that the extremely wealthy, and often eccentric, go about. But usually these people would build the biggest tallest structure within miles, with giant glass windows that looked as though they stretched into to the heavens. A home that smacked of affluence and the American dream, of the ability to conquer the land and sky and anything else the heart desired.

This house was different.

It had been built fairly recently and it was obvious to the naked eye that no expense had been spared, but it still managed to exude the feel of an old-fashioned farmhouse. Albeit, a large and expensive one.

Another sharp shove planted right between the shoulder blades knocked him off balance and brought Eddie back down to earth, quite literally. He landed hard at the foot of wooden steps leading up onto a large open porch that wrapped around the far corner of the house. The hard gravel pack ran small but intense scratches into the palms of his hands. He managed to haul himself up just in time to take another shove in the back that propelled him up the steps and onto the porch. Eddie found himself standing in front of a large door that had been painted red. Somewhere in the deep recesses of his mind he recalled a snippet about red doors helping to ward off evil. He couldn't be sure but he had an idea this might be somebody's idea of a joke. Dead center in the door was the perfect, true to form, gold doorknocker. The shape of the knocker, however, caused a cold chill to spill down his back.

The house was indeed a beautiful nod to, and a representation of a time in our culture that may be lost. A time when the word neighbor still meant more than just someone who lived in a close proximity to you, but the skull and cross-bones that comprised the knocker, shining golden in the moonlight, spoke to the truth of the danger within.

He saw the door waver in his vision a second before he realized that he was about to faint. His mind, still with no reasonable explanation as to how the hell he had even come to be here, was giving up the ghost and shutting things down. The guy with the cologne caught him and held him up with a strength Eddie wouldn't have expected. He could feel his breath, hot and close, on the back of his neck. It made him want to vomit.

"Go on in, Eddie. No need to knock," the guy said from behind him, and Eddie could hear the wicked smile that he was unable to see.

He opened the door and stepped into the front hall.

It looked exactly as he might have expected it would from the exterior. No house of horrors the second he crossed the threshold. Not even close. Candles were burning, warming the front hall. A modest, yet elegant, dining room with a table set for eight opened off to his left. To his right a stairway led away to the next level, complete with an ornate blue and white runner on the stairs.

He was prodded down the hall but the force and malice that Baldy had displayed earlier seemed to have lessened. At the end of the hall the kitchen opened off to the left. Here Eddie saw the floor to ceiling windows that had been absent from the front of the house. They did not enter the kitchen but went to the right, down a short flight of stairs to a landing that then turned left onto another short flight of stairs. These stairs opened onto a room that was enormous. Eddie realized that from the front of the house you had no idea how far it sprawled. The room looked as though the design was based on a medieval great room. Dominating the focal wall was a giant fireplace surrounded by bookshelves. In front of the fireplace, a plush fur rug and two high-backed chairs.

"Ahh, our guest has arrived." The voice came from one of the high-backed chairs. The voice was rich, warm and inviting, but the warm tonal qualities did not help to keep Eddie's blood from running cold.

"Come sit."

Eddie looked to Baldy who seemed far less imposing in this room. He motioned for him to take the seat opposite the voice. The walk across that expansive room lasted an eternity. Eddie found his way to the chair and sat, at first unable to even hazard a glance at the chair across from him. For a moment he watched the fire and soaked up the power of the heat and the dancing colors of the licking flames. Then at last, he turned and faced the man.

Eddie was well beyond having any rational expectation of the situation he found himself in, but still he was caught off guard by the well-dressed man seated before him.

"Welcome, Mr. Watson. I assume that your trip here was satisfactory?" the man asked.

Eddie was glad he was sitting or he was certain he would have fallen over. He was reeling. His mouth was dry which would've made speech difficult even if he were able to think of anything to say. The dancing shadows from the firelight made it hard to focus.

"Would you like something to drink?" he asked, after what must have been a long silence. Eddie's sense of time seemed to be slipping on him as well.

"That would be great," he managed. His throat felt scratchy and it hurt to talk.

"Mr. Mason, would you please prepare a tea for Mr.

Watson?"

"Sure thing, boss." Baldy replied from the doorway then he disappeared back up the stairs towards the kitchen.

The man stood and crossed over to the fire. He reached into a bin to the right of the fireplace and produced a log that he then tossed onto the fire with a precision only possible from a practiced hand. Eddie stared at the sparking embers that exploded from the bed of coals and then drifted up the flue.

"I'm sure you have many questions for me," the man said still standing by the fire, lost in the flames for a moment it seemed. "And maybe you will get some answers, although most of the answers you are likely to get will be for questions you don't even know you have yet. Does that sound like a riddle? Perhaps it won't for long." He paused but never looked away from the fire. The flames snapped and crackled and drew Eddie's confused attention as well. "Unfortunately, any answers you get are incidental. What will be vital to your well-being are the answers you give to me. My name is Sullivan or at least it will be for the purposes of any business between the two of us. My apologies for any mistreatment you may have had to endure on your way here. Mason is not always the most nurturing soul, but he does always get the job done and in your case we had to take a few precautions."

There was no illumination as to the necessity of said precautions and Eddie was still not able to muster any coherent questions, nor the fortitude to ask them. The man went on.

"I intend you no harm. I want you to know that and I hope you can believe me. I'm not a cruel man. However, I need some things from you Eddie, and I intend to get them."

The warm, ingratiating tone never left his voice but the malevolence beneath it was clearly apparent.

"I don't see how I can possibly help you." Eddie managed to squeak.

The man, Sullivan as he was to be known to Eddie anyway, watched him intently for a moment. A look of genuine curiosity marked his gaze. Eddie had no clue what was happening behind those eyes. Much to Eddie's dismay the curiosity faded and was replaced by a malicious, knowing grin.

"Eddie, do you know who I am?" His voice held a lilting, conspiratorial, *we're just old buddies* quality, but Eddie knew right then that no matter what happened or what this man said, he was not to be trusted, ever.

"How could I?" Eddie asked, his voice grated but it was coming back a bit at least.

"Maybe you couldn't, but then again maybe…" He trailed off but his eyes never left Eddie's, the shadow thrown by the fire danced on their faces.

"I'm sorry, I don't understand." Eddie said feeling weak under Sullivan's gaze.

"No," his eyes remained on Eddie, full of scrutiny. Then he turned back to the fire. "I suppose you wouldn't."

Mason stepped back into the room with the tea and set it down next to Eddie. Then he stepped back to his post by the door. Eddie eyed the tea with an unveiled yearning. Sullivan gave him a slight nod and Eddie picked it up and sipped. It was warm and soothing, a welcome contradiction to the last twenty-four hours or however long it had been. Sullivan said nothing for a long time, just stared down at the fire. Eddie drank a majority of the tea down in the first few gulps. He watched the fire as well and began to get lost in it. His thoughts began to drift.

"I love fire. I could watch it for hours," Sullivan said in a voice almost as soothing as the tea. Eddie took a few more quick sips, nearly emptying the cup while he stared into the fire. His eyelids grew weary and started to droop. "You could get lost in the fire couldn't you?" Sullivan asked in that same soothing voice.

"Yes." Eddie said, his voice coming from far away.

"Are you getting lost in the fire, Eddie?"

He nodded.

"Good. Are you feeling a little sleepy?"

"Yes." Eddie's voice was distant now even to his own ears. His brain felt fuzzy. He struggled for a moment to find the words he was looking for but eventually snagged them.

"Something…in the tea?"

"Yes, Eddie. It's called Amobarbital. It will help relax you. Help you to remember."

"Remember what?"

"All in good time." The firelight danced in front of them continuing to hold their attention. "Can I ask you a few questions, Eddie?"

"Sure." Eddie was alert but felt outside his body. He was still mentally aware that this man was not to be trusted but he seemed to have shrugged off all stress.

"What's your name?"

"Eddie Watson."

"Good, what do you do for a living?"

"I sell cars."

"Very good." Sullivan paused and they both stared into the fire for a piece. In the space between, Eddie's breathing slowed and his eyelids grew heavy. Sullivan turned his hard quizzical gaze upon Eddie but he hardly noticed. He was drifting and was far too distant to realize that Sullivan's focus had intensified upon him. Had he been more alert he may have even noticed that those hard, hateful eyes were veiling a slight anxiousness as Sullivan voiced his next question. "Can I ask you about your uncle?" Eddie nodded, slow and deliberately. "Did your uncle ever tell you about a man called Plundering Pike?"

A childish smile broke on Eddie's lips. "Of course."

"What do you know about him?"

"He was a pirate."

"Indeed he was." Now Sullivan's lips curled slowly back into that wicked grin. "What did he tell you about this Plundering Pike?"

"We talked about him a lot when I was little. It was my favorite bedtime story. Pike had a treasure. It was hidden somewhere on the North Shore. I always wanted to find it when I was a kid."

"Your uncle talked about Pike's treasure?"

"Yep…"

"What did he tell you about it?"

"He said we could never go looking for it because the North Shore was dangerous." The smile slipped from his face, his eyes were barely open but a look of consternation had shadowed his features.

"What's wrong, Eddie?"

"I never remembered that before. He thought the North Shore was dangerous. That's why he didn't want me to go to Duluth for college." His tongue was getting thick and speech was becoming difficult.

"See, I told you we could help you remember. What else did he tell you? Did he ever talk about how to find Pike's treasure?" Eddie nodded, but now his head bobbed as he lost motor control. A terrifying grin spread across Sullivan's face but Eddie didn't see it. His eyes had slipped shut. "What did he tell you, about how to find it?"

Eddie managed to raise a finger to his lips. "Shhh. It's a secret. We don't talk about secrets."

"What do you mean? What secret, Eddie?"

"I told you we don't talk about secrets." Again he managed to raise his hand. This time he attempted a snap. "Poof, now the secret is gone."

The grin slipped from Sullivan's face.

"What are you talking about?"

"Secrets are like treasure. They need to be hidden." Again he attempted to snap but with even less success. "Gone…"

"I don't understand."

"My uncle took the secrets. He took them and he hid them." With a very deliberate effort Eddie tapped an unsteady finger against his temple then his hand fell to his lap.

Sullivan sat back in his chair and eyed a barely cognizant Eddie. A look of frustration drifted across his features as he realized what Eddie was saying. "Are you sleepy, Eddie?"

"Yep."

"Good. Go to sleep." His voice was sharp, no longer soothing.

And Eddie floated away but as he was slipping under the blanket of sleep he heard Sullivan say one more thing, presumably to the man he had called Mason but who Eddie still thought of as Baldy.

"I think his uncle told him what we need to know but he used hypnosis to bury it. You're going to have to get it out of him, by any means necessary."

There may have been more but Eddie didn't hear it. The darkness came for him and he slipped down beneath it.

He opened his eyes in the utter black, again.

It might have been the fifth or sixth time he had returned to consciousness in such a fashion. Reality was askew. Time had slipped and somehow become inconstant.

Any possible measure of days had been lost. The only demarcation of time was the occasional appearance of his captors. It wasn't just the lack of light that was keeping his head fuzzy either. When his captors did show their faces, it was usually Mason and he never came without the tea. At first Eddie had spit it out but when you learn something the hard way you learn it fast, and Eddie never spit it out again. There was no shortage of tea it seemed and also no shortage of questions. The questions varied but at some point they would always return to Plundering Pike and his treasure. The obsession with some children's story was beyond him. But so was everything else that was happening.

He sat up on his cot but then stopped short. Something within his environment had changed.

The darkness was complete as always but some indecipherable quality of his senses was differing from the norm. He settled on the quality of sound, it was all he really had to go on. He realized that there was no one outside the door of his cell; he had become accustomed to the small sounds a sentry would make out there. Then what had roused him?

A gunshot.

And then another, followed by the return of fire. It sounded far away, but moments later he heard running on the decks above him. More gunfire, again it stopped and the quiet fell once more. Eddie sat still and waited.

Then he heard movement.

Someone was descending below deck. He could hear them moving down the corridor, moving towards his cell. Whoever it was stopped outside his door. On either side of the metal door they both listened to the absence of sound from the far side. Then the latch was thrown, the door swung open and Eddie saw a new silhouette in sharp relief of the light behind it. It was Jacobs' silhouette but Eddie wouldn't know that for some time. The glare from the hall split through his head like someone had taken an axe to it and he passed out again.

4

Morning, June 6th
Itasca State Park

Jacobs had never been late before.

He'd picked a hell of a time to break with tradition. Seeing the guy in the fishing hat, Mr. Plaid Shirt from the bar in Duluth, outside his window brought Eddie around to the realization that they had found him. Why hadn't they attempted to take him yet? He realized that was probably precisely what was happening at this very moment. All at once his head was assaulted by converging thoughts, all screaming at the top of their lungs, demanding attention. Eddie had been standing at the window watching the guy in the hat pass. He stepped back and let the curtain fall back into place just as the guy glanced right up at where he had been standing a second before.

He stood, pressed tight to the wall at the side of the window. He couldn't bring himself to look again, not just yet. He tried to regain control of his breathing.

The door swung open behind him.

He whirled fast bringing the gun up as he spun. His instincts and reflexes had improved by quantum leaps over the last few weeks, but still, he never stood a chance. Before he could even process who or what had come through the door, the gun was ripped from his hands.

He found himself staring down the barrel of his own weapon.

His eyes moved slowly from the gun, up the arm, and finally resting on the pearly white teeth of Jacobs' smile.

"Come on, Eddie, you don't really want to kill me do you?" Jacobs asked. Eddie wavered as the deceleration of adrenaline left him reeling and his limbs feeling like jelly.

"I think it's the other way around, you almost gave me a heart attack." He managed to sputter.

Jacobs' smile faltered. "Why do you have the gun?"

"The guy in the fishing hat outside...I know him."

Jacobs stepped to the window and scanned the area. His body and movements were loose and fluid per usual, but his left hand had crept towards his right ribcage. "He was out here?"

"Yeah, he was right... He's gone?" Eddie stepped next to Jacobs at the window.

"You know him?" Jacobs asked.

"I don't actually know him but I've seen him before. The same guy was sitting at the bar I was at the night they took me."

Jacobs thought for the briefest of moments and then he engaged. "We're leaving right now. You ready?"

"My stuff...."

"Forget it. Anything else I need to know?"

"There was a Yukon that drove by," Eddie said in a daze. "It made me nervous." He felt there was more to add, but he didn't know what. Instead he just shrugged.

"Okay, pay attention, Eddie. This is happening right now. I'm going to walk out that door, straight out to the road. You stay right behind me. If anyone moves to you, tell them to stop and let them see the gun. Once, only once, and if they don't listen, shoot them."

Before Eddie could find his voice to say anything, Jacobs turned to the door and unbuttoned the three buttons of the Hawaiian shirt he was sporting over his undershirt. He swung open the door and with an easy comfort, walked out towards the road. Eddie told his legs to move but like his mouth, they also seemed to be the victim of some faulty wiring. After an interminable amount of very weighty seconds, the order went through and Eddie stepped back out of the cabin and into the sunny morning.

Seconds after Jacobs walked onto the road the white Yukon screamed back around the bend. In one fluid motion Jacobs flipped back his shirt and drew two semi-automatic Glocks from the crisscrossed shoulder holsters that had been hidden by the loose-fitting Hawaiian shirt. It stopped Eddie short. He looked at Jacobs standing, guns drawn, in the middle of the road. The picture of serenity, he looked so calm and peaceful, except for the guns.

The quiet, vivid, picture-perfect morning moment hung on for another second. The sound of the Yukon's engine seemed far away. The call of birds was crisp and clear in Eddie's ears. He could not force his mind to accept what his heart knew was coming.

Then the serenity was broken.

The brakes of the Yukon screamed as the driver locked them up. The air filled with the acrid smell of rubber burning on the asphalt drive. As the truck came to a screeching halt the driver's door and the right rear passenger door swung open. Jacobs did not flinch. Eddie took it all in, unable to move.

The thunder of gunfire filled the air.

Eddie's body shook. He was flinching with each resounding report. He knew he should move, do something, but he was paralyzed. He couldn't even take cover. Thoughts of cover made him feel like a coward as he watched Jacobs standing tall unloading into the Yukon. The sounds of shattering glass were everywhere now as well. Jacobs had done his best to train Eddie well, and Eddie had been catching on, taking well to the training, but this was too much. There had not been enough time to be prepared for something like this.

Just as suddenly as it had started, the gunfire stopped and an eerie silence fell. Eddie could see the driver of the Yukon slumped on the ground not moving, blood pooling around him. He could not see anything on the far side of the truck. Jacobs was still standing in the middle of the road, guns extended but silent.

Eddie tried to take a step but he couldn't move. He tried to call to Jacobs but nothing came out. Jacobs lowered his weapons and that was when Eddie heard the crashing in the bushes to his left.

He managed to rotate his body in that direction enough to see the fisherman pounding up the trail. In his right hand the metal of the blade on the knife he carried, gleamed. Eddie didn't know quite how to feel as he realized that the guy was angling towards Jacobs and not him. It was like a wave of momentary relief, then being baked in pure cowardice. Jacobs spoke, clear and calm, but all sounds were coming off amplified to Eddie.

"Eddie, you've got to take him."

Eddie felt and remembered the gun in his own hand at the same time. It felt heavy, too heavy. Eddie heard Jacobs' empty clips clanging to the ground as he tried to reload.

Eddie saw the fisherman.

Eddie saw Jacobs reloading. Still calm, still cool.

He was not going to make it. The gap was closing too quickly. The knife was coming up. Eddie finally found himself. In spite of the seemingly absurd weight of the weapon he managed to raise it. He leveled it and lined the sight.

At 9:53 a.m. the gun bucked once in Eddie's hand.

Interlude

An excerpt from
'Mysterious Waters:
Tales of the Great Lakes'

Shiver Me Timber
Lake Superior

On a quiet summer night, small waves lap at the sides of a solitary luxury sailing yacht. It is the only vessel for miles atop the vast, silent, freshwater lake. The name adorning the stern of the boat is 'Shiver Me Timber'. The slightest of lake winds breeze across the empty deck and there is not a soul in sight. None of the lights in the cabin below are illuminated. While there may be no lights ablaze down in the cabin, emanating from the dark are more sounds of lapping water. It's only about ankle deep but gaining depth as the boat takes on more and more of the advancing lake. It sloshes against the cabinets in the beautiful galley but is not yet deep enough to submerge the two dead bodies on the floor. A man and woman lie amidst the slow flood filling the cabin, their blood mixing with the water as it rises up to take them under, into the depths of Mother Superior.

To begin to grasp what may have happened aboard the Shiver Me Timber that fateful night we must go back, back a generation to another night and another ship sailing that same lake. Back to a cargo freighter called the Angelina.

The Angelina was a freighter owned by timber baron D.B. Allan. It was on the last leg of a journey from the port of

Rochester on Lake Ontario through the chain of great lakes and on to Duluth. While in the service of her owner the Angelina carried all sorts of cargo, but on this night she was transporting a particularly precious freight. On board was a young French woman named Amelie who was on her way from France to Minnesota to be wed to Allan's son, D.B Allan Jr. But the Angelina never reached Duluth.

The journey was interrupted by a marauder known as Plundering Pike.

Pike was somewhat notorious throughout the great lakes region. He was a thief and a smuggler; a pirate. Pike and his crew sailed the lakes in the early half of the 20th century collecting their booty. But they weren't stealing gold or jewels or any of the other treasures normally attributed to pirates. Plundering Pike was plundering lumber. He was a Timber Pirate. While the thievery of trees may sound absurd it was actually quite a lucrative trade. Pike and his crew would clear-cut tons of acreage, from both federal and privately owned lands. Then they would ship their haul to an illegal saw mill that he owned located in Michigan's Upper Peninsula where it would be processed.

For years Pike had been feuding with the Allan family and stealing their timber. Pike began attacking some of the family's other business interests as well, not restricting his plunder to the timber trade. The two factions waged a war of sorts back and forth for almost a decade. But something changed the night the Angelina was taken.

Pike used a tactic called 'Moon-Cussing' to take the freighter. Moon-Cussing involved rearranging guide lights in order to get ships to run aground. The Captain of the Angelina realized that they had been duped, but not until it was too late. He changed course and moved back out to deeper waters but the hull had been breached and the ship was taking on water. The crew was in a frenzy attempting to handle the situation when Pike and his men boarded. Pike used the ensuing chaos to his advantage and took control of the ship. They pilfered the cargo as was to be expected, but did allow everyone on board to evacuate including the younger Allan's wife to be. The crew was also permitted to offload all of Amelie's belongings as well, all except for a painting by Dutch artist Piet Mondrian.

The stealing of the painting was mysterious and out of character. It was the first and only time that Pike had resorted to the theft of personal property in his feud with Allan. Whatever his reason for taking it, stealing the painting set an unfathomable and historic course of events into motion.

The Mondrian was Amelie's most prized possession. It was a parting gift from her father who had remained back in France and losing it broke her heart. She was able to convince her new husband that if he were to set aside the feud and help her campaign for the return of the painting through the media, she would then be able to curb Pike's targeted attacks on their businesses. One might wonder how Amelie thought she would be able to appeal to Pike and quell his rebellious nature toward them, but Allan did acquiesce. A very public effort to have the painting returned commenced. For several months the attempts to acquire its return seemed futile. Pike did not respond at all. But after some time it turned out those attempts had not been made in vain. And not only were they not made in vain, but Amelie delivered on her end of the bargain as well.

On an early fall night Pike appeared in public for the last time.

In a harbor barroom in Grand Marais he met a man named Brian Anders. For several hours the two men engaged in intense conversation and then left the bar. Roughly two weeks later, without explanation, the Mondrian was returned. And not only did Pike never steal another thing from the Allans following the painting's return, as far as anyone knows he never sailed again.

Later when it became clear Pike's marauding days were over, that he had effectively retired, such a turn of events began to raise questions. Not the least of which were surrounding the man he had met in the bar that night, Brian Anders. The Anders family had long been heavily involved in the visual art world, brokering deals for galleries, developing relationships between patrons and artists, and sometimes commissioning works themselves. That Pike would meet with Anders before returning the Mondrian, based on the reputation that his lineage boasted, followed a certain strain of logic but in the end only raised more questions. One popular rumor was that perhaps Pike had somehow commissioned a fake painting to be returned to the Allans, but there was no proof to corroborate such a theory and it did nothing to alleviate questions as to why the painting might have been important to him in the first place.

Brian Anders, unfortunately, was no help in bringing any clarity to the situation. It took some time to come to realize that Pike's Great Lakes reign had ended, and by the time anyone thought to ask Anders about their last conversation he was nowhere to be found. Apparently he had picked up and disappeared not long after that meeting with Pike.

While not a satisfying ending to the tale, for many years it seemed that was, indeed, how it ended; unresolved. The Allans asserted that they had no insight as to why Pike had retired and the only other players who may have been able to shed light on the situation were gone. Pike had become a recluse, his whereabouts unknown. Anders had vanished, and the Allans had moved on with their lives and with their business.

But it seems that the story may have continued on after all. The narrative was picked up many years later and only after the sinking of the Shiver Me Timber. Again, the many questions raised, outnumbered the answers. The yacht and the unfortunate souls that had been aboard were recovered by the Coast Guard not long after the boat was sunk. The bodies were initially difficult to identify but authorities were eventually able to determine that they were a married couple from Grand Marais. Little else was known about them. They seemed to be loners, no friends, not even any real acquaintances. While their solitary lifestyle may have originally seemed odd but little more, it quickly became much more intriguing.

The same night the 'Timber' sank, a small massacre had taken place in the office of a lawyer named Victor Leland. The office had been ransacked and three of his staffers present at the time were murdered. Leland himself was not among the dead but was nonetheless never heard from again.

An investigation into that case later revealed that the couple murdered on the yacht had once retained Leland to be their lawyer. Leland had aided the couple in changing their names but no information regarding their identities prior to the name change ever came to light. This allowed some conspiracy theories to begin hatching. When it came out that another former client of Leland's was the man known as Plundering Pike, those theories caught fire. It was quickly assumed that the couple aboard the yacht had been Pike's son and daughter in-law, and that their deaths were connected to what happened at Leland's office.

Adding to the rampant, wildfire speculation was the Shiver Me Timber itself.

The sailing vessel had been reported as stolen little more than a month earlier by none other than D.B. Allan Jr.

Had Pike's son and his wife, been murdered on a yacht owned by the family's former rival? Had they stolen the yacht to resurrect old animosities and been killed by someone connected to the Allans for their efforts? The name of the yacht itself generated mysterious theories of its own. The Allans were a timber family but 'shiver me timber' was a phrase long associated with pirates. Did one have anything to do with the other? Was the name of the yacht a coincidence or some macabre joke by the Allans who had concocted the theft of the boat in order to finally put an end to an old smoldering feud?

There was never any plausible proof to back any of these stories (some of which were floated in the press but many more as gossip at elitist cocktail parties) and today they remain tall tales. Whatever transpired leading up to that night, and the reasons behind it, we'll never know or understand. Shortly after the sinking of the Shiver Me Timber, D.B. Allan Jr. was killed in a car accident. Allan was gone, the Pike legacy had come to a brutal and abrupt end, and Victor Leland and Brian Anders were missing and presumed dead.

What remains are many questions with few answers and Mother Superior is generally reticent to whisper up her secrets. It seems that whatever led to the tragedy aboard the Shiver Me Timber that night will forever remain a Great Lakes Mystery.

Part 3

Plundering Pike, Brigand's Woods and Old Farmer's Road

1

Death hung about him like a foul scent.

An odor a dog might pick up, but then cower from. Tucking tail until the owner of the dank smell passed. A human might not actually smell it but they would be aware of it just the same. He was the kind of man that always earned a wide berth on a sidewalk, the sort of man that might cause one to cross to the other side of the street for no reason but to avoid him.

It was nothing in his looks.

His appearance was normal as those things go. He was a large man, maybe a bit intimidating at first glance, but he dressed well, kept his hair cut close and his face shaved. It was not his appearance that put one off but the sense of the darkness underneath the façade. You may not actually be able to smell or see it, but he had blood on his hands, the blood of many. It was a stench that couldn't be washed out. So he carried it always, but today it was fresh.

The boys he'd left at Split Rock were young, neither of them probably twenty. They were innocent and did not deserve to die. But die they did. Sometimes being in the wrong place at the wrong time got you a slap on the wrist, other times it got you killed. It was all the same to Quentin Bellows. He had his orders and orders were followed. Those kids weren't the first to be poking around in the woods.

The story of Brigand's Woods and Old Farmer's Road had been a whispered legend in these parts for decades. Long before Sullivan had brought Quentin or any of the others to this godforsaken place, kids had poked around these woods chasing legends or tail or both. It was how it went with the young. They came and they went, playing their silly games, never knowing how close death was. Never knowing that it watched them always, marking their progress to be sure they never got too close to any of the secrets that were actually hidden out in those woods, at the end of Old Farmer's Road.

Those boys hadn't the first clue about what they were doing. They were fumbling around hunting half-truths, but they had found more than they ever should have. No one should have gotten as close as they did. Sullivan was none too pleased to find out that a bunch of teenagers had stumbled upon them.

Quentin was large in stature. He bore death in his own hands and a blade he had carried since he was a young man. And still he shuddered at the thought of what Sullivan's reaction would be to the fact that one of those teenagers had gotten away.

These were the thoughts that darkened his demeanor as dawn broke on June 7th. The motion of the boat rocked him in his bunk. Normally the sounds of water slapping the hull and the seesaw created by the soft rolling waves would have been comforting, but this morning it bore only stress as it shook the anxiousness outward from within him. Loose ends were meant to be tied, and somehow he had left a whopping dangler.

It had been easy to find out who the other kid was. When it came out yesterday that two of his best friends had been killed and he hadn't come home, Jimmy Swansby's parents hitched a ride on the circus train that was the media and told anyone who would listen, who their son was, and what he looked like. The 'who' of the missing third kid was easy.

The 'where' on the other hand was not so simple.

He hauled himself out of his cramped berth and went up on deck. Morning's first light was slowly creeping on the eastern horizon. It was nothing more than a lighter shade of black where the darkness of the lake met the darkness of the sky, but still a sign of the day to come.

Jimmy Swansby.

A damn kid.

A damn kid who had been smart enough to disappear after what he'd seen. Quentin had put a guy on the Swansby kid's house in hopes he'd come home like a frightened bird back to its mama's nest but so far there had been no sign of him.

The anger began its slow pulse deep in his veins.

It made his head hot and his forearms burn as he clenched his fists down on the deck rail. No one made a fool out of Quentin Bellows, or at least no one that lived for long afterward. The kid was going to have to die. He unsheathed the knife from the scabbard tied tight around his massive thigh. It was the same knife that had carved the sign of Plundering Pike into the arms of the two young boys just barely one day ago.

An X with a dagger stabbed down through the middle of it.

Like Quentin himself smelled of death so did the knife he held in his hand. The heft of the hilt was reassuring as the anger poured through him. The blade shined in the dull, first light of the day. Not a trace of blood could be found on it for Bellows cleaned and cared well for his tools. A small joy bit through the anger as he thought about the sharp edge of the blade sliding easily through the skin of Jimmy Swansby's neck.

He was reassured.

The knife slid home in its sheath. The same as it had one day ago, after dispatching the two young men. The same as it had six years ago when he finished with Richard Devlin.

The thought of Devlin simultaneously chilled his blood and made it boil, for he had gotten the best of Quentin Bellows. Devlin had traded in secrets. The secret he sold was that of Old Farmer's Road, the myth, the two-bit fantasy known to every high school kid north of Duluth.

The real secret, the secret he kept, he had worn on a chain around his neck every day of his adult life – a skeleton key. But on his last day alive when Quentin shook the life from him with his bare hands, the chain and the key were absent from his person and never found. An unfortunate circumstance for Bellows as the key was necessary to unlock the real secret of Old Farmer's Road.

His boss was bound and determined to have that which had eluded him for many years, so they had returned to Brigand's Woods. This time they had come with much less and had already lost more. The Swansby kid had seen the old farmhouse and still escaped with his life.

Bellows took a deep breath, letting the fresh lake air fill his lungs. He did not look forward to seeing Sullivan again. He wanted to have something to take to him, something to ease the anger caused by his mistake.

His phone chirped, pulling him back to the present. He didn't need to check the ID. There would only be one person that would be calling him.

"This is Bellows," he said, answering the phone.

"You have our latest acquisition?"

"Of course."

"Good… bring him to me."

The line went dead.

He smiled as he terminated the call. There had been no mention of Swansby. For the moment it was going to be let go.

He went down into the storage bays buried in the bow of the boat. There were four bays and the smell of aged rot was heavy in the air. He released the lock and swung open the door of one of them. It was dark inside but he could still see Kirk Hanlon's wide, horrified eyes.

He met them with a terrifying smile.

2

Eddie woke and physically peeled his eyelids apart. He had slept hard and they had adhered to one another. He rubbed the crust from his eyes and sat up in bed. For a moment he couldn't recall where he was or how he had come to arrive in such a foreign spot. The room was well kept but the dated wallpaper betrayed its age. He blinked away the foggy remnants of the night's hold and he began to make sense of his current whereabouts.

Jacobs had delivered him to this little cabin after they had somehow escaped Itasca and the carnage they had left behind there. Jacobs had brought him here, to another cabin, in yet another wood. The call of the surrounding forest was soothing though and he sat that way, still half tucked into the bed, and took it in.

After a moment he pushed the covers back and stepped out of bed. The floors creaked along with his bones. Yesterday had taken its toll on him. He walked gingerly into the main room of the cabin working out the initial aches and pains of waking. The cabin was small and Eddie knew at once that he had it all to himself.

Jacobs was absent again.

A small shudder shivered through him, he was not up to a repeat of the previous day so he could only hope the similarities to the start wouldn't play out to the same violent end. Whatever the situation turned out be this morning, it was too much to digest before coffee was given an opportunity to spell the clutches of sleep. He crossed into the small kitchenette off the main room of the cabin and saw the note taped to the coffee maker.

'I shall return' signed J.

Comforting, just as long as there would be no maniac

gunmen arriving on the doorstep intent on killing him in the interim.

On the tail of that last thought he heard the sound of an approaching engine cut the quiet solace of the morning.

It would be Jacobs returning, of that there was little doubt but Eddie stepped back into the bedroom and grabbed his 9mm just the same. He walked back to the front door and pulled the shade on the window next to it aside and watched the vehicle approach.

It was indeed Jacobs, or at least it was the car he had left in. Eddie caught a glimpse of him behind the wheel before the sun caught the windshield, effectively converting it into a mirror. He also had noticed that there was someone in the passenger seat but couldn't make out who it was before the reflection blinded him to the interior.

He unlatched the door and stepped out onto the porch. The gun hung loose at his side but he remained cautious, ready if necessary. The car pulled to a stop just before the steps up to the porch where Eddie stood. He put his arm up, the one that was not attached to the hand holding the gun, in attempt to cut the glare from the windshield. The driver's door opened and Jacobs's familiar face came into view. He was smiling. The passenger door opened and a woman stepped out.

It was another familiar face.

"Hi, Eddie," she said.

Words eluded him. He stood on the porch stupefied and gawked at the pretty young woman standing at the foot of the stairs. The pretty young woman that had once lived in the apartment opposite his in a life that now seemed to have happened a lifetime ago.

Shannon.

Sitting at the small, sturdy, wooden table where their duo had just become a trio, confusion dominated Eddie's thought process. He looked from Jacobs to the woman who used to be his neighbor. He was attempting to demand an explanation but the words would not come.

At least her name was actually Shannon.

At some point, and it was probably just a defense mechanism, he had been able to accept the sudden appearance of Jacobs in his life without further question. It was all so unreal, his abduction, the abuse, and the arrival of his heroic savior. It was a storybook plot line and somehow acceptable to his remaining mental capacity. At this juncture however, the appearance of someone he associated with his old life in this terrible fairytale was not computing.

She reached across the table and tried to take his hand, a gesture he would have fallen all over himself to have received not so long ago. Now he yanked his hand back by sheer reflex.

"Eddie, listen..." Jacobs started but Eddie cut him off.

"I'll listen but the only thing that I'm going to be listening to is explanations. Do you hear me? I want to know what the hell is going on here. What the hell is she doing here?"

"Calm down, Eddie."

"Don't tell me to calm down."

"It's okay," the woman, Shannon, said to Jacobs in an attempt to diffuse the growing tension.

Jacobs sat back for a moment. "Alright, what do you want to know?"

"Just what I asked. What is she doing here?"

"Eddie, this is Shannon Bentley. I work for her, or more specifically for her father."

Eddie shot a look her way. She returned his gaze with ease and an air of confidence. She smiled the slightest of smiles.

"Shannon's father is the head of security for a company called Loeffler and Son's Incorporated. Ever heard of them?"

Eddie shook his head.

"Well, you might not know them but they know who you are. The people that run Loeffler have a very keen interest in your safety."

Nothing that had occurred in Eddie's life over the last few weeks made any sense. This latest bit of information remained consistent if nothing else. Another thing that was remaining consistent was Eddie's inability to speak.

"I moved in across the hall from you to watch over you," Shannon said. "We misjudged the immediate level of threat they considered you and how aggressive they would be and for that I do apologize. It was an absolute lapse on our end. You never should've had to endure the things that you have."

Eddie continued to struggle to find his voice but eventually managed the only question he could fully formulate. "What are you talking about? Who could possibly consider me a threat?"

"The proverbial 'they' in this case is a company called Hawking Inc.," Shannon went on. "The people that abducted you work for them. They're corrupt and have been since their inception. They are lately involved in the business of putting us, Loeffler, out of business. And even though you don't know it, you're the one person that might be able to stop them."

The ability to put voice to thought or opinion was out of Eddie's control once more. An uncomfortable quiet filled the cabin. After an eternity he was able to speak but the sound of his voice was thin, gut-punched.

"How is that possible? What does any of this have to do with me?"

Neither of them said anything for a moment then Shannon spoke. "It's not just you, Eddie. It's actually your entire family."

"What are talking about?" Eddie asked, bewildered.

"You know that the man you call your uncle wasn't your biological uncle, right?"

Eddie nodded. "He adopted me after my parents gave me up."

"I'm afraid that's not actually true. Your parents never gave you up and your 'uncle' never officially adopted you." Eddie's eyebrow arched but he said nothing. "Your parents were murdered and your uncle would have kept you as far away from any official agency as possible."

"What…? Why…?" Eddie asked his voice little more than a whisper. She gave him a long look that was hard but seemed also to bear some empathy.

"Because keeping your existence a secret was of the utmost importance. The man you consider to be your uncle was actually a man named Victor Leland. He was once a lawyer and one of his more prominent clients was a man named Pike."

The blood ran from Eddie's face leaving him with a ghostly pallor.

"You've heard of Plundering Pike?" Jacobs asked.

Again Eddie nodded. "Sullivan seemed very interested in him for some reason."

"I'll bet he was."

The conversation ground to a halt and the dead space crept from the corners filling every inch of the small cabin before Shannon spoke.

"The reason Sullivan was so interested in him is that Plundering Pike was your grandfather, Eddie. All the trouble that you've found yourself in is because you are now the sole heir to his inheritance and some very bad people would like to make sure you never see it. Their very existence depends on you never getting your hands on Pike's treasure. And when I say treasure, I'm not talking about children's stories and pieces of gold in little treasure chests that are hidden along the North Shore…"

Eddie sat stunned and silent across from them.

"While your inheritance inevitably *is* money, Eddie, what Pike plundered for you is so much more than *just* money. It's power."

3

Just before dawn, June 7th
Lake Superior

The smell of the place was terrible. It was dank and moldy but that wasn't the worst of it. This place had the rotten smell of blood spilt. Previously Kirk Hanlon never would have had the capacity to comprehend the violence and hate these people were capable of. Now he couldn't get the images out of his head. Some indeterminate amount of time after leaving the library and then being abducted, his captors had shown him photos of Bellows handy work. They felt it would aid in making his call to the police more convincing. Their tactics had worked. Somehow, trapped between sheer terror and utter disgust, Kirk had managed to spit out the message he was forced to relay.

It had been the young deputy, Tremely, who had answered the call. He wondered what Tremely had done after getting that call; he wondered how the Sheriff and Ryan were fairing.

He wondered about those poor kids.

Carved with the Plundering Pike.

Just like Richard Devlin.

What in the name of all that's holy have I gotten myself mixed up in?

He could feel despair working its way through his body. He fought back tears and tried to maintain some level of composure, infinitesimal though it may be. Forces beyond his comprehension were at work here, but mentally fracturing would be of no advantage to him.

He was lying on a dirty sheet, on a thin dirty mattress, on a rickety old cot. He had been here for hours, how many he couldn't be sure. He figured it to have been at least a day. It felt like so much more than that, time playing the funny games it's apt to play when you're locked away.

2 days ago –

The mid-afternoon sun was falling across the rows of books in bars, let in only by the long slender windows reaching up the greater part of the library walls. Kirk had just recently returned to his post, returned from his lunch with Sheriff Gurley.

He was unsettled and distracted from the meeting but

he still noticed the man walk in and Kirk knew at once that he didn't belong. It was in the way he walked, the way he carried himself. Small town living does something inexplicable to your posture. Not that it gives you a slouch necessarily, but you do uncoil a bit. City folk hold their tension in a different way.

Kirk watched the man disappear into the long rows of bookshelves and for the moment let him slip from his mind. A few minutes later, when all of the traffic at the checkout desk had dispersed, the man returned. Kirk tried not to stare at the scar below his right eye as he plopped a book down on the desk. Kirk turned his attention to the title.

Mysterious Waters: Tales of the Great Lakes.

"Ever read this?" the stranger asked.

"Sure, it's a fun little read." Kirk responded. He turned to his monitor and began typing the code from the back cover of the book into the computer.

"Yeah, I'm especially interested in the story about Pike."

Kirk's eyes shot up to the man across the desk from him. Remnants of his recent awkward discussion with the publishing company employing him and his not quite comfortable lunch with the Sheriff were still fresh in his mind. The stranger smiled and it alleviated some of his sudden tension. Kirk tried to remind himself that plenty of people could be interested in Pike without having ulterior motives. This man's interest was probably a coincidence, but that scar made his smile hard. "Yeah, that's a good one alright," Kirk muttered as he finished punching in the code.

"You remember that story?" the guy asked.

"I do, I'm pretty fond of the Pike legend myself."

"I had no idea there was so much piracy on superior. Who would have thought stuff like that was happening right here on the North Shore?"

His innocent excitement continued to set Kirk at ease and after all, he could relate. Who was more excited about the Pike legend than he was? "Do you know much about Pike?" Kirk asked.

"A bit," the man said. His smile was still in place. "What really fascinates me though is the part about him meeting with Brian Anders. The story says the Anders family was involved in the art world. With Pike stealing that Mondrian painting from Allan's wife, there's got to be a connection. I'd love to find out what he and Brian Anders were up to."

"Yeah, me too. I'm afraid you may find that difficult though."

"Why's that?" the man with the scar asked.

"To tell you the truth, I think that part of the story is a bit of creative writing on the author's part. I've done some pretty extensive research on the subject. They're right about the Anders family being heavy hitters in the visual art world, but I've never found any record of them having a son. I believe the reason that no one was ever able to locate Brian Anders again is because Brian Anders never existed in the first place."

"What if I told you that you were wrong?"

Kirk looked up at the stranger again. He was still smiling but it had lost that innocent quality. Now it bore a sly, knowing quality and was not at all comforting. In fact it set Kirk right back to being on edge. "What do you mean?" he managed to ask, but his voice sounded reedy and thin.

"Listen to me, Kirk. I need you to listen very closely to what I'm about to tell you, do you understand me?" The last traces of his smile had faded and his voice was as hard as the smile had been.

"How do you know who I…" Kirk stammered.

"How is irrelevant. I do know who you are and you're in trouble. More trouble than you can possibly comprehend. That publishing company you are working for, they don't give a damn about your book. They are owned by a corporation called Hawking Inc., and they want information. They need to find out what you know about Pike and his family and they intend to get that information by any means necessary."

"Why do they care about Pike?" Kirk managed.

The man brandished the Mysterious Waters book. "Nothing was ever resolved between Pike and D.B. Allan. Not even after Pike's death. Not only did the feud go on, but it is *still* going on and it's coming to a head. The Allans purportedly sold their family business and since then it's been sold a few more times, but if you were to dig into those sales you'd find that every buyer was a shadow corporation still technically in the family. Eventually it was sold back to Allan's wife, Amelie, and she still owns it today. It's nearly impossible to trace. They laundered the name like it was money, but D.B. Allan's former company is none other than Hawking Inc. You are being employed by the Allans and they'll kill you to get what they want."

Kirk was stunned into silence.

"I can help you, but I need you to help me too. The painting that Pike stole from the Angelina was important, important enough for both Pike and Allan to put on a public farce of putting their troubles behind them. Pike aligning himself with the Anders family and their specific area of expertise had to be significant. I think the reason you, and anyone else who would care to look, thinks Brian Anders didn't exist is because that's how Pike wanted it. I believe he was real and whatever happened to him is the real link to the Pike mystery.

"You have to find out what you can about Anders. Take the rest of the day off, call off sick or whatever, but do not go home. Go find a discreet motel somewhere and meet me at two p.m., the day after tomorrow at Devil's Kettle. Do you know it?"

It took a couple seconds to register and make sense of the question but Kirk did know it. It was a natural anomaly, a waterfall that had become a tourist attraction just north of Grand Marias. After an interminable silence he gave an awkward jerk of his head meant to be a nod.

"Good." The man started to leave.

"Who are you?" Kirk sputtered, finding his voice if only just.

"Who I am is none of your concern. Your only concern is Brian Anders. Find out what you can about him. Your life literally might depend upon it."

Without a further word he turned and walked out of the library leaving the book sitting on the corner of the checkout desk. After a moment Kirk fought through the shock and scooped Mysterious Waters off the desk. He called someone over to cover the checkout for him. With a sense of urgency he walked back into his office and closed the door, trying not to slam it as nervous excitement attempted to unravel him.

Once seated behind his own desk he found himself momentarily unable to function. The book sat there staring back at him. Where to begin? He'd spent plenty of time searching for information on the Anders family so how was he all of a sudden going to come up with new information? He decided to start the old fashioned way.

He shook the mouse to wake his computer and started plugging things into the search engine.

The searches returned a lot, but nothing that was new to Kirk. He had already scoured most of the websites and stories that popped up at least once during his previous studies. He kept at it though and eventually settled down as the comfortable nuance of investigative research settled over him. As before, he found no mention of Brian Anders, or of the Anders family ever having a son. He searched D.B. Allan and the Angelina but found nothing of note.

He searched 'the Angelina' and 'painting'. It returned nothing about the Mondrian that was supposedly aboard the Angelina but he did get a few hits that made mention of a painting titled Angel at the Rock. That particular painting was semi-famous locally and had actually hung in the Split Rock Lighthouse once upon a time, prominently displayed along the curved stairway ascending to the lantern room. It depicted the Angelina running aground on the rocks below the lighthouse. The geographical location of the shipwreck was incorrect, Allan's freighter had not run aground by the lighthouse, but that had not kept Angel at the Rock from being a reasonably popular piece of art. Kirk was familiar with it. In fact he had a book on a shelf at home that contained a picture of the painting.

Angel at the Rock was not really what he was looking for but sometimes the surreptitious route is the road that takes you home. He often found that when you don't know what exactly you're looking for, sometimes following any lead would eventually lead to pay dirt. He plugged 'Angel at the Rock' into the search engine just to keep things moving.

Again, most of the returns bore no fruitful information. The painting had been displayed at Split Rock, which he knew. It had been commissioned anonymously, which he also knew. He scrolled through pages and pages of returns looking for any oddity in the results that might seem interesting. A couple things caught his eye and he clicked on them but each time a quick review of the site was all he needed to realize there was nothing there. He was about to abandon this particular avenue of investigation when one result piqued his interest. The line in the tease that caught his attention was about the original dedication ceremony of the Angel at the Rock to the Split Rock Lighthouse. He clicked the link.

It initially looked to be a complete dead end as he was redirected to some high school kid's personal page that featured his term paper, the subject of which was the history of Split Rock. He scrolled quickly through the paper and was about to close it when an attached image halted him. The picture was a newspaper photo of Angel at the Rock hanging in the lighthouse that had been taken during the dedication ceremony. In the picture there was a plaque below the painting but the text engraved on it was illegible. He attempted to enlarge the image but all he got was a pixilated mess.

He opened a new window and did an image search hoping to find one where the text on the plaque was legible. He was sure to use enough key words so that he wouldn't be inundated with literal renditions of Angels perched on rocky tableaus. His screen filled with the images he'd been hoping for, actual shots of the painting hanging on the wall in the stairwell at Split Rock.

The first thing that struck him as odd was that there was no plaque in any of the images that appeared. Something seemed off about the painting too, nothing he could put his finger on but for some reason all of the images seemed to differ somehow from his recollection of it. Whatever it was about the pictures that clashed with his memory continued to elude him, it was nothing specific and so he moved on. As he started to move through a few pages of results a small spark began to kindle in his chest. He might not know yet what it was, but he thought he may have stumbled upon something. The fact that not one of the pictures of the painting he found included the plaque that was in the newspaper photo seemed to perhaps be of some import.

He searched 'missing plaque Angel at the Rock'. None of the returns were helpful in regard to the plaque but the overwhelming lack of information only continued to lead him to believe that he may have stumbled upon a path worth investigating. While the plaque was absent from all the results, he did find a story about the painting itself going missing so he scanned through that.

The painting had once been stolen, that was another tidbit that he was already familiar with. In fact the photo of the painting in the book he had at home was from after it had been restored to the lighthouse. Angel at the Rock was never displayed again after being returned, which meant the photo in his book came from one of the last public displays of the painting.

The story he had found was about the return of the painting. A man named Aaron Anderson had stumbled upon it at a thrift store and happened to know what it was. He had contacted the proper authorities and was able to get it restored to the lighthouse. Kirk found all of this of some interest but it was not what he was looking for. He re-opened the page with the kid's term paper and looked at the image of the newspaper photo again. While the text on the plaque was illegible, the date and edition of the newspaper were not.

Now he decided to actually tackle it the old fashioned

way and headed over to the archive room to scour the microfiche for old copies of the Duluth News Tribune. The library had begun the laborious task of trying to update its database and get things onto the computer. But collating so much information was a slow process due to a lack of resources. He looked for the edition corresponding to the date in the photo and after a bit of trial and error, eventually found it.

He loaded it and moved the tray around until he had the photo in focus. He found the plaque and zoomed in on it as best he could. The resolution was not perfect but he was able to read it. That kindling feeling in his chest caught and ignited.

The plaque stated that the Angel at the Rock had been commissioned anonymously, but had been dedicated to the lighthouse by none other than the Anders family. It went on to name them: David, Jennifer, and their son…Brian.

Brian Anders did exist. But other than in Mysterious Waters his existence had been relegated to the pages of this long antiquated newspaper. Somehow, most likely by Pike's doing, he had been erased. He was gone except for a name on a plaque in an aged lost newspaper. So now Kirk had verified that he was real, but that did nothing to advance the narrative he was trying to piece together. What was it about Brian Anders that was so important? What piece of the puzzle did Anders hold that made him worth the trouble of removing him from history?

Kirk closed his eyes and leaned back in his chair rubbing his temples. The quiet but present sounds of the archive room rolled over him. He tried to relax and not force thought but to let it come to him instead.

Suddenly, with a reflexive speed he opened his eyes and sat up straight in his chair.

Something had clicked. It was nothing tangible but perhaps a thread to be pulled. It was the name of the man who had returned the painting to the lighthouse, Anderson. The similarity in names between Anders and Anderson was perhaps just a bit too convenient.

There was a computer in the archive room, meant to help track information in newspapers that had been banished to everlasting life on microfilm. Kirk made his way over to it and pulled up the story about the return of the painting. It took some digging but after a few minutes of searching he was able to ascertain a date range of when Anderson had returned the painting to the lighthouse. There had been some sort of glad-handing ceremony upon its return. He went back to the microfiche and searched out the date in question, again it took some time but the reward was that which he sought and more.

He moved the tray around until he settled on another image from the Duluth News Tribune. This one was of a man, presumably Aaron Anderson, with two young boys. The kids looked like they were twins. He focused the image as best he could but then stopped short. His hand slipped from the tray.

There were very few photos taken of Plundering Pike but if they were out there, Kirk had seen them. Seen them, and committed them to memory. He knew the man's face like he knew his mother's. The visage in the photo wasn't quite the face he had burned into his memory but it was damn close.

The man identified as Aaron Anderson could only be Pike's son.

And if he was Pike's son, that would make the twin boys in the photo Pike's grandchildren.

Plural.

One of which would be Richard Devlin, now deceased. But whoever that other kid was, he was Devlin's twin brother and now the sole heir to Pike's Plunder.

For the next ten minutes Kirk did not move. He sat utterly still in the archive room of the Castle Danger Library and tried with minimal success to keep his wits about him. The man with the scar had told him that the feud between Allan and Pike had never ended. That he himself was currently employed by the Allan family and that they would kill him to get the information they sought. And now he quite possibly had information that could bring about such an end.

As if all his muscles suddenly began working at once he jerked to his feet and collected his things. He found one of his assistants and managed to convey the fact that he suddenly wasn't feeling well, his pallor certainly aiding to alibi his story. He left the library and made his way to his car but sat behind the wheel for another long stretch attempting to regain his composure.

As he sat there something strange occurred. A calm cool stole over him, arresting the rising panic. It was the painting, the Angel at the Rock. He had felt that in all the images he had pulled up of the painting on the computer, something had been wrong.

No. Not wrong, but missing.

He couldn't quite put his finger on *what* was missing but the longer he sat, the more certain he became that a vital piece had been omitted from the images he had found today. Or at least he was convinced that the picture of the print that he had at home was somehow different than those he had viewed online. And so, against his better judgment he turned the key, started the car, and headed for home.

He arrived at his house. His heart was pounding hard in his chest as he stepped through the door into his living room.

The house was silent.

A brief inventory of the main rooms convinced him that the sanctity of his home had not been violated since he had left that morning. He went to his study and dropped the Mysterious Waters book on his desk. He pulled the book containing the print of Angel at the Rock off the shelf and rifled through the pages. Never had he treated a book with such abandon but he couldn't help it. At last he found the page he was looking for. The book fell open and he stared at the photo of the painting. That little 'something' that had been missing was right there staring right back at him.

His mouth was agape. The caption explained that the shots had indeed been taken when the painting was returned to the lighthouse. That it had never been displayed again was the likely reason no one had ever taken note of the small change.

It wasn't that something had been omitted from the images he had found on the computer. Rather, in the period of time that the painting had been missing from the lighthouse, something had been added to it.

He had no idea what had become of the Angel at the Rock and perhaps it didn't matter, because the location of Pike's Plunder was right there on the page in front of him. It had been cleverly denoted on the painting, and thanks to a photo in some obscure book, Kirk now knew where it lay.

He stumbled to the kitchen and made some tea then he sat on his couch staring out the window at the road letting the adrenaline fueled excitement and confusion wash over him.

He was interrupted almost immediately.

The nondescript black sedan that rolled slowly into his view on the street in front of his house could only mean one thing. They were coming for him. He didn't wait to see if it would pull into his driveway, he already knew that it would. The man with the scar had warned him.

He jumped up spilling his tea and scrambled to his study. He grabbed the book and, no longer concerned at all with the treatment of the thing, he tore out the page with the photo of Angel at the Rock. Then he dog-eared the previous page in the book. He put it back on the shelf facing the wrong direction. He sat down at his computer and jammed out one quick line of very basic code. He killed the monitor as the pounding on the door started. He heard them enter his home as he was hiding the photo. He finished throwing a few maps over the Mysterious Waters book and as nonchalant as he could hope to be, he stepped out into the hallway and found himself staring into the cold blackened eyes of Quentin Bellows.

Now –

Bellows crossed the little cell in two long strides and dragged him up from the dirty cot. He was hauled up onto the deck and into the beautiful sunshine of June the 7th. The boat was docked at a long pier. He was shuffled down the gangplank, along the pier, and then his feet were back down on solid ground. He was put into the backseat of one of those very nondescript sedans and driven off.

Kirk was quite certain he knew where they were taking him, who they were taking him to see. Not so long ago he had sat across from the man in the offices of a publishing company that was owned by Hawking Inc., owned by Amelie Allan. Exactly how long ago that may have been, he could not be sure.

From where he sat in the backseat of the car he could see Lake Superior receding in the rear-view mirror. He thought about the fact that once upon a time Pike had sailed those waters and feuded with the people now holding him hostage.

A small smile rose to his lips as he thought about the fact that he now knew where Pike's plunder was located. But it slipped from his face as he thought about trying to hold on to that secret in the face of the adversity that was sure to come.

4

Late morning, June 7th
The Gurley residence

Forever the phone rang, down the line. It echoed in his ear as Bob's impatience mounted. He squeezed the handset tight, waiting. Until, at last, sweet relief as Ryan answered.

"Hello?"

"Ryan, it's Bob." He faltered for a moment. They hadn't spoken since they left the station the night before. The previous evening in many ways was a lifetime ago.

He was spared an awkward moment as Ryan spoke.

"Hey boss, how's life on the other side been treating ya?" His tone was light, but forced.

"I don't need to tell you that it's been hell, but listen, I need you to get over here as quick as you can."

"Is everything alright?" Ryan asked.

"We'll see. You did some encryption work in the service right?"

"That's right. Why?"

"I'll show you when you get here. Now, giddy-up."

He put the phone back on its cradle, all the while staring at the little piece of paper in his hand.

A page torn out of a duty notebook.

Yesterday –

After a horrendous and lengthy day he had finally arrived home.

He and Ryan had both been put on administrative leave following the disaster at Kirk's house. It was standard operating procedure. After the debriefing, in which he did his best to explain why he'd been at Kirk's house, he had put on some old civvies that he'd kept in his locker at the station and handed over his soiled uniform for processing. On the way out he had retrieved a bag with any personal belongings that had been in his uniform, keys, wallet, etc. He tucked the bag under his arm and stepped out into the thick humidity. If it didn't rain soon, it would become suffocating.

He spent the rest of that night in a fog. His wife did her best to attend to him but he was a wreck. Jessy was dead and, for the moment at least, he lacked his badge and the identity that had for so long defined him. He was adrift.

The next morning was not much better. Norma made breakfast and they sat as they usually did at their weathered kitchen table. They had spent many comfortable silences at that little table but the usual serenity had been replaced this morning by an anxious angst. Bob was a man being tormented, not only by grief but by inactivity as well. Eventually he excused himself and went out to sit on the porch.

He sat there for several hours deep in reflection but found little comfort. He stayed that way until shortly after eleven thirty when Norma stepped out on the porch and asked him what she should do with the bag of personal effects he had brought from the station. He took it and thanked her. She lingered for a long moment before letting the screen door slip shut as she returned to the house. He removed the items from the bag and found the little scrap of paper.

It was a page from a duty notebook, but he knew at once that it wasn't from his own. He unfolded the paper and found a jumble of letters and numbers.

6u4 r4g9pe o466p4   630 –k i8j4 e4g4j6u

At first it meant nothing, it was just a bunch of nonsense, but then a thought occurred to him.

Jessy said Kirk had left a code.

He had forgotten all about it in the aftermath of what he and Ryan had walked into at Kirk's home.

How did it end up in my pocket?

But then he knew, the memory was there, so fresh and raw, tearing at him.

He had thought Jessy was trying to hold onto him as he thrashed, living out his death throes. But in fact, he had been attempting to stick this folded page from his duty notebook into Bob's pocket. And he had succeeded. The fact that he hadn't originally noticed it did not altogether surprise him. He had been out of sorts to say the least when he received his personal items, but it should have caught his attention. The little piece of paper was pristine. There had been so much blood, it was everywhere in that room. The fact that Jessy had been able to pass it off to him under such circumstances, and unsoiled, seemed to be on par with divine intervention, if he even believed in such a thing.

His religious beliefs aside, he did believe in redemption and breaking the code might just lead to finding some.

He nearly knocked over the little wicker table as he launched himself out of his chair and went through the door in as close a fashion to 'racing' as a man his age could muster. Once inside he went straight for the phone. One of the other things Bob Gurley believed in was Ryan Tomlinson.

Now –

Fifteen minutes after Bob had hung up the phone, Ryan pulled into his driveway. Bob met him on the porch and nearly dragged him into the study.

"Jessy told me on the phone that he thought Kirk had left some code. I'd forgotten all about it but I found this in with my personal stuff." He said handing over the paper to Ryan.

"How'd you end up with it?"

"Jessy somehow managed to get it jammed in my pocket. I thought the kid was trying to hug me…" Bob drifted off, pride, intermingling with sorrow, evident in his voice.

"And this is the code he was talking about?"

"I guess. I don't know what the hell else it could be. You think you can do anything with it?"

"Maybe. It looks like it's supposed to be words right, the way the sections of characters are broken up?"

"I'd guess so." But Bob sounded unsure of himself.

"Well, we can start with the three letter words. There's a solid chance one of them is 'the'. And we have two words of the three letter variety that start with a six, so for starters let's assume that 6 equals 'T.' That would make either '630' or '6u4' equal 'the'. Wait a minute…" Ryan seemed to have made some connection. Bob was anxious to press him but worried that interjecting might break his train of thought. Just as the moment had stretched out too long for his fragile psyche and he was about to say something, Ryan picked up the thread of his previous thought.

"I need to see your computer," he demanded more than asked, and Bob acquiesced. He opened the cabinet that housed his desktop. Bob Gurley had not yet embraced the laptop much less a tablet or any other such device.

"Here ya go." Bob stepped aside and let him sit. Ryan did nothing more than look over the keyboard for mere seconds, then a small laugh escaped him. "What is it?"

"The code is simple. '6u4' is 'the' and '630' is 'two'."

"How did you figure that out so fast?"

"Once you know what you're looking for it's easy. I figured Kirk wouldn't leave a code that would be hard to crack, not if he left it hastily in hopes someone might figure out what happened to him. Some sort of keyboard code seemed like it would be reasonable. Now look at the numbers running across the top of the keyboard."

"Ok."

"Start with '630' and look just below and a little left of the 6."

"It's the 'T' key."

"Now do the same thing for the 3 and the 0."

"W and O, I'll be damned it's 'two' alright."

"If you look below the 'U' and the 4 you'll find it spells 'the'. I think he just moved his fingers from the base keys up one row and one letter to the right and then just typed normally. It'll take a second but we can just work backward from each letter. Do you have a pencil?" Bob grabbed one from the other side of the desk. Ryan put the page from Jessy's duty notebook out on the desk next to the computer. He filled in the two words they already knew then started on the rest. The message appeared below the nonsense on the page.

6u4 r4g9pe o466p4   630 –k i8j4 e4g4j6u
The devils   kettle   two pm june seventh

"Devil's Kettle," Bob said lost in thought.

It was a tourist attraction just north of Grand Marais. Both men were familiar with it. It was a waterfall but what made it interesting was that the flow of water split as it fell. There was a high part of the falls that fell into a cavernous hole in the rock. The rest of the water rushed on and over the bigger part of the falls and down to the river below. The notable thing was that no one knew where the water that fell into that hole went. The state park service had attempted dying the water to see if they could find where it ran its course but were never able to determine the outlet. A north shore point of interest was secondary to the second part of the code though, the time and date.

Ryan looked at his watch. "It's a little after noon. It looks like he was telling us to be there at two, right?"

"That's how it'd seem to me."

"Then it would seem to me we need to get a move on."

"You have a personal weapon at home, I assume?"

"Of course I do. And my permits are all in order, Sheriff." Ryan said, a small smile playing across his features."

"Well, get on home and get it then, and throw on something inconspicuous."

"What? You don't think this 'Castle County Sheriff's Department' t-shirt will fit the bill?"

"I know very little about what we're going to be walking into but the one thing I'm sure of is that announcing ourselves as cops probably won't work in our favor."

Ryan's smile faltered. "I guess we're not really cops right now anyway."

"I only hope we can be again when all this is over, but right now we've got to help Kirk. Hustle home. I'll be right behind you to pick you up."

5

Late morning, June 7ᵗʰ
The house in the woods

Sullivan paced the floor of his study awaiting the arrival of Kirk Hanlon. He was hoping that June 7th would play out more to his liking than the 6th had. Between the debacle at Itasca and what had transpired at Hanlon's house with the cops, yesterday was a complete mess. While Hanlon's house had been a disaster and he didn't want to think about it, the former was worse. He did not care to linger on the events that had played out at Itasca.

At Hanlon's house his men had killed a cop. That was not good. It was not a situation that Sullivan saw as insurmountable but it did not bode well for his cause. It raised the stakes and much quicker than he would have liked. They would have to make haste and at the same time show more caution than they had thus far.

The bodies were beginning to pile up and it would be harder to keep these incidents separated. It would be imperative that he get what he needed from Hanlon. He could not afford to add more bodies to the growing count without gaining something useful.

And he would need those answers soon. Today was Eddie's thirtieth birthday. Today he became a serious liability

The front door opened and closed. He could hear Mason conversing with the new arrivals. A moment later Mason led Kirk Hanlon into the room. The man looked skinnier than he had when they had taken him. It didn't seem possible but then Sullivan had seen plenty of the odd physical manifestations of fear.

"Have a seat." He motioned Hanlon to the same chair Eddie had sat in the day he was in this room. Thinking of Eddie made Sullivan's blood run hot, though he didn't let it show.

"My apologies for your accommodations since you've joined us, and that it's taken me so long to get around to seeing you. I had a very full day yesterday." He didn't mention that what had been occupying his time was the fallout of multiple homicides that had taken place in Kirk's home. "I bet you're surprised to see me again so soon."

Kirk continued to uphold the silence he'd been keeping since entering the room.

"I had a feeling we'd be seeing each other though, after our last conversation in Minneapolis. You sure seemed to get antsy when our interest in the Angelina came up." Sullivan threw him that wicked grin. "But maybe that was just coincidence. Coincidence is a funny thing isn't it?"

Still Kirk said nothing.

"You see a few coincidences aside this would probably be just another conversation in a nice plush conference room downtown Minneapolis. If you had told me what you knew about the Angelina and its connections to Pike, our publishing company would've cut you a generous check and everyone would've gone home happy. But then there's coincidence. It's a coincidence that you and Sheriff Gurley happen to be friends. It's a coincidence that he realized your affinity for the tale of Plundering Pike. And it's a coincidence that he got you involved in Richard Devlin's murder."

Kirk remained silent but his silence did little to mask his fear.

"Funny enough, all of that makes it no coincidence that you became nervous when you realized that the only thing we were interested in was the connection to Pike."

Sullivan stepped over to one of the bookcases and pulled a book from the shelf. Kirk recognized it but this particular copy was in much better condition than the library's tattered version. Mysterious Waters: Tales of the Great Lakes.

"You had a copy of this book on your desk, why?" Sullivan asked.

"Just research." Kirk managed but his voice was hoarse and his throat cracked.

"I guess we can chalk that up to another coincidence then."

"I don't know what you…"

Sullivan cut him off with a wave of his hand.

"Let's not dig ourselves into holes we can't crawl out of, Kirk. The fact that you did have it is enough for me. I know that you know a lot about Pike. It's why we hired you. I could care less about some tourist book about the Great Lakes. As I'm sure you inferred at our little meeting the other day, my interests lay elsewhere. With the Angelina for instance and her related history. With the Mondrian painting that Pike stole from Amelie Allan."

Kirk said nothing. He could summon no words.

"I don't know exactly what you know but I'm going to fill in some holes for you. And then, hopefully, for your sake, you are going to fill in some holes for me." Let's start with that stolen painting. It was a piece by Piet Mondrian, what do you know about him?"

"Mondrian?" Kirk asked. Sullivan nodded. "Not much," he said after a long moment. "He was a painter, associated with Cubism, I think."

"Cubism, that's exactly right, very good." Sullivan said. "His style was straight lines and minimal blocks of color, spectacular only in its minimalist subtleties. Many of his paintings from this period contained small oddities such as lines that didn't reach all the way to the end of the canvas, but fell just short, so close that one might never notice if one weren't looking for just such a thing."

Kirk had returned to the aforementioned realm of silence. Sullivan went on.

"Mondrian lived in Paris for some time before World War I and while he was there a man named Jean Paul Pesquidox took quite an interest in him. Pesquidox was a small time art dealer and gallery owner. Whether they ever knew each other is for some historian to decide but Jean Paul collected a number of Mondrian's paintings. He always tried to display at least one in his gallery.

"It turns out Pesquidox was part of a Secret Alliance that was attempting to draw the U.S. into joining the war. He would doctor whichever Mondrian painting he was currently showing. In those small spaces where the lines didn't quite reach he would mark the canvas. These markings were very difficult to see if you didn't know what you were looking for but they were codes, codes that contained information.

"His most important assignment as far as we are concerned, was passing information that led to the sinking of the Lusitania, a British passenger vessel that was carrying many Americans when it was sunk. Pesquidox provided the Germans information about munitions that were supposedly on board in order to convince them to sink the ship. Afterward Woodrow

Wilson was left with little choice and the U.S. was eventually drawn into the war. While it could never be announced publicly, Pesquidox was considered a hero within his secret circles. He retired content to live out his days quietly and raise his new baby girl, Amelie.

"And now coincidence puts in another appearance. There were indeed munitions aboard the Lusitania, over 4 million rounds of Remington .303's. There were also a multitude of cartons dubiously marked as cheese, butter, and oysters. Much of this cargo was explosives, shells, powder, gun-cotton, and had been manufactured by none other than D.B Allan Sr.

"Some twenty years later, D.B. Allan Jr. having taken over the more legitimate aspects of his father's company namely the timber production, took a holiday to France. He met a pretty young girl in a small Paris nightclub and he fell for her.

"Her name was Amelie.

"She was not much interested in him but he was not one to be easily deterred. A man bred of that kind of wealth is used to getting what he wants. You can imagine his surprise when he came to discover that his new love's father had sold out the U.S. and killed American citizens, not to mention destroyed some of his own family's product, for the purpose of coercing the U.S. into a war. You might think he would be angered or offended, but he saw an opportunity. He wanted Amelie. And so, the blackmail commenced.

"Allan Jr. demanded that Pesquidox turn his daughter over and that they be married or he would expose him. Pesquidox and Amelie had no choice but to acquiesce. But as the dirty secrets that beget blackmail can pass one way so can they swing the other. Pesquidox had discovered that the Allans had also supplied munitions to the Central Powers during the First World War, essentially making D.B Allan Sr. a traitor. He didn't have enough evidence to prove it, but what he did have was damning.

"He instructed his daughter to take the information he

had unearthed and use it to destroy the Allans. He sealed these documents in the backing of the original Mondrian, and sent it and his daughter off to America. She arrived in New York, and via the great lakes chain made her trek to Minnesota, aboard the Angelina.

"And then Pike entered the picture and stole the Mondrian. You can see now why it was so important to her to get that painting back. Without it, and the contents sealed in its backing, she would be destined to a life of little more than indentured servitude being married to Allan. Had Allan known he may have been less adamant about the return of his new wife's most prized possession."

Sullivan finished and a smile crept across his face. He pointed to the table where Mysterious Waters sat.

"You know about Anders and about the other painting, the Angel at the Rock?"

Kirk nodded his assent.

"Did you know that Pike commissioned the Angel at the Rock himself?"

"I didn't." Kirk said. His voice was scratchy and his face paled a bit at the mention of that particular painting and what he had recently realized about it. Sullivan gave him a long look, but then moved on.

"Any guess as to why he would do that?"

Kirk shook his head not trusting his voice.

"Perhaps the content of the painting was a little joke. As you may well know it seemed Pike was partial to such little jokes. But the real reason for commissioning Angel at the Rock was to disguise a contract that he had previously penned on the back of the canvas."

Kirk was unable to hide his surprise. While Sullivan had already told him a number of things he hadn't known, the revelation of a contract hidden on the back of Angel at the Rock was information that he was not prepared for.

Sullivan went on.

"It took her some time, but with Allan's name and wealth behind her, Amelie was able to make contact with Pike.

He agreed to return the Mondrian to her but not without compensation. Once Allan was ruined and Amelie was able to take control of the company, he wanted half of it. She was not motivated by money but by revenge, she already had all the money she needed, and so she agreed. Pike was getting older and it would take her a number of years to orchestrate the elaborate plan. She would need to get Allan to leave everything to her and then depose him as the head of the family. They agreed that Pike's son would work with her on the transferring of shares in the company when the time came. That's what the contract on the back of the Angel at the Rock was about. It contained the truly damning details of Amelie's plot. It may not have been legally binding but it would be enough to cause a boatload of trouble for Amelie if it were ever to come to light. What do you know about that contract?"

"Nothing, that's the first I've heard anything about it." Kirk was able to answer honestly.

"And yet your face paled a bit when I mentioned the Angel at the Rock. Now why would that be?"

Kirk could say nothing, all the saliva in his mouth had dried up and his lips would not move. Terror paralyzed him.

"Why didn't you tell me you knew about the painting when you were in Minneapolis and we asked you about the Angelina?"

"I…I didn't know then." he stammered but it was the truth, and the truth somehow helped him to find his voice.

"Come on, Kirk, don't bullshit me. I know someone's been feeding you information."

If there had been any color left in Kirk's face it was gone now. He was a sunken mask, as white as a sheet. He knew he had to say something or he was going to die. He found his voice.

"He didn't approach me until that afternoon, after I had met with you."

"What?" Sullivan asked his voice sharp.

"He came to the library that afternoon."

Sullivan sat back into his chair and stared at him for a

good long time. His hands were tented in front of him, his eyes piercing. Finally, after an eternity, he spoke.

"What did he look like?"

"Tall, salt and pepper dark hair, muscular, and he had a small scar on his right cheek."

"Did he now?" Sullivan's demeanor changed. His face split wide with a smile that seemed genuine. Such pure joy seemed an awkward emotion to be worn by such a man. Then he actually laughed. "Oh Kirk," he said as the laughter expired, "I wasn't referring to the man with the scar, I was actually talking about Victor Leland. I know that once upon a time he had your ear."

Kirk's eyes went wide.

"You didn't know? Well it's true. The man you considered to be your 'source' was actually Pike's lawyer, Victor Leland."

The shock coursing through him squeezed, crushing him, expelling his breath as its vice like grip left him speechless. Victor Leland had been his source? The pieces fell into place. Leland had absconded with both boys, the twins. He separated them, probably for their own safety, leaving Richard with his friends Myron and Willa Devlin and keeping the other himself.

"I'm not really sure what his motivation was for feeding you information, but it hardly matters now," Sullivan went on. "He's dead."

"Dead?" Kirk managed.

"Yes, a house fire I believe. A terrible accident." But Sullivan didn't really seem to find it terrible. In fact, he seemed to be enjoying himself. "I'm much more interested in his 'nephew' or maybe you thought it was his son? Either way, the boy is the real prize."

Kirk, still without his wits about him, tried his best to mete out his answer appropriately. "I don't know anything about a boy." He tried to gauge Sullivan's acceptance of that answer. His movements measured, Sullivan leaned in close to Kirk.

"I don't really care what you know about him. The man

with the scar knows about him, not least of all, his current whereabouts. You're going to help me find them."

"I don't know where…"

"Shut up." Sullivan barked cutting him off. Whatever you do know, you're going to tell me. One way or the other, I'll know what you know."

And with that, Bellows stepped into the room.

Sullivan swung open one of the bookcases lining the western wall and entered his personal study. The secret door was his own design and it was one he insisted on. Anyone who is up to no good should have a secret door behind a bookcase or so Sullivan thought.

The man in the expensive suit rose from the chair behind the desk as Sullivan entered. He lit a cigarette, a gold bracelet jangled loose around the wrist of the hand holding a platinum plated Zippo. He inhaled and blew the smoke out quick through a set of perfectly, straight, white teeth. He was a man with expensive taste. His suit was tailored to precision at no small expense.

"What did he say?" the man in the suit asked.

"Not what I expected him too."

"And he's still alive?"

"There's a wrinkle."

"Isn't that why I pay you lots of money, to smooth wrinkles?"

"And smooth it I will. Someone unexpected contacted him."

The man took a long drag on his cigarette and let it out slowly, jetting the smoke through both his nose and mouth. Then he spoke.

"Who?"

"I don't know precisely *who* he is, but apparently the guy has a scar on his right cheek." Sullivan said.

The man's eyebrow rose. "The guy at the pier?"

Sullivan nodded.

"The guy that stole Eddie from us." It was a statement

from the man in the suit, not a question, but Sullivan nodded his assent anyway. "And he knows where they are?"

"They've set a meeting. He'll take us there."

"He told you this?"

"Bellows didn't even have to touch him, Devil's Kettle this afternoon."

On the tail of another jet of blue smoke, those perfect white teeth flashed a Cheshire grin.

6

Early afternoon, June 7th
The cabin near Grand Marais

Eddie sat alone in the stifling humidity on the front porch of the little cabin. Jacobs and Shannon were inside preparing to leave. The two of them were due at a rendezvous soon. They had a meeting with a man he had never heard of, and that man probably knew more about Eddie than Eddie knew about himself. But that seemed to be true of just about everybody as of late.

He watched the trees across from the cabin. Their branches hardly moved in the thick, still air. Eddie had been moody and brooding for the better part of the last few hours, the result of being suddenly reacquainted with a new family tree, a tree that had strange and gnarled branches. He'd come out here to think and to attempt to square himself with his new found familial situation. It was slow going. It would take him some time to absorb.

His parents had been murdered. His uncle was not who he had purported himself to be. And his grandfather was a man named Plundering Pike.

After dropping those bombshell revelations, Shannon and Jacobs had tried to provide Eddie some background as to how they were connected to the situation that he now found himself in. They had explained that Shannon's family had worked for the Loeffler family for generations and at some point the Loefflers and Pike had done business together. Any business dealings between the Loefflers and some pirate were of little interest to Eddie. He was still too busy trying to reconcile the fact that he was apparently a direct descendent of the pirate in question.

They had also made an attempt to explain how Eddie fit in to this mess but his current mental state made the information incomprehensible. Talk of some sort of inheritance and a pirate treasure that was not money but some corporate currency that could potentially bring about the fall of titans of industry had thudded flat on the dulled edges of Eddie's shaky comprehension.

He shook his head trying to clear his thoughts. He was slowly digesting it, but a shadowy lineage that had been kept from him for so long and all the dramatics tied to it was proving a tough pill to swallow. He stood up from the porch and took a deep breath. He was still feeling lost, adrift, but too much time knocking around in one's own head could be dangerous at times. He turned and opened the screen door to the cabin. He stood there for a long moment looking back out at the trees before walking through and letting the door slip shut behind him.

Jacobs and Shannon were just standing up from their seats at the breakfast nook.

"Is it time to go?" Eddie asked.

Jacobs gave him a long look. "You still want to come with us?"

"The last time you left me alone in some crappy cabin I had to kill a man and almost got killed myself. Yeah, I think I'll stick with you."

To that Jacobs had nothing to say. He nodded his head then walked past Eddie and out the front door. Shannon went out behind him. Eddie took a moment to look around the cabin then he followed them out into the heat.

They stopped at Sven and Ollie's in downtown Grand

Marais on their way out of town. Eddie waited in the car while Jacobs and Shannon ran in and grabbed lunch from the take-out counter.

Eddie was lost in thought, still grappling with the onslaught of information that had been unloaded on him. He saw the dusty old Ford Ranger that pulled in to a parking spot next to him. He saw the two guys in feed caps get out and walk towards the restaurant, but they paid him no mind and he afforded them little more.

A few minutes later Jacobs and Shannon returned with the food. Shannon stayed tight to the car as she got in. That dusty Ford Ranger had parked a little close and she didn't want to rub against it. It made Eddie smile, just a little. Then she was in the car and they were on their way, headed north. About ten minutes into the twenty minute drive, Eddie had finished his lunch and finally felt like he was ready for some answers.

"So who is this guy we're going to meet?"

"His name is Kirk Hanlon," Jacobs answered from the front seat. "He's the librarian down at the Castle Danger Library. He's a Pike aficionado."

"And I suppose he has information for you?" Eddie asked.

"I hope so. I've asked him to try and find out what he could about a man named Brian Anders. Anders was enlisted by Pike for a job a long time ago but we don't know what that job was. If we can discern what the nature of his business with Pike was it's possible we'll find the..." he paused, "the answers that have otherwise eluded us." Eddie had the distinct impression that Jacobs had intended to use the word 'treasure' and went with 'answers' for his benefit.

"And so we'll find these 'answers' at Devil's Kettle?" Eddie asked.

"I certainly hope so."

"Why Devil's Kettle, did you feel you needed to get some exercise today?"

Devils Kettle, quite likely thanks to its intriguing name and stunning landscape was a popular spot to those touring the

North Shore. While popular, it was not exactly easy to get to. The only way to take in its wonderment was to hike up a mile and a half of trails intermingled with twelve-hundred wooden stairs built onto the face of the hilly landscape. The daunting trek provided some privacy while still staying in a public place.

"Devil's Kettle is the perfect place for this kind of meeting, a secret meeting."

And now it was Eddies turn to stay silent, for he was no expert on the protocol of such things.

Seven minutes later they pulled into Judge C.R. Magney State Park, home to the Devil's Kettle. Three minutes after that they pulled into the parking area and stopped. Jacobs parked in the back row facing out towards the lot, and the exit. They all got out of the car and stood taking in the pleasant scenery and breathing the thick, humid air.

The path that led up to the Kettle started about a hundred feet from where they were standing.

Jacobs and Shannon checked their weapons. It wasn't as if Eddie had really known her back when Shannon had lived across the hall from him, back when she had been 'watching' him. But seeing her handle a firearm with such an ease and dexterity unsettled him. Jacobs turned to him.

"Your 9mm is in the glove box Eddie, I want you take it and keep it close until I get back."

"Am I going to need a gun?" Eddie asked.

"I hope not but I want you to have it, just in case."

"Just in case of what?"

"Anything." With that he turned to Shannon.

Eddie walked around the car and sat down in the passenger seat. He popped open the glove box and removed the gun. He held it and remembered. He remembered the way it kicked. The way it felt to shoot a man. He felt weak as he stood up and slid it home in his belt.

Shannon and Jacobs finished up a quiet conversation. They nodded to each other, looked to Eddie, and then Jacobs hit the trail.

Shannon glanced at Eddie and smiled. He walked over and stood next to her. For a moment the silence reigned. Eddie pushed some gravel around with his foot. After a moment he spoke, a small smile curling the corners of his mouth.

"I've gotta tell you, I always kind of wondered if we'd ever hang out a little but this is *not* what I had in mind."

"Believe me, Eddie, it's not what I had in mind either." Her eyes scoured the tree-lined landscape but Eddie got the sense that she did that by instinct, that behind those eyes she was far away at the moment. "I'm still not entirely sure how it happened, how they found you and took you from right under my nose."

"Well I don't know much about this whole business, but the one thing I have learned is not to be surprised by the ruthlessness that those people are capable of."

"It's still no excuse. You're abduction is on me." Her exterior demeanor did not change but there was little mistaking the bitterness that her words carried.

They sat quiet for some time, leaning against the car listening to the rustling of the leaves as a heavy afternoon breeze began to pick up. He mentally cursed himself for wearing a black t-shirt, the humidity was causing it to stick. He pulled it away from his tacky skin and exhaled.

Back at the cabin when the subject of his time at Sullivan's hands came up, he was on overload but he thought maybe he could process a little more now.

"So, explain to me again how I'm involved in this fight between your companies. Loeffler, and what was it called, Hawking?"

He was on her left leaning against the car. She nodded then looked at him over her shoulder.

"Pike's so called treasure, your supposed inheritance, isn't exactly money. It's a contract of sorts I suppose…" She stopped and looked back over her other shoulder. He followed her gaze but she was looking at nothing, listening he realized. A vehicle was pulling into the lot. She craned her neck further for a better view of the entrance. "Shit!" She expelled in a toneless breath as she slumped down against the car grabbing Eddie and dragging him down with her.

A truck had just pulled in, a dusty Ford Ranger.

"What is it?" Eddie whispered.

"That truck was parked right next to us when we were at the restaurant earlier. Someone has been following us." They watched two men in feed caps exit the vehicle. Shannon didn't recognize either of them as Sullivan's men but she didn't miss each of them discreetly checking weapons before hitting the trail.

"Alright Eddie, I'm going to have to follow those guys." She looked around and settled on a spot in seconds. "I want you to go around that corner in the lot, over by that informational signage. If you see anything that you feel is a cause for concern I want you to hit the woods and find a place to hole up." Eddie nodded. "You feel comfortable with that thing?" she asked indicating the gun. Again, Eddie nodded. She returned the nod then ran for the trail. Eddie didn't linger long; he headed around the bend in the parking lot.

It was not a moment too soon.

A second later he saw a dark sedan pull into the lot and he was certain that being out of its view was prudent.

Eddie drifted into the cover of the trees, deep enough to see the new arrivals on the far side. The right rear door of the sedan swung open and a man whose name he did not know stood.

Eddie did not need to know his name.

He knew the face. That face had brought him terror and pain in the days he had been kept captive, the days before Jacobs.

Quentin Bellows stood and stretched.

Bellows scanned the tree line and Eddie slumped down against the nearest tree. He could never have been seen from his position but Bellows inspired a level of cold terror that most men could not equal. Eddie was not ready for a confrontation with him. But then, in a heartbeat, everything changed and confrontation seemed inevitable.

Bellows shot a quick glance around the parking lot, his gaze then settled on their car as if he knew what he was looking for. Eddie made a whistling sound as he took a sharp intake of breath. No one was close enough to hear it but still, the sound was loud to Eddie's ear. Bellows had looked right at their car. It took Eddie a long moment to ascertain how the man knew what car he was looking for but then it dawned on him.

It was the way that the car was parked, alone on the backside of the lot, with a full visibility of the parking lot. Backed in, facing the exit for a hasty escape. It was the perfect spot, but to Bellows it must have been conspicuous. He walked right to it.

Eddie held his breath.

Bellows was cautious not to touch the car but he looked in the windows presumably checking the locks. They were disengaged of course, to hasten a retreat. He stepped back and looked at the ground around him. Eddie groaned. He felt as if he could see everything Bellows was seeing. He imagined him looking down into the dirt tract of the parking lot. It wasn't muddy exactly, but somewhat malleable from the humidity. Tracks would be visible and there would be two sets, one heading up the path and the other off to this little stand of trees. As if Bellows was now in his own head, he looked up to the path leading to the Kettle, then directly at where Eddie was crouching in the trees. Eddie startled and almost tumbled over backward.

He saw Bellows stand and start walking in his direction.

Eddie drew his gun.

His hand was sweating. Bellows couldn't have actually seen him from his position but Eddie was afraid that Bellows was skilled at relying on more senses then just his sight. He knew he had to move. If Bellows got much closer it would be over. Just as he was about to move deeper into the woods the doors of the car opened again. Two more goons stepped out into the afternoon sun. They were accompanied by a smaller, skinny man, who looked as though he had no business being there.

It could only be Hanlon, and he was in the company of nefarious men.

Time was now speeding and it was difficult to keep up. Eddie realized, and perhaps a moment too late, that he had lingered too long. Bellows hadn't reached the copse of trees in which he hid but something changed in the set of his body and Eddie knew why. He'd seen enough nature shows on television to understand that the hunter had just scented its prey.

Eddie turned to the woods at his back, and he ran.

Kirk was hauled out of the vehicle and noticed Bellows examining a car on the far side of the lot. Bellows looked up and then off to a stand of trees jutting out into the parking lot from the main bulk of the forest around them. Then Bellows stood and started in the direction of the trees.

"He's going the wrong way." Kirk said to one of his escorts. The man replied not with words but with a sharp rap to the side of Kirk's head. It didn't hurt so much as it just stung but it achieved its desired effect. Kirk Hanlon shut his mouth.

And then his mouth was open again. Not to speak, it had dropped open in shocked disbelief. He didn't dare let his gaze linger for long. He didn't want to create suspicion. He was filled with intermingling sensations of shock, dread, terror, and a twinge of hope as he walked past the dusty, blue Ford pickup. Eddie and Shannon had no point of reference for the truck, Kirk on the other hand did and his heart redoubled its efforts to pump.

He had seen it often over the last few years. It was a 'kicking around vehicle' that belonged to the Sheriff of Castle County. Kirk allowed himself the slightest bit of optimism. It was Bob that had discovered and translated his code. He fought the urge to look everywhere, scan the tree line for signs of his friend, he knew better. The men whose company he kept at the moment would pick up on the slightest change in his demeanor. He continued to hang his head and walk on, but a glimmer of hope was on the rise.

They walked out of the clearing and entered the woods following the path to where the stairs stretched, off and up, into the distance. From there they began the climb.

It was a healthy bit of hiking before the roaring water could be heard somewhere still well above them.

Jacobs stood atop the stairs, the slightest sheen standing out on his forehead. Even he was not immune to the humidity after such a climb. He stood on a small platform facing back toward the stairs, leaning against a large rock at his back that seemed almost to grow from the ground toward the sky. On his right the water rushed by, most of it falling down and over the rocky outcropping where it would then rush off to Lake Superior, but some of it fell directly into a craggy hole in the rocky topography and disappeared, the mysterious anomaly for which this spot was named.

The sound of the rushing water was almost, but not quite, loud enough to mask the approach of people clambering their way up the steps. Not knowing whether the newcomers were an expected party, enemies, or just tourists, Jacob stepped around the large rock he had been leaning against. A small trail ran around it, he followed it putting the rock between him and whoever was arriving. He found a vantage point that gave him reasonable sightlines of the landing without awarding much of a visual to his spot.

He did not recognize the men in the feed caps then, but he noted right away that they carried weapons. The first arrivals to his meeting carried guns and were not Kirk Hanlon. That did not bode well. He was still behind the rock weighing his options when he heard another set of footsteps coming up the stairs. The tread was light and he heard it well before the two men in the feed caps did, but when they did hear it they practiced little restraint. The guns came out in a hurry.

Shannon was not one to be caught unprepared though and she came around the last corner with her weapon already drawn. And that's how the morning's stand-off began, with Shannon and the no longer active portion of the Castle County

Sheriff's Department training their weapons upon one another.

Before things could escalate further from there, Jacobs stepped out with both guns drawn and told the two men, in no uncertain terms, to stand down. They initially chose not to acquiesce.

"What are you doing here?" Shannon asked them.

"I might ask you the same thing." The older of the two replied.

"Why don't you be a gentlemen and tell the lady first." Jacobs said from behind him with a weapon aimed at his head.

The younger of the two men also currently had his gun trained on Shannon. He shifted his weight as if to turn but both Jacobs and Shannon caught it.

"Don't." They both said in almost perfect tandem stopping him short.

"I'm going to ask you another question and I suggest you answer this time." Jacobs said. "If you choose to keep your silence, you'll keep it forever so let's not jack around. Where's Hanlon?"

The older one gave a slight jerk at the sound of the name and then whirled on Jacobs regardless of repercussions. He lowered his weapon but was still lucky to be alive long enough to voice his question.

"What do you know about Kirk?!" the Sheriff spat.

Jacobs' recognition registered as soon as the man turned on him. He'd built a file while researching Kirk Hanlon and Bob Gurley was a big part of it. That would make the younger of the two Ryan Tomlinson, no doubt.

"I need you to settle yourself, Sheriff. I think we're on the same side."

For a moment Bob was dumbfounded. "How do you know who I am?"

"I'm the man that Hanlon was supposed to meet up here. I'm guessing by the appearance of you two, something has gone amiss."

"I think he was abducted." Bob said reticent to just hand over the information but not seeing another option at the moment. "We found a code that led us here."

"A code? When did you find it?"

"Yesterday." Bob was still not sure how forthcoming to be with this man.

"Where did you find it?"

"Who are you?"

"There will be time for those sorts of questions once we know Kirk is not dead. Where'd you find it?"

"It was at his house, on his computer," Bob offered but his response was not whole-hearted.

Jacobs looked to Shannon "He went home, damn it."

"Do you know who would've taken him?" Bob asked.

"Maybe, but who took him is of less import than where they took him."

As if to punctuate, a rapid succession of gunshots peeled, and echoed up the hill from below. Shannon and Jacobs shared a glance. In an instant it was as if the Sheriff and Ryan were no longer there. Again they spoke in perfect unison, one word.

"Eddie."

Then they were bounding down the steps. Shannon was down and around the corner out of sight in a heartbeat. Jacobs slammed past Bob and Ryan and disappeared as well. Ryan and Bob shared a look, they had no idea who these two were or who 'Eddie' was but they knew something about had happened to Kirk. A second later Ryan gave Bob a nod and they gave chase down the steps.

Another couple of shots rang out.

It took about half the time to descend the stairs as it had to get up them, but to Jacobs and Shannon it felt like eons. The whole time they were careening down, both half expected to take a bullet at any moment. They were watching the woods as best they could but at the speed they were running, they were unable to give it their full attention. There were no further shots fired. Maybe it was a good sign but then again maybe it was very, very, bad. Every second that it took to reach the parking lot could mean they had lost everything. As they got closer to the bottom they could hear cars peeling out and a lot of shouting. Trouble was afoot. That much was very evident. They passed a body along the path, it was noted, but it wasn't Eddie so its implications could be managed later. Eddie was the only concern.

Chaos greeted them as they reached the parking lot.

More people had arrived and the lot had filled up. The would-be tourists were now running in all directions, many taking refuge in the trees. Both Shannon and Jacobs scanned the lot. Eddie was nowhere to be seen. They both called out for him but received no response. Shannon spotted a woman standing amid the fleeing people who seemed more in control of herself than most of the others still present and walked up to her.

"Are you alright?" Shannon asked the woman.

"Fine, for the most part."

"Can you tell me what happened?"

"We heard what sounded like gunshots from the trail over there. Everyone down here was still standing around, you know, trying to sort out if that's what it was. A few moments later a couple of men came out from the path, one of them had a gun, he fired into the air a couple of times and that's what sent everyone scattering. He pushed the two guys that were with him into a car and they took off."

Jacobs had joined them by this point. "What did the two men that he pushed into the car look like?

"One was skinny, had glasses."

"Hanlon." Jacobs said to Shannon. "And the other?"

"About your height I guess," she said indicating Jacobs. "He was wearing a black short-sleeved shirt."

"Shit!" It was Eddie.

"Will they kill him?" Shannon asked Jacobs.

"Not until they can get what they want out of him. They don't know how much he knows, only that it's more than he knew the last time they had him."

The Sheriff and Ryan reached the parking lot. They both carried their personal weapons. There were not many people still lingering and the appearance of two more gun-toting men cleared those few remaining stragglers to the woods, including the woman that had helped them with Eddie's whereabouts.

Shannon stiffened, her head angled slightly.

"What?" Jacobs asked.

"A car is coming." She paused. "And it's coming fast."

Jacobs turned to Bob and Ryan, without the necessity of words they both nodded to him.

"We'll form a loose line across the entrance."

The four of them drifted into a line across the lot facing the mouth of the driveway.

The rumble of the engine became louder.

"If you're still within the sound of my voice I suggest you head deeper into the trees." Jacobs hollered for any by-standers who still hadn't gone completely to ground.

Silence descended except for the rising drone of the approaching vehicle's engine and the light rustle of the weighty warm breeze through the trees. Bob glanced to Ryan on his left. The nerves he was feeling were apparent on his face. He then glanced to the right and was not sure which was more unsettling, the anxious and slightly scared look of Tomlinson or the calm, cold, murderous look of Jacobs on the other side of him. He steeled himself and faced forward.

They stood like that for another couple of seconds, spread across the parking lot. Tomlinson on the far left then, Bob, Jacobs, and Shannon bringing up the far right. Jacobs took up the command.

"You're Tomlinson, right?"

"That's right." Ryan responded.

"How you holdin' up?"

"I'm alright," and so he sounded but only time would tell if that would remain true.

"If you see Shannon break and run, you do the same, alright? Make an angle for the trees as far back and to the left of the vehicle as you can. Fire every bullet in that gun while you go. Sheriff, you follow behind him. Don't shoot unless he fires himself dry. We clear?"

"Clear." Ryan called back.

"And, fellas?"

"Yeah?"

"Try not to get yourselves killed."

If there were any further instructions to give it was too late. A jet-black Yukon rounded the bend and pulled a hundred feet or so into the lot. An odd sensation of doubling came over Jacobs as he was reminded of the ordeal the day before at Itasca. They all waited as the vehicle slowed to a stop about three car lengths in front of them.

Both of the front doors swung open. The driver and his passenger took shooting stances in the crux of the open doors. Mason, Sullivan's portly henchman, stepped down out of the back seat and walked with an easy gait around to the front of the vehicle. Although his demeanor seemed easy and care free the fact did not escape any of them that he was very careful not to put himself in the line of fire of either of his men. His focus was on Jacobs.

"We come in peace." Mason said, his voice lilting, mocking. Jacobs said nothing. "We're gonna pack up and head on out of here, I suggest you do the same, and I mean all the way out of here. Let these nincompoops go back to Castle Danger." He said indicating the Sheriff and Ryan. Bob's fury spiked but it chilled as Jacobs shot him an icy glare. "I'm serious," Mason continued, again fixing Jacobs with his intense gaze. "I don't know exactly what your business is here and I don't really care. We can all start killing each other but that hardly seems sensible. It'd make a lot more sense if we just went our separate ways."

Tension hung in the air between them.

"We would be happy to get out of here, except it seems you have our friend," said Jacobs.

"Eddie is not a 'friend'. He's a commodity. I know it. You know it. So let's not shit each other."

"If you say so, but then I guess you've got my commodity."

"Possession is nine-tenths of the law, so they say." Mason spoke through a clenched smile.

"I'd say the law has very little to do with any business we have between us." Shannon spat.

Mason dropped the clenched smile.

"Get out of town. I'm not fucking around. I don't know who you are. But I do know that we will kill you if you stick around long enough to give us a chance." And with that he walked back around the open door and the gunman planted there and climbed back into the truck. As soon as his door was shut the two men slipped fluidly out of sight back into the car pulling their doors shut as they did. The Yukon backed out of the lot to the bend in the road then turned around sharply and peeled out of sight, spitting dirt and gravel in its wake.

The silence was held between the four. For a moment they just listened to the sound of the big engine receding in the distance. Shannon and Jacobs exchanged a glance. Both Ryan and Bob slowly lowered their weapons to their sides, neither spoke. Jacobs broke the silence.

"We better bug out. Police will be here soon."

"We are the police." Ryan said his voice distant.

Jacobs turned and looked at both of them.

"Not anymore you're not, not until this thing gets sorted out anyway. For now you're one of us. Let's go."

7

Late afternoon, June 7th
The house in the woods

Eddie watched Sullivan's fist descend the arc that ended at his jaw but he was helpless to defend himself. He was not bound but his spirit was broken. The fist connected and the pain was instantaneous. Eddie's lower lip mashed against his teeth drawing blood. He watched it spill in tendrils, a lazy drool, soaking into Sullivan's carpet. All hope felt as if it had been wrung from him. He had been through so much and yet here he was, back in this same room.

Blood hung in sinewy strips from his mouth and still Sullivan said nothing. Kirk Hanlon sat in a chair across the room staring into space, his eyes unfocused, blank.

The clock ticked.

The hearth was dark, no fire burning now, not in this heat.

Eddie reflected. At the moment the past was more enticing than the present or the future. He let his mind unwind.

2 hours ago –

Branches were snapping, the sound ricocheting. Twigs were cracking and leaves were crunching the way they do only when silence is of the essence. He was surrounded by a cacophony, leading Bellows on easily, he was sure.

Running hard with no concept of where he was headed, he burst through some dense foliage into a clearing that ran between two sets of the wooden stairs and he ran right over one of the men leading Hanlon up the path.

The man yelped as he fell. Eddie was going down too, but time had slowed for him. As he continued his awkward descent, Eddie looked to the other man still standing next to Hanlon. He watched the man going for his gun, and realized that he was already holding his. Eddie fired a round in the general direction of the man and was rewarded when a fine red spray exploded from the guy's shoulder, misting Kirk Hanlon's wide eyed face in a regal scarlet.

Two things happened at once.

Eddie smashed into the ground and the man he'd just shot started screaming. Eddie watched the man, the second man he had shot in two days, stumble for a second and then attempt to raise his weapon. Again Eddie found his body a step ahead of his brain. Still lying on the ground, he had already brought the gun up for another shot. His pointer finger tensed on the trigger and the thunder rolled. The man in front of him clutched his gut, dropped his gun, and went down in a heap.

He was hollering now in a profanity laden, inarticulate chant. Kirk looked like a blood-stained scarecrow, standing there, eyes as big as saucers and mouth agape as the blood settled on his face. His arms were held out at length as though he was disgusted to even touch himself. Eddie regained his feet and looked to the man he had run over. He was up on one knee having not yet gotten to his own feet. Eddie aimed the pistol at him and was about to pull the trigger when something caught the corner of his eye.

Bellows.

Just off on the left, leaning against a tree watching him. At the sight of him the fight went out of Eddie. They both held guns. Eddie's aimed at the guy crouched in front of him. Bellows' not trained on anything at all, just dangling at his side. Still, Eddie knew better than to think he could still hold the upper hand in this fight.

"Drop the gun, Eddie."

Eddie did as he was told. The man Eddie had shot had ceased screaming but was emitting guttural whining sounds.

"Help your new friend, Eddie. He looks a little shaken," Bellows said referring to Hanlon. "Walk him back the way they came on the path here. We're done with this adventure for the day."

The man in front of him got to his feet and Eddie stepped over to Kirk. He put his hand on his shoulder. Kirk jerked at first but it seemed involuntary. His mind was still a million miles away. Maybe it would be back, maybe not. Eddie got him turned around and headed back up the path.

A shot rang out behind Eddie's back and the moaning stopped. Bellows and the other guy hustled them up the path to the parking lot. They got both of them back into the cars and sped away. He showed no concern for the man left behind.

Now –

The blood in the carpet pooled, gained a small surface

tension, and Eddie came back to himself. Sullivan had asked him something just before punching him in the mouth. Eddie couldn't remember even now, what the question was. He could only assume, judging from his aching jaw, that whatever his response, it had been insufficient.

Hanlon still sat, pie-eyed in the corner. He didn't seem to realize where he was, that this could actually be happening to him. Eddie could sympathize. He had felt much the same the first time he had sat in this room. Now he no longer enjoyed the luxury of disbelief.

From faraway he heard the front door slam. For a moment everything stopped then Mason appeared in the doorway. He made a motion with his head and Sullivan followed him out toward the kitchen. Bellows remained, leaning nonchalant, just to the right of the door. Eddie could hear the soft rumble of low voices from the other room. He looked to Hanlon who seemed to be even more confused about how he had ended up in this mess than Eddie was.

Sullivan walked back in and threw a towel at him. He didn't look at Eddie just took his usual seat across from him. Hanlon looked down at the floor as if finding something of sudden, profound interest there. Eddie dabbed lightly at his mouth but recoiled. The pain was excruciating to the touch.

"Let's have a chat about your new friends, Eddie."

"Fine by me." Eddie mumbled over a fattening lip, and thick tongue. "I don't really know anything about them."

"I'm sure that's probably true. They are difficult people to pinpoint. Fortunately for me, I'm interested less in what you know about them and more about what they might have known about you."

I'm sure you are. Eddie thought, but had the good sense not to say.

Eddie knew this was a subject he probably didn't want to broach with Sullivan. The last time he had been here he had known nothing. The fact that he knew just a little more now, seemed very dangerous. Jacobs and Shannon hadn't told him much but the little bit they had would be easy for Bellows to get out of him. Convincing these two that the little he knew was *all* that he knew would prove a bit more difficult he feared.

"The man with the scar, what's his name?"

Eddie decided this was not the time to hold out. His aching jaw wasn't up to any more push back. "Jacobs," he said.

"And how much was your friend Jacobs able to tell you about your past, how much do you remember now?"

Eddie weighed his options. The fact that Sullivan seemed to be unaware that Jacobs was employed by Loeffler should work in his favor but he didn't know yet how to use that information to his advantage. What he did know was that any delay in answering right now would look like an attempt to lie. These first few seconds would determine the direction and intensity of his interrogation. He didn't know much, might as well go with the truth.

"I know that my grandfather was the pirate known as Pike."

It wasn't new news, not to anyone present but putting the admission out there into the open, took the air out of the room if only for a moment. Even Kirk seemed to come back somewhat, from whatever vacation destination his rational mind had made a break for.

"Did they say anything about his treasure?"

"There was mention of it, yes."

"Did they tell you what it was?"

"No. Only that it was not what that word might lead you to believe." It wasn't exactly a lie but not exactly the truth either.

"Good Eddie, you're doing quite well. Now, and this is important, did he tell you about, or ask you about the key."

"The key?" Eddie asked dumbfounded.

Sullivan nodded.

Eddie tried to keep his face blank as his mind took off like it was strapped to a rocket. The key. Those two little words put a healthy crack in the levee holding back the repressed memories that Sullivan had been after the last time they sat in this room together. It wasn't complete recall but in an instant, moments of a life forgotten began to return. It was all he could do to keep the recognition from registering in his face.

The key.

His birthright. A gift from parents that he no longer remembered. It was just a glimpse of an image, his father covering his small hand with a large one and placing the key in Eddie's palm. *When you are old enough this will bring you your inheritance.* His father's voice, nothing more than an ancient memory. It was just a snippet of his past.

Then Sullivan's angry voice.

"The fucking key, Eddie. Did he talk about the key or why it's important?"

"They never said anything about any key." Eddie replied, he was still technically telling the truth. Jacobs or Shannon never spoke of a key but he was being bombarded by these fragmented memories. Trying to process the information while keeping his outward appearance neutral, made him dizzy.

"There is a key with some sort of phrase engraved on it, and for some reason, it is very important. It's the only piece of this whole fucking puzzle that I'm still missing." He wasn't precisely yelling, but the line had become very fine.

Eddie forced thought and reasoning from his head and with as much innocence as he could muster, he asked the question again.

"A key?"

"Yes, a key! The key Richard Devlin, your goddamn brother, wore around his neck most of his adult life. The key he spouted off about, telling anyone who would listen to him that it was the key to his inheritance. That it was going make him rich someday. The key that was conveniently absent the day Bellows here beat the goddamn life out of him!" He was screaming now, but despite Sullivan's anger Eddie no longer had to feign innocence, he was at a complete loss.

"I had a brother?"

The anger boiled over and Sullivan was on him. Eddie didn't even see him come out of his chair but in an instant he was there before him, raining punches down on Eddie's head.

His already tender lip split wide, and through the pain he could feel the hot flow of blood covering his chin. He curled himself into a ball on the chair as tight as he could, and covered his head with his arms. The punching stopped but then his side exploded as Sullivan planted a boot into his exposed kidney.

Sullivan stormed out of the room.

Hanlon made some very small whimpering sounds from his spot in the corner. Eddie wheezed and sputtered and did his damnedest in spite of the pain, to continue breathing. Bellows remained relaxed at his post by the door. He hadn't moved an inch during the entire onslaught. Eddie was a disaster of different pains but what worried him the most was *how* Sullivan had reacted. Sullivan did not seem the type to lose it, and that he had, was unsettling to say the least.

Sullivan walked back into the room. Hanlon tried to make himself small. Sullivan knelt in front of Eddie and picked up the towel that had slipped to the floor during the assault. He dropped it on Eddie but without malice. Somehow Eddie forced his eyes to meet Sullivan's. The anger was still there but it was back under control.

"You did have a brother, Eddie, and Bellows there killed him. Your very being allowed me the luxury of killing him. If you were to show up in the real world alive, regardless of any fairytale pirate treasure, you would be a very rich man. Even if you were to show up dead, you could destroy my employer.

"I can't have that happen.

"One way or the other, you and I are going to find that key."

8

Afternoon, June 7th
The Cabin near Grand Marais

The return trip had been made in silence. Jacobs and

Shannon were in one car and Bob and Ryan were in the old Ford Ranger trailing behind them.

They arrived back at the rented cabin and settled in, unsettled.

Sitting in an untenable quiet they stared at one another, no one quite sure how to move things forward. At the moment the strained silence was about to turn and curdle, Jacobs spoke up.

"We need to target possible locations that they might have taken Eddie."

"Well I'd still like some answers as to what the hell just happened." Bob said referring to the stand-off at Devil's Kettle. Jacobs turned a hard, cold stare upon him but Bob didn't wither beneath it, just returned it. "Look, we're all a little riled up here and it doesn't seem to be getting us anywhere. Maybe if you can take a step back, tell me how it is that you came to know Kirk and what you know about those people that have him, it's possible that we could actually help each other. If we're more informed we may be better able to help you find your friend."

Jacobs let out his breath slow and steady and dropped his pointed stare. "Kirk was working on a book for a publishing company owned by a corporation called Hawking Inc. Were you aware of that?"

Both Bob and Ryan nodded.

Shannon jumped in picking up the narrative. "Hawking gained most of its strength and power from devouring its competition by any means necessary, means that quite often were not entirely legal. Hawking has grown to a point where its influence is no longer restricted to the private sector. They have become a very strong lobbyist in Washington. They are working tirelessly to manipulate corporate governance regulations and if they are successful they could effectively demolish our company and other competitors."

"So how does Kirk figure in?" Bob asked.

"We think he can help us prove that the majority owner of Hawking Inc. is responsible for the murders of at least a half dozen people."

Bob and Ryan turned to each other. They shared a long look before Bob spoke. "And Kirk can help you prove that?"

"We hope so."

"How?"

"He can help us find Plundering Pike's treasure."

That statement was met by silence.

"You see, Pike's treasure is not really a treasure at all," Shannon went on. "It's a contract forged long ago between Amelie Allan and Pike's son that would, one day, transfer holding in the company that she had taken control of over to Pike's grandchildren."

"His grandchildren?" Ryan asked.

"Richard Devlin," Bob said his voice little more than a whisper. Something was happening in his head, some unknown connection being made.

"That's right," Jacobs said to Ryan before turning his attention to Bob. "Not just Richard but his twin brother Edward as well."

"Richard and Eddie are twins?" Now Bob's voice was hardly audible at all. Any color in his face was draining leaving him ghostly and pale; his voice mirrored his complexion as he went on.

"The woman at the window, she was pregnant with twins…"

Every set of eyes in the room turned to Bob.

"The woman at the window…" He said again before trailing off, giving no further enlightenment as to the meaning of this cryptic sentence.

Three confused sets of eyes scoured him but Bob was not present. His own glazed eyes made it clear he had departed for some distant locale in his mind. He looked as if he was lost in another place, or perhaps another time.

"Old Farmer's Road." he muttered into the stretched quiet, as long repressed memories were triggered and began to envelop him.

"Old Farmer's Road?" Ryan asked confused. "Isn't that

some old urban legend?"

"What are you talking about?" Jacobs asked.

"I have an idea where Eddie might be." Bob said staring off into nothing.

All eyes still remained on Bob and yet his own remained far away.

"What do you mean?" Jacobs snapped.

"I'd bet that they took him home..."

"Could you clarify please?" The edge of his tone sharpened.

"They took him home, to the house at the end of Old Farmer's Road. It was where Eddie grew up, I think. And I was there once, a long time ago."

39 years ago –

They were sitting on the Gurley's back porch. It was Bob and his best friend Sam Madison, Sam's girlfriend Gina Lynn, and Bob's steady, Barb Polinski. Bob was not sure how the afternoon had taken the turn that it had, and he was a little rattled by the way he felt, a swirling combination of fear and excitement. The story of Old Farmer's Road had been all the rage around school the last few days, but sitting out on the porch as he and Sam told the story to the girls, it set something off in him that he couldn't quite put his finger on. It made his blood run hot and cold all at the same time.

Sam was goading the girls, asking if they truly dared to hear the terrible tale of Old Farmer's Road. The girls were giggling and begging him to tell the story. Bob was looking across his large backyard. The sun had just begun its lazy descent to the western horizon, but he couldn't shake the eerie feeling that had started tickling at the back of his neck.

Sam had teased the girls as far as he thought he could before they would turn angry, and he launched into the tale that would haunt Bob Gurley's dreams for decades, whether he remembered them or not.

Her name was Eileen Beckinsale, Sam started, and his

audience of three was rapt. *She was from out east, at least that's what everyone said because of the way she talked. She arrived on the Superior shores, young, pretty, pregnant, and alone. It was cause for a lot of talk around town. There was never any mention of a husband, she didn't wear a ring and she never implied any previous matrimony. 'Minnesota Nice' kept the town ladies from asking her any questions directly about her condition or position and she never volunteered any info. But the ladies who were made for the art of idle chatter were more than happy to create stories of their own.*

Eventually the talk about her died down as she became more a part of the community, but the curiosity never really went away. The baby was born and gifts were delivered. The ladies from the rumor mill took their opportunities, however short, to poke around her home while the gift basket they'd brought was being examined. She kept a comfortable, modest, home. Nothing out of the ordinary, nothing to gossip about. The old biddies were deflated.

Many months passed, and then…

Sam stopped talking and stared out across the yard, it was like he was thinking hard about something, like whatever came next would be hard for him, personally, to tell. The girls bought it hook line and sinker. Bob couldn't be sold Sam's crap anymore, maybe when they were ten but not now. He still enjoyed hearing his old pal spin a yarn though, just like he did when they were ten. Having had enough of the suspense, the girls urged him on. Sam, never one to disappoint, indulged them.

Nobody knew what she was doing out there that night, although it certainly raised the level of mystery about her tale. She and the baby were out driving on Old Farmer's Road. There was nothing out there, no conceivable reason for her to be there and yet she was.

Old Farmer's Road is somewhere northwest of Castle Danger. Only a few folks actually know how to get to it. You'll know once you get there though. The road itself cuts through the woods until it comes to a stream big enough to be called a creek. There is an old iron truss bridge, only big enough for one car to pass, and that bridge is the beginning of Old Farmer's Road.

It had been raining and while it must have made most of the journey down that muddy road a mess, it made the bridge slippery. It was the beginning of the end for Eileen Beckinsale.

The car skidded on the wet grated decking and smashed into the guardrail. Nobody knew why she was there in the first place so no one knows why she needed to be going so fast. From the way the safety rail looked, she must have been flying. It was bowed way out where she had hit it. The noise of the crash must have been huge and scary too, but she checked her baby boy in the backseat and he was fine. The car was a different story. It fired when she turned the key but it wouldn't start up again.

Gina Lynn interrupted him. She wanted to know how Sam knew all the little details as though he was there with her when it happened. She was being playful but the look Sam gave her was hard. This was supposed to be fun. Bob was uneasy because he couldn't really interpret his friend's look. Before he could say anything Sam went on.

This is where things really stopped making sense and started going extremely wrong for this lady. She got the baby out of the car and started to walk. There were no lights anywhere, not as far as she could see. It wasn't pitch-black though. The moon wasn't full but it would be before the week was out so it threw some light. Just enough to make shadows dance and make the mind play tricks. Up ahead something caught her eye. It looked like a white flag floating at about eye level in the trees just to the right of the road. When she got closer she realized it wasn't a flag but a homemade wooden box, painted white. The strokes of paint were fat and lazy and didn't cover the rotting wood underneath very well. There were quarter-sized holes here and there punched into the stale wood and a few old streaks of faded red disappearing into the shoddy white paint job. She didn't want to think about what the red stuff might be.

She pushed on. The woods were eerie and silent around her.

What came next is almost too much to be believed and as far as I know there is no physical evidence to back it up because no one has ever found the old farmhouse.

But she did.

It was the only place she'd seen since she ended up out on this crummy little road. She walked up and the house loomed at her from the dark. There looked to be a bit of light coming from behind one of the shades but then again it may have just been a trick of the soft moonlight. She rapped on the door and waited for what felt like forever. Finally the door was opened by an older guy. He was in his late seventies maybe. She saw that she had been right about the little bit of light. The house was completely dark except for the lone candle he carried with him. She explained her story to the old guy and all the while she talked, his eyes were darting around the dooryard. The second she finished, he ushered her quickly into the house. She stood there, feeling crammed into the entryway, clutching her baby boy to her chest. He said he'd walk her back to her car and have a look at it. Then he disappeared into one of the other rooms and Eileen was left in the darkness of the entryway. She could hear him rooting around in the other room and a few seconds later he returned. He was still carrying the candle in one hand but now in the other he was carrying a rifle. Her breath caught in her throat and she knew he heard it.

He told her not to worry, that it was better to be safe than sorry. He told her there were things in the woods, things they didn't want to go messing with after dark. The words chilled her to the bone as she recalled the unnatural silence on her journey so far.

They started the walk back to the car under the half-light of a pale moon.

All was well for most the way. No reason to worry and why should there be? She wasn't superstitious. She didn't believe there were monsters lurking in the woods. About the time they reached the white, wooden box though everything went wrong.

Sam stopped and stared across the yard. The girls were both holding their breath. Bob waited. When Sam resumed his voice carried the lilt of a man selling his story. Bob liked this better than the far away tone he had been affecting for a time there.

Who knows what really happened out there, if there was actually some faceless evil in those woods that caused the old man to go nuts or if he just snapped. But he went crazy alright. Grabbed the baby and knocked the lady down. Then he put the baby into the box, closed the lid, stepped back and emptied the rifle into the thing. The woman was screaming, hysterical. The old man dragged her all the way back to the house, she screamed into that unnatural quiet the whole way there. Back in his yard he veered from the house to his little garage. Terror consumed her, but not for long. He threw her up against the garage and without a word or any fanfare raised the rifle and fired.

Sam stopped and the tale was done.

It was a nice bit of storytelling, a little grisly there at the end for Bob's taste, but a good yarn, nonetheless. Both girls had lost all their giggling bubbliness.

"That's a stupid story, Sammy Madison," Gina Lynn said as she whacked him with her purse. Barb was quiet and Bob took the opportunity to slip his arm around her and provide some comfort. The sun had fallen low in the sky during Sam's story and dusk was upon them.

"Well, what next?" Sam asked trying to change the subject. It was Bob who surprised them all with his answer.

"We wait til' dark and go down there obviously."

"Oh no, Bob Gurley." Barb said standing up. "I am not going into those woods in the middle of the night." Her tone implied however, that she would be going and that if her Bobby wanted to keep that comforting arm around her that would be fine too. And so the mood was lightened. They waited until the darkness began its crawl and then set off.

They swung by Sam's place so he could try to steal some of his old man's beers out of the fridge in the garage. He ran in and could hear his dad on the other side of the wall, sitting in the backyard, catching the Twins game on the transistor radio. He would be sitting in his deck chair, beer in hand, and a crushed soft pack of Pall-Malls on the table next to him. By the time the Twins went down in the ninth Sam's daddy would be six sheets to the wind and would never miss the beers that Sam made off with.

And so with darkness laying its reign across the land, the four made their way to Old Farmer's Road.

Most of the way was just as one might imagine it, rock music blaring from the car's speakers, teen-age boys and teen-age girls playing their games of give and take. Flirting then turning the cold shoulder. It's a dance that has worked itself out among the young many times before and it was no different for them. The girls laughed every time the boys seemed to have gotten them lost, then quieted in an instant as soon as the correct path was rediscovered. This happened a time or two during the journey into the woods. The country roads were long and dark and drew out for what seemed like forever.

Then something changed.

In an instant the darkness enveloping them was complete. Their skin began to crawl, half from fear and half from anticipation. It was this feeling that they had come out here for. It was the adrenaline buzz they all desired. And then the bridge appeared in the pale glow cast by Sam's headlights.

He let the old Buick roll to a stop.

The metal was an aged brown color.

Sam and Bob shared a quick glance. It was held no more than a moment but in it, much was said. Both boys had heard the stories and liked the idea of a terrifying unknown. They liked the thought of bringing their girls out into a dark wilderness with wild stories running about in their heads.

But now they were here. Was this really such a good idea?

Too late.

"What are ya waitin' for Sammy?" Gina Lynn ribbed from the backseat and Sam, as a boy standing on the threshold of being a man, had no choice but to make a move. Whether it was floundering or not, stalwart or stupid, Sam Madison dropped his old Buick into drive and Bob Gurley was introduced to the bridge that was the gateway to Old Farmer's Road. It wouldn't be the last time he crossed it. Sometimes it would be in his sleep, but cross it again he would.

As they passed at a very slow idle, the bent out section of the bridge where Eileen Beckinsale supposedly crashed with her baby, oxygen felt absent from the car. Bob knew he needed to breath but nothing was happening. He could see on the faces of his friends that they were experiencing the same thing. He also knew nothing supernatural was happening here, that he and his friends were merely being slapped in the face with more fear than perhaps they'd ever been subjected to before. The old Buick rolled ahead, bucking and grating over the bridge and crunched into the dirt and gravel on the far side. Sam let the car roll to a rest and at once they all could breathe again. They all sucked air from any pocket they could find. Each of them did it, yet each of them tried to down play it. They were on Old Farmer's Road now. It wouldn't do to be scared, or certainly not to show that they were.

The Buick rolled on.

It hitched and jumped on old divots and ruts on the half gravel, half dirt road. Bob wondered how this old cart path actually came to be here. He didn't voice his question though; there was no mood for chatter in the car. Branches hung low over them as they drove. The road had not been traveled it seemed for a fair amount of time.

Or someone went to great pains to make it look that way.

That thought was like an ice cube being dropped into Bob's pants. And to make matters worse they had just rounded a bend and in the distance, on the right, just off the road, something white in the shape of a box caught his eye. He looked at Sam to see if he'd seen it. Their eyes meet, Sam had seen it too. He let his foot off the brake and the car rolled to a stop.

"Why are we stopping?" Gina asked from where the girls were sitting in the backseat. Barb hadn't spoken but she reached her arms up around Bob in the front seat and was gripping him so tight that she was cutting off his wind. Then Gina Lynn saw the box. They all saw the box. The car took on a terrible silence. Bob Gurley, at age seventeen, who many years later would take an oath of office and become the Sheriff of Castle County, knew that this was on him.

He gently removed Barb's hands from his midsection and stepped out of the car. He was assaulted by night sounds, a constant humming drone. Bob heard the driver side door open then close and he knew Sam had joined him, but right now he couldn't tear his eyes away from that box. It hung from a tree a mere fifteen feet from the edge of the road. Bob stepped off the road into the brambles. The swashing sound of his pantlegs against the roughage made an ugly awkward sound.

He reached the box.

It was tethered to the tree at about eye level on him. Sam was beside him. Bob didn't hear him come up from behind, the pounding of his heart was blocking out all sound. The two boys shared another look then both tossed a glance back to the girls in the car. Neither said a word, but their terror was evident, written all over their faces. They couldn't stand there all night doing nothing. Bob steeled himself and reached for the lid of the box.

He flipped it open in one quick movement.

The grinding sound of old rusty hinges trying to swing, coupled with the smacking sound the lid made as it flipped open and crashed back against the tree, caused the boys to jump back and the girls to let loose a short scream.

Then the woods were quiet again except for the sounds of agitated nightlife all around them.

Bob and Sam stood back a few steps from the box, neither daring to step forward and peer over the edge into whatever awaited them inside. Bob could tell that Sam, for all his talk, had probably had enough for one night. He could tell by the rigid way he was holding his body. If anyone was going to look it was going to be Bob.

And they hadn't come all the way out here to turn around now.

Bob stepped back to the box. His gaze became fixated on the holes driven into the sides and the grisly reddish hue that, now faded, ran from those holes. At this close distance Bob had no question that they were bullet holes. He'd been going hunting with his dad since he was ten and he knew what it looked like when a bullet punched through cheap pressboard. The inside of the box, behind the holes, was black.

He leaned close so he could peer into the foul darkness. Teetering over the rim of the box his mind was full of imagined horrors that could never have been put into words. The darkened interior was so complete that at first he saw nothing. His breath caught in his throat as his eyes adjusted and he took in the horrors of the box for what they truly were.

"Shit!" Bob barked in a pinched whisper.

Sam made a quick move toward the car but then forced himself to hold his ground. From the car came a short burst of shrieks.

"What the hell is it, Bobby?" Sam asked, his voice was breathy and scared. Bob turned slowly to him, his face blank. Then an ugly grin stole across his face.

"Absolutely nothing." He started to laugh.

"What do you mean?" Sam was still not entirely sure what he'd witnessed.

"I mean nothing. Go look for yourself. It's some kind of an electrical box. It's filled with wires and crap. There was never any baby in there."

Sam slowly inched over to look, and sure enough, it was true. There had never been anything in that box but electrical equipment. The bullet holes and red paint were nothing more than someone's idea of a joke and possibly target practice. Sam had to catch himself to keep from falling as his muscles relaxed.

They returned to the car. Old Farmer's Road had not let them down. It had provided excitement, a moment of sheer terror, and had resolved itself to be nothing more than legend. They continued on down the road looking for the farmhouse but the mood had changed. It was light and good-natured. Now that they had disproved the myth the rest of the story carried no weight and was basically forgotten. They drove on trying to get each other to jump at shadows and the sounds of laughter filled the car. They saw no farmhouse.

Eventually they left Old Farmer's Road that night and returned home. The boys kissed their girls goodnight and all four of them went to sleep in their own beds. As that fall passed, they made the trip back several times. Sometimes they would initiate new people, sometimes it would be just the four of them.

The night they found it, it was again just the four of them.

Most of the drive passed just as it had every time

before. Sam knew the way now without missing a turn. So did Bob. They drove right to the bridge but no matter how many times they came to this place the heebie-jeebies took over as soon as it was in sight. Certainly that was part of the allure of a place such as this. The girls would squeeze them tight as the car bucked on the grating of the bridge or as they slowly rolled passed that decrepit old box. Then like every other night that they'd been out here, they drove on, telling stories and listening to loud rock and roll music. They never really thought about finding the old farmhouse anymore. They had driven this road enough to have determined that the house was just a piece of the folklore.

That night they quit early.

On previous trips they had been much further down the road. Tonight there was other action back in town and they had decided to make an early night of it.

Once past the bridge, Old Farmer's Road was more like an old cart path than an actual road. There was a swath of area cut through the trees the size of a road but the surface itself was just ruts.

That night Sam swung his Buick around on those old ruts, his only intention was to turn his old boat around and head for home. Something caught Bob's eye as the car turned perpendicular to the road. It was nothing more than a glimpse, caught in the splash of the bouncing headlights but he made Sam stop nonetheless.

The boys got out to examine the situation. The tall grass stood high on the sides of the road, a solid six feet. The boys noticed though, that behind the high grass there was a definite break in the tree line at that particular spot.

It was about wide enough for another road.

Bob's mouth filled with a coppery taste as all the feelings he had had the first time they were here tried to consume him. He dared to hazard a glance at Sam hoping to find a little more control in the face of his friend but the grim set of his jaw was telling. It was as if they both knew, right then, that whatever it was that had so drawn them to this place it was not going to let them go just like that. It had its claws in them and didn't want to release.

The girls were beginning to get restless. They had been here enough to have caught the shift in mood of the two boys who had brought them out here under the pretext of being men.

"You want to tell them to hush up before they start hollerin' at us or should I?" Sam asked in a loud whisper, his lips drawn tight together. "Cause I don't know about you, but I suddenly got the feeling we should keep the volume down."

For the moment Bob said nothing.

Without warning Sam took a quick swing with his arm at the tall grass in front of them. As it wavered the headlights of the car illuminated some sort of structure beyond the grass.

Bob and Sam both instinctively hopped back a step.

"Did you see that, Bobby?"

"Hell yes."

"Was it the farmhouse?"

"I don't know. I don't think so. It wasn't big enough, but it was something alright." It was then that the ladies had officially had enough and decided to make their presence known.

"Sam Madison, I don't know what you think you are up to, but I've had enough and I want to go home."

"Gina, shut your damn mouth right now." From Sam's mouth those words might as well have been a slap in the face. He had never spoken to her in such a manner before and it had a sobering effect on them all. "What do we do, Bob?"

Bob was not particularly eager to take charge of this situation but he did anyway. Whether it was in him from the start or this was a defining moment on his road to becoming Sheriff, he could not be certain, but in retrospect it seemed likely. He assessed the situation with the shrewd eye of the man he would become. Bob Gurley took the reins.

"Girls stay put. We're gonna go about a hundred feet into this brush and see what we find. We'll never be out of earshot and we'll come right back."

"Bobby…" Barb started, but he stopped her with a smile. "We'll be right over there and then we'll be back. Just promise me now, that you won't start screaming or anything for no reason."

"How long will you be gone?"

"No more than three minutes and we'll just be on the other side of this brush. Then we'll be right back."

"Do you promise me, Bob Gurley? Promise me that you're coming right back."

"No more than three minutes. I promise." He had taken her hand, now he let it fall. He turned to Sam then started to wade into the tall grass. He saw Sam squeeze Gina Lynn's hand as well. The future Sheriff waded into the tall grass and Sam Madison, like a faithful deputy, followed.

Seventy-five feet in, give or a take a few, the tall grass ended and an opening began. Due to a moonless night it was hard to tell how big the open area was or even what the shape of it was. There was a dim cast in the tall grass behind them from the headlights, but on this side of the wall of greenery there was nothing but the deep black of night.

It took a moment for their eyes to adjust but as they did the boys were able to make out a shed or garage-like structure directly in front of them down a small path that ran through the break in the line of the trees. It must have been what the headlights had reflected off of when Sam had turned the car.

The boys moved closer.

They walked slow and hesitant. Even as their eyes adjusted they couldn't make out the garage until they were right up next to it. Bob looked to Sam and saw a deep mixture of anticipation and fear. Had they found the mythical farmhouse? Well, it wasn't really a farmhouse, being basically a garage, but it was enough to incite the excitement that they hadn't achieved since their first night out here.

Bob signaled Sam to stay quiet and follow him.

They moved along the side of the structure. The darkness was still so complete they couldn't see more than a few feet in front of them. They moved around the front of the garage and something hit Bob's face.

A cloth substance was suddenly wrapped around his head. He panicked and fought trying to remove whatever it was. He wanted to scream. He wondered what the hell Sam was doing while he was being attacked.

Then he felt Sam's hand on his arm and heard him whisper.

"Mellow out, man. It's just a flag."

Bob relaxed, and felt the cloth let go and slide easily off his face. It was indeed just a flag, hung low so that as he came around the corner of the garage it caught him right in the face. His relaxation was short-lived however. He heard Sam's sharp intake of breath as he took in the flag. It settled in the light breeze, flat, so it could be viewed in its entirety. Neither knew what to make of it only that it made their skin crawl.

The Jolly Roger's gaping grin stared back at them.

The flag slapped lightly against the side of the garage as the breeze lifted for a moment and then faded. Both boys stood rigid and still, but their hearts were pounding loud in their chests and ears.

It was a miracle they didn't scream when, from the darkness, a light came on.

It was just one, on the main level of a house that until now had been too deep in the dark to see. The house sat atop a small hill off to the left of them. Bob dropped to his stomach and dragged Sam down with him. He waited for what seemed like an eternity, about ten seconds. When no one came out on to the porch, Bob decided it was coincidence that the lights had happened to come on while there were interlopers in the yard.

"Let's get the hell out of here, Bobby." Sam whispered from beside him. He knew it was the right thing to do. This place was creepy, legend or not, and at the very least they were trespassing. People had been shot for less before. Yet Bob couldn't quite bring himself to quit the adventure just yet.

"Go back to the car, keep the girls calm and for the love of God kill the headlights."

"What are you going to do, Bob?"

"Just a quick little investigation."

"Bob, don't do this. We've had enough foolin' around tonight. Let's just go."

"I won't do anything stupid. I just want a closer look."

Sam gave him a hard look but then without a word he turned on his tummy and sniper crawled back to the tall grass. For a moment Bob caught sight of the headlights as the grass wavered in the wake of Sam's passing. He turned his attention back to the house. He had never been so scared. He wasn't worried about a ridiculous legend anymore, but something about this place just felt like…well, it felt like danger. The windows where the lights came on were covered with drapes. Bob began to move toward the house.

He had just crawled past the porch steps into the angle formed where the steps met the porch itself when he heard the front door swing open above him. He made himself as small as he could squeezed into that little corner. The underside of the porch was walled off with lattice so he couldn't sneak underneath. He could only hope the darkness would provide him enough cover. Heavy boots crunched on the wood above him. One step, then two, then they stopped.

Bob pulled into himself in as tight as possible. He didn't dare look up but he thought he still had cover from whoever was on the porch. Another step or two though and he may not be so lucky.

Time was on its own meter.

It no longer seemed bound to any sort of rules. It made its own way, and its way was slow and plodding. Then it snapped back and the clomping of the boots receded back into the house and was followed by the slam of a screen door flying unimpeded to the jamb.

Bob took a deep breath, then another.

It was time to go, to get out of there before trouble had a chance to make its way too him. Maybe he would have done just that too, if he hadn't caught sight of how the curtain in the window nearest him twisted on the bottom and gave way into this mysterious house.

That was something Bob could not pass up.

He was fully aware that he was now working outside of his rational senses. It bore no weight however. He crawled out from his spot in the angle of the porch and around in front of the steps.

One…Two…Three stairs leading up to the landing. It looked like a mountain.

He stood, hunched over and put his hands on the floorboards of the porch then he lifted the weight of one foot onto the first step. It groaned and in Bob's mind, echoed across the yard. He took one moment to think about Sam and the girls back at the car then he crawled up the steps quickly, thinking it was the best way to go about it.

He made it up onto the porch and waited for the door to swing open again while he sat huddled in front of it like some kind of troll. It didn't happen and Bob moved to the window.

From what he could see the room was sturdy, and moderately furnished. It was not elegant or elaborate but it exuded class. Directly in Bob's line of sight was a beautiful, very pregnant woman sitting in a rocking chair.

Her belly was so swollen that he thought to himself that she must be having twins.

She was conversing with a man that Bob could not see. He couldn't make out their words either. The conversation was no more than a steady cadence of mumbles.

He knew every second that he sat there, huddled on the little porch, that he was just asking for trouble. He knew he should turn on his heels and high-tail it out of there, but every second that he waited the words drifting through the wall were becoming more discernible.

Then the man stepped into Bob's line of sight and Bob saw something incredible.

The man wore a tattoo on his right forearm. The ink was the aged faded blue of sailor's ink. The symbol was something he would see again later, and not remember. In fact he would see it again a number of times in a number of different ways. He would see it in a charcoal rendering, as well as in the crude scabbing on the forearms of multiple dead bodies.

The Plundering Pike.

A pirate dagger stabbed through an X.

He had seen enough. He scurried off the porch as quiet as possible and ran back to the car. It had been a jarring incident, one he would think he could never forget.

And yet he had.

Now –

Bob leaned against the mantel of the darkened fireplace having said his piece. In the cabin their ruminations echoed between them while outside the walls, birds called back and forth to each other.

"We need to find that house." Jacobs said finally.

"Don't know that I can. Brigand's Woods is a big damn place." Bob's voice was weary and distant from the remembrance, and in turn the telling of it. "The landscape has changed a lot over the years. I don't know that I could even find the road anymore much less the house."

"The road would be a start," Shannon said, but the words just hung there in the silence, drifting to nothing like dust motes in the sun.

No one spoke. Bob was standing there, now silent and resigned. It was obvious that he was working internally with no small amount of desperation to latch onto any recall. The conscience of the room stayed focused on Bob but the stillness was stretching out, becoming weighty.

"I'll be damned!" Ryan snapped from his forgotten corner of the room. A hard realization was dawning behind his eyes. His detective skills had come late to the party but they were there now and for the first time since they had left Kirk Hanlon's home, he was feeling like a cop again.

"Robbie Anderson's friends knew how to find Old Farmer's Road, and so did he. And I'd bet dollars to donuts that the reason those boys died is because they found the farmhouse too."

"But even if Robbie can tell us how to find the road, he can't tell us how to find the house. He didn't go out there with those boys." Bob said.

"He might not be able to tell us where the house is, but I've got an idea of who could." All eyes were on him, scrutinizing, but that was fine because now he had the answers. "I think Jimmy Swansby could tell us."

"But we don't have the first clue where Jimmy is." The expiring of any modicum of hope was audible in Bob's voice.

"I'm not so sure that's true." Bob's head jerked up to look at him. The other three had all stood. "I can't believe I missed it." Ryan began to pace. "I knew something was wrong when I was at the Anderson's place. It was the open window in Robbie's room even though they had the A/C on. I saw it but I didn't see it. There were smudges on his closet door too, little signs."

"Ryan, what the hell are you talking about?"

Tomlinson looked up. All eyes in the room were on him.

"Robbie Anderson knows where Jimmy is, or at least he did yesterday because Jimmy Swansby was hiding in his closet while I stood not five feet from it."

9

Late afternoon, June 7th
Sullivan's private study

The man in the expensive suit lit the cigarette dangling from his lips, inhaled and then sent smoke billowing across the room.

"So we have Eddie?"

"We do." Sullivan answered.

"But we also lost more men, and in public."

"That's also true." Sullivan's response was measured, his anger veiled, but only just.

"That's a lot of bodies over the last few days."

"I'm aware of that."

"This has to end soon."

Sullivan eyed him warily. "If you came here to have a conversation about the obvious, I have better things to do."

"The man with the scar that Hanlon was going to meet, the man that had Eddie, his name is Evan Jacobs and who do you think he works for?"

"I don't know. Too many people hate you for me to make an educated guess."

"He works for Loeffler."

Sullivan shot him a serious look but said nothing.

"That's right," the man in the suit said. "If anyone other than me gets their hands on those contracts this is not going to end well, and if Loeffler gets a hold of them, we're screwed."

Sullivan let go of any remaining anger. "I've worked for you and your mother for a very long time. I may not have as much invested in this mess as you, but I'm still in pretty deep myself. The sole reason for my employment is to keep your family safe and out of jail. I have always done my job in the past, and I expect to continue to uphold my duties until whenever it is that I retire. You don't need to worry. I'll do my job."

The two men sat in silence for a long moment, the weight of a treacherous past settling on their shoulders.

"What are you planning to do with Eddie?" The man in the suit asked.

"We'll take him to the farmhouse. He grew up there. Devlin was in those woods when we found him. That place contains answers. We'll take him there and we will make him remember."

Amelie's son, D.B. Allan III, exhaled a streak of smoke across the room.

**

He wanted to ask where they were going but somehow Eddie had drawn the unlucky lot of having to sit next to Bellows. His attention was elsewhere at the moment and as long as it remained that way, Eddie did not care to disrupt it.

Night was coming on out in the woods, but it was coming early. The fall of the darkness was premature as thick clouds, pregnant with rain, began to slip across the sky. The quiet cloud cover provided a false twilight that cast its pallor across the landscape. From somewhere still far off came the faint sound of thunder rolling.

The road they were travelling had ceased to be much of a road at all. A giant oak tree lay across their path a hundred feet up ahead. With the dense heavy trees lining each side of the road it seemed they were on a dead end, but then the driver turned right, into the thick forest cover. They easily parted the low hanging leaf cover of a giant weeping willow that Eddie hadn't even noticed. The tree had blended seamlessly into the rest of the foliage along the road. But now under its umbrella, Eddie could see that it had been cleared by man and for a reason. It opened onto another well-worn road that ran parallel to the real road for a bit then came back out to the main thoroughfare well beyond the fallen tree.

"Well I'll be damned," he said aloud momentarily forgetting himself. He drew Bellows' gaze but the ogre did not speak. Eddie said nothing more and after a moment that seemed an eternity Bellows turned and looked back out the window.

Eddie stole a glance back over his shoulder at the fallen tree laid out across the middle of the road. It looked natural enough but it was obviously a deterrent to keep anyone who happened to be driving out here from continuing on down the road.

Leaving the fallen tree behind them they came around a bend and Eddie's blood ran cold.

The monstrosity before them towered against the backdrop of the oncoming clouds. Up ahead was the old, iron, truss bridge that was the gateway to Old Farmer's Road. Lost memories, surprise revelations and overwhelming emotion were about to become the norm for Eddie but the shockwave that coursed through him at the sight of it demanded the entirety of his focus for the moment.

They broached the mouth of the bridge and passed under the girders. The car kicked and bucked as it traversed the grated metal decking. Eddie's stomach turned caused only in part by the jouncing motion of the vehicle. The stunned feeling that had gripped him at the sight of the bridge intensified as they passed the bowed out guardrail. It compressed in his chest but then they were clear of the bridge and Eddie's breath came a little easier.

After crossing the bridge they drove on for another five minutes or so. The driver then veered off into another hidden path. Nothing had blocked the road here. It would have been entirely possible, if not probable, to keep rolling right past and miss the turn.

As so many kids had.

All of them in fact until Jimmy Swansby and his two dead friends had found it.

For much of the youth of this region it was the pot of gold at the end of the rainbow, and just as unattainable, the farmhouse at the end of Old Farmer's Road.

The black sedan carrying Edward Pike III rolled out of the woods into a clearing, past a small garage on their left, and came to a stop. A second car, bearing both Hanlon and Sullivan rolled in directly behind them.

The house stood, majestic, atop a small hill in the faux twilight. Someone had absolutely been manning the upkeep. The wooden siding looked as though it had very recently received a fresh white wash. Flowers were blooming in planters on the large wraparound porch.

Edward Pike, formerly Eddie Watson of Duluth, felt something in him trying to shut down. So much information flooded him at once that his brain acted like a circuit breaker. The breakers were tripped and connections were lost. For the moment nothing new was being processed.

In the distance thunder rumbled again.

Eddie stumbled out of the car and stood staring at the house.

He was in too much turmoil right now but very shortly, when those circuits were reconnected, a few things would begin to come together for Eddie. Those wisps of ideas that Sullivan had tapped with the mention of the key would begin to solidify.

Eddie would remember.

Pike's treasure did exist, and Eddie had a key of his own.

The door of the second vehicle swung open and Sullivan stepped out into the coming night. He stretched for a moment then dropped his arms and turned to Eddie.

"Welcome home, young master Pike."

10

Early evening, June 7ᵗʰ
The Anderson Residence

Chuck Anderson stood his ground on the porch above them.

Neither Bob nor Ryan had tried to mount the stairs to the porch yet. Chuck didn't want to tell them that they weren't welcome up those steps but if push came to shove he wasn't entirely sure that they were. This morning that might have been a different story, but now it was just that, a different story.

He had been surprised enough when he pulled the shade aside to watch the Sheriff, who had been at least temporarily relieved of his duties, pull up the driveway. Surprise began to give way to fear as a second car pulled in. He watched two strangers get out of the vehicle and both were carrying weapons. For reasons he couldn't have entirely explained, he had told Mindy to grab his rifle from the bedroom closet and leave it inside the door.

News about Jesse Tremely's death combined with the

death of the other two boys, his son's friends, had made the Anderson family and many others in the small town of Castle Danger afraid and suspicious.

He realized Bob was speaking to him.

"We just need to speak with Robbie for a second, Chuck, then we'll be on our way."

"Ryan was up here and talked to my boy already. What more do you need from us?"

Ryan stepped forward. "We just have a few more follow up questions for him."

"He's been through enough since yesterday, Deputy. I don't want to put him through any more than need be."

"You're not going to have much choice in a minute." It was Jacobs. He had strolled a few feet up onto the lawn to the left of the porch, and Chuck Anderson. Bob shot him a quick, frustrated glance. This was his situation to handle.

"Who's your friend, Sheriff?" Chuck asked. His tone and inflection on the word 'friend' was anything but friendly. Bob tried again to diffuse the situation.

"Chuck, I need you to understand that I'm giving it to you straight here. Who these folks are is none of your business. We just need a few minutes of Robbie's time then we'll be off your porch and on our way."

"How am I to know if you're giving it to me straight, Bob?" His voice was strained as he spoke. "The TV news said you had taken a leave of absence as of this morning, and yet here you are asking to see my son who, by the way, has been scared half to death ever since this whole thing came out yesterday."

"Times up."

It was Jacobs again. He started to move in on the porch. At his first step, Chuck took a step back and opened the door retreating into the house. He found his old .22 leaning against the jamb. As he grabbed it the realization was dawning on him that he was about to take up arms against a man he had known for years, the Sheriff. At least he had been the Sheriff until last night. The whole world seemed upside down at that moment. He swung the stock of the rifle up to his shoulder and stepped back out onto the porch.

Both Bob and Ryan remained where they were. Chuck could see the weariness in their eyes and the downtrodden expressions they wore. It was almost the last thing he ever saw. He registered the fact that in the mere seconds that he had stepped inside the door, the two newcomers had flanked him and drawn their own weapons.

He knew that he had misjudged this whole situation. That he had let his emotions get the best of him. That he had made all the wrong decisions since they had pulled up the drive, but now the thing was in motion and he wasn't entirely sure it could be stopped.

He heard Mindy as she opened the door behind him. He yelled for her to stay inside but it was too late, she was coming. His eyes darted back and forth trying to gauge his adversaries' positions and their intent. He had exacerbated the situation by bringing out his weapon, he knew that, but he also knew if anyone of them pulled the trigger and hit Mindy he would not stop firing until they gunned him down too.

Thankfully, it never came to that.

It happened very fast for Chuck Anderson, but Shannon and Jacobs were professionals. Maybe if Chuck would have accidentally squeezed off a round everything would have been different, would've turned disastrous, but he didn't. Robbie chased his mom out onto the porch and everyone stopped. He stepped up behind his dad and put his hand on the barrel of the rifle nudging it towards the porch floor. Robbie looked at Bob and then to Ryan.

"I guess I knew you would be back."

For a moment no one said anything then Ryan spoke breaking the silence.

"Can we ask you a few more questions?"

Robbie shrugged and then looked all the way around his yard taking it in for the first time. Shannon and Jacobs were no longer aiming their weapons but they still held them loose by their sides. "Yeah I guess, come on in." He said finally.

Ryan followed the stunned and terrified Andersons back into their living room. They disappeared into the house and a palpable quiet fell over the yard. Bob shot Jacobs a look that was hard to read. After a second his features softened but he turned and directed his next statement to Shannon.

"Why don't you all head back to the cabin. It'll help soothe Chuck's mind a bit to have you out of his front yard. We'll head back as soon as we've got something."

Jacobs nodded. "Okay, Sheriff. Just find out where that farmhouse is before Eddie runs out of time."

Bob didn't look at him, just shook his head and walked up to the Anderson's porch. He heard the car start behind him and the gearshift drop into reverse then he was across the threshold and into the house.

The Anderson's living room was dark, the first clouds creeping past the sun as it was making its long, slow dip towards the back of the house. Chuck stowed his rifle in the corner and hung there a moment, not wanting to look these guys in the eye. It was partly shame at raising a gun on two men that were, not only the law, but also neighbors. More than that though he was still harboring some anger at the men who *were* the law and *were* neighbors coming to his house and piling on to the stress that his son was barely handling as it was. Mindy vanished off to the kitchen to put coffee on, her natural instincts told her to be a host above all else. That left Robbie to stand and face Bob and Ryan. Ryan spoke.

"We need to talk to Jimmy Swansby, Robbie. I know he was here before, hiding in your closet last time we talked." Robbie's face lost some of its color but he didn't deny it. "I'm sure he's scared, but we know a bit more about what went on out there in the woods the other night and those people that were outside can help us protect him."

"Speakin' of, who are they?" Chuck asked turning around and joining the conversation.

"Look, Chuck," said Bob. "I know it sounds like a load of crap but the truth is you really don't want to know. All that matters is that they are on the right side of the law and can help." Chuck had more to say on the subject but before he could get it out, Robbie stepped forward.

"You promise he'll be alright?"

"Promise." Ryan said. Bob nodded his assent as well.

"Cause he's awful scared. He was right there when Billy and Scott were killed."

Both Bob and Ryan could see the distress in Robbie's eyes. The last few days had aged his young face. It left them to wonder what state Jimmy Swansby might be in.

"We can take care of him and get him back to his parents."

Robbie looked hesitant, like he still needed a bit more convincing. He was in a hell of a spot and he was still just a kid. Before any further convincing could be done the Anderson's old stairs creaked.

A moment later, Jimmy Swansby came down the steps. Bob took in Chuck's reaction and there was no question that it was genuine. He had had no idea that this kid had been holed up in his house.

Jimmy took the stairs slow, favoring his right leg. Robbie had obviously provided him some clean clothes but it was just as obvious that he hadn't risked being discovered by taking a shower. He may have had access to a washcloth but his nails were dirty and grime stood out thick at the base of his hair. Small cuts marred his arms and face.

Ryan stood.

No one spoke.

Tears rimmed Jimmy's eyes and slipped down his cheeks, tracking through the light sheen of dirt.

"If you can tell us how you came to be out there, it would be of great help." Ryan said, starting slow.

They had gotten Jimmy settled in Mindy Anderson's big rocking chair. She had tried to fuss over him at first but his responses were despondent. She gave up and left him to the questions posed by Bob and Ryan. Up to this point he had only given yes or no answers so the likelihood of them receiving a pertinent cognitive response seemed nil, but then he spoke.

"We went to find the farmhouse at Old Farmer's Road."

The adults in the room shared a quick glance. The two youngsters did too, feeling the weight of a ridiculous legend receiving credence.

"Go on." Ryan prodded, knowing time was of the essence but also aware that to push him could be to lose him.

"We'd been out to the old road a bunch of times, and it was fun but we never found anything resembling a farmhouse. Until the other night, that is. Billy and Scott said they had been out there earlier and had found a turnoff that had been hidden. In the daylight they hadn't dared check it out, but once night fell they couldn't get over it. So we went. The hidden drive led right to a garage and there was the house, just sitting up on this little hill. None of us would've admitted it, but we were scared. Excited too I suppose."

Mindy returned with a cup of coffee, his manners were intact but his actions were desperate and greedy. He grabbed the mug and slurped. He pulled his lips back up on his gums combating the heat and they all had a glimpse of the old man he still might yet become.

"What happened next?" Bob asked.

"A couple of guys came out of the house and we hit the deck." He paused and took another sip of the coffee but displayed more caution this time. "We were still in the darkness down by the garage. I thought maybe the sound of the van was what had brought them out but then they started talking."

"And you could hear them, could hear what they were saying?"

"Yeah, the one guy said, clear as a bell 'if we don't get Eddie back soon I swear he's gonna kill us all'."

"Eddie? They used that name, Eddie?"

Jimmy nodded and sipped his coffee with continued deference.

Bob and Ryan shared a glance. "Then what happened?"

Ryan asked, trying to urge him on but again trying not to push.

Jimmy gave a little laugh. It was grim and without humor. "Scott farted, a little squeaker like a balloon deflating. I know it sounds dumb and it was the stupidest thing that could've happened but it did and that's the truth. Then it got all silent, the guys on the porch stopped talking. We were huddled down by the garage, but then Billy got the giggles.

"One quick, short, little bark of laughter, then dead quiet for a second, then they started shooting. No warning, no nothing, just started shooting.

"The windshield of the van blew out and I heard Billy yell 'run', and I did. I never looked back. I never saw which way Scott and Billy went. I never saw them again. I just ran." He stopped talking and stared into space trying to deal with the reality and failing. It had been a continuous cycle since finding his way out of the woods and to Robbie Anderson's window. The world he knew no longer seemed to make any sense.

When it was clear he was not going to go on, Ryan spoke.

"Jimmy, I have to ask you one more thing," he paused. "Do you remember how to get to the farmhouse? Do you remember where that hidden turnoff was?"

At first it seemed he wouldn't speak, almost as if he hadn't heard the question at all, but then he did.

He said, "I won't ever forget it," and a distant sadness came over him. "No matter how hard I try."

11

Late evening, June 7th
The farmhouse at Old Farmers Road

Eddie wandered the home of his youth.

Outside thunder rumbled, still distant but approaching.

He laid his hands on knick-knacks and old memories. There was an abundance of both in this place of his past. He marveled at the capacity of the human mind to simply set aside the things it desired, important things that could be relegated to the shadowy corners of the brain.

The house was basically as it was all those years ago. Every few steps he would find some new piece of nostalgia that would bring on another flood of forgotten images.

The men that had dragged him out here, now waited patiently. Mason and a man he didn't know stayed by the door. Sullivan sat in the living room and waited. For now he applied no pressure. This part was something Eddie needed to do himself, at his own pace. His recollections of this place were central to them getting what they wanted, so they kept themselves in check and let Eddie take it in as it came back.

He knew the second they had pulled into the driveway that it was the house that he grew up in. A few things had snapped together instantaneously. The house. The yard where he had played with a brother he could barely recall. And the keys that his father had given them, the recollection of which, he had so far been able to keep to himself.

They had received the keys shortly before his father's death. What had happened to his parents was still shrouded, but he remembered clearly his dad sitting them down in the living room and handing them each a key on a chain. He had explained that those trinkets would unlock their inheritance. He had told them that keys were symbolic, but would also be necessary. Exactly what that meant though, was still a mystery to Eddie.

What he did know was this:

There was significance in the fact that there had been two keys. What that significance was remained a mystery as well. Just out of his reach, but it was important. Of that, he was sure.

He also remembered where his key was hidden, and it was right there in the house, or had been anyway the last time he saw it. This was information he had opted to keep from Sullivan until it became detrimental to his health to continue to do so.

Eddie had already made a quick tour of the second floor, where his bedroom had been. The room was still intact and seemed to be, for the most part untouched. His recollections were little more than fragments of a whole that was still coming together, but he saw the box on his top shelf right away. That box was one memory that was not escaping him. He remembered putting his key there the night his father had given it to him.

He did not linger, but strode down the hall surveying the other rooms as he went. Recall came slow, the memories hanging back in the shadows but the dulled edges were sharpening as clarity attempted to find its way. He was unsure how much Sullivan knew already, but he intended to keep any new findings on his part to himself for as long as possible.

Keeping his head straight though was proving a tall task. Every room he passed brought forth a new onslaught of images that he had buried deep. Images of his parents were swimming in and out of focus. He could see them as they were back when he was a child, his father strong and sure; his mother poised and beautiful. It cut him deep to realize how much he had blocked out. Quiet, tender moments with his family; wrestling on the floor with his brother, other moments that should've helped to define who he became.

He moved back through the main level with old ghosts nipping at his heels. He knew he had to push the memories aside and focus on devising some sort of plan. Hanlon was in the main sitting room with Sullivan, waiting. Sullivan looked relaxed but Eddie knew he was taking in every slight nuance of the situation as it unfolded before him. Bellows had been wandering the house as well, keeping tabs on Eddie.

How to reveal his newfound knowledge of the key, and what would come next? These were the questions most pressing at this point. Sullivan must believe that he knew what the key would open or why would they be going through this whole charade. Eddie wracked his brain trying to remember what lock the key would fit. He had known, once upon a time, of that he was certain. Now it remained elusive, stuck among the clutter at the corners of his mind.

Sullivan's phone began to ring and everything stopped. Sullivan reached into his pocket, removed the phone and answered it. The house was silent but for the ticking of the old grandfather clock. Sullivan listened, nodding here and there but not saying anything. Eddie realized he was holding his breath and let it out in a light, slow sigh, wanting to make as little noise as possible. Sullivan continued to listen but he was watching Eddie. His gaze made Eddie uncomfortable and after a long moment he looked away. Sullivan had his phone to his ear but he was still looking right at Eddie. He wasn't about to miss a beat, not right now. Eddie glanced toward Hanlon. Kirk looked less lost now. In fact he was watching Eddie with a look in his eye that Eddie couldn't quite decipher.

Sullivan ended his call.

"My employer says we're running short on time, Mr. Pike." Sullivan was wearing a slight smile but his voice carried a cold chill.

"I don't think I would like to be called that." Eddie responded, not knowing what to say but feeling it necessary to fill the void. To kill some time.

"Come grab a seat, Eddie." Sullivan motioned to the armchair directly across from him. "You've walked around this house now and you've done a fine job of keeping up a neutral façade, but I'm not buying it. I think things are coming back to you. You better start telling me what I am interested in hearing or this situation is going to start getting very ugly for you very fast."

Both Kirk and Eddie registered the fact that Bellows had just walked back into the room. It was as if there was now less air available in what was already beginning to feel like cramped space. It was like his mere presence was sucking up a majority of the oxygen.

"Eddie, where is the key? It's here somewhere."

Eddie had never been a poker player. The nuance concerning the right time to fold was not a skill that was known to him. Eddie did not fold.

He bluffed.

"I don't know what you're talking about."

Eddie saw Kirk cringe before he even realized what was happening. Bellows stepped in and grabbed his left wrist and flipped it over, exposing the underside of his forearm. Bellows was so fast that Eddie didn't even really register the pain until he was almost finished. A long slash down, a quick one across and X to mark the spot. He had just carved the 'Plundering Pike' into the youngest Pike's forearm. Eddie's reprieve from the pain only lasted for those first few seconds and then he was howling. Kirk turned away, Sullivan's gaze never wavered. As soon as Bellows had finished he produced a towel and Eddie quickly wrapped it around his bloody forearm. From elbow to wrist, his arm was a throbbing, sinewy mess.

Eddie pulled himself back into some semblance of control. He raised his head and met Sullivan's eyes.

"Upstairs in my room, on the top shelf, there's a wooden box with a false bottom. The key is in there."

Sullivan nodded his head towards the stairs. The nod was almost imperceptible but Bellows started off for the stairs and disappeared. Sullivan continued to keep his eyes riveted on Eddie. His guys had been over everything in that room, as well as all the others. He could hardly believe something as little as a false bottom had kept them from finding the key on their own.

They could hear Bellows clomping around upstairs. He moved around in Eddie's old room then there came a string of banging sounds followed by a string of expletives. Sullivan glanced towards the stairs and in the brief respite of the man's glare, Eddie couldn't help but smile. He knew why Bellows couldn't open it.

Bellows came down the steps carrying the little wooden box. Ever prudent, Eddie wiped the smirk off his face before anyone had a chance to catch it. Without a word Bellows tossed the box to Eddie. He bobbled it and almost dropped it still trying to keep the now blood soaked towel wrapped around his forearm. He was about to ask Bellows what he was supposed to do with it but the smart-ass comment died in his throat.

Common sense advised against it.

The keepsake was the size of a small jewelry box, five inches or so across and three or four deep. Eddie took stock of the room. Hanlon was rapt and made little effort to hide it. Eddie was sure Sullivan felt the same but managed to keep any physical manifestation to a minimum.

He flipped the box upside down. The bottom was covered in a rough felt, and it had four little legs. Eddie looked at the underside of the box for a long moment then he grabbed the little leg on the upper right corner and gave it the slightest clockwise twist.

A compartment popped open. The rough felt had obscured the lines of the little door. Eddie flipped the box back upright holding his hand underneath it.

A silver key on a silver chain dropped into his hand.

Eddie looked at the key in awe.

More memories flooded over him and these were the ones that counted. The little mysteries were coming clear now. Etched along the length of the key were the words 'Atop the sea we sail....' The phrase was familiar to him. It was the beginning of a rhyme he had once known quite well, words that he now remembered hearing slip from his father's lips long ago. He read it aloud but then continued on from memory.

"Atop the sea we sail, and always keep a watch-ward eye..."

"...and to the locker when we bed for a pirate soul don't die." Sullivan finished the second part of the couplet. Eddie stammered for a second.

"How... how did you know that?" he finally sputtered.

"Another man, also in a very dire situation, spoke those words to me once."

"My father...?" Eddie's voice was little more than a whisper.

"That's right. I assumed it was of some import seeing as it was the last thing he ever said."

"You killed my father?"

Sullivan took the key from him and then removed his

weapon from the shoulder holster where he had it stowed. He racked the slide hard, chambering a round. It was a brazen, showy act. He didn't care. He wasn't trying to be subtle. He was putting punctuation to the situation. The shock and confusion that already mired Eddie's visage deepened.

"I think I'll ask the questions from here on out Eddie." Sullivan lowered the barrel of the gun to right between Eddie's eyes. "Where's the lock that fits that key? And don't you dare tell me you don't know or you're dead."

12

Time traipsed on as it always does.

The unlikely quartet of corporate security forces and suspended members of the Castle County Sheriff's Department were reunited and were sitting on the porch of the cabin waiting out the light.

Jimmy Swansby had given them what they needed in terms of a location and directions. Now they waited for night to fall. The thickening cloud cover would hasten the timetable. Soon they would make their move, but they wouldn't be going together.

"You're sure you won't need us?" Ryan asked.

"It's for the best that we leave you out of whatever happens at that farmhouse. And if you think there might be something at Kirk's house that can help us locate those contracts then you should go and try to find it."

An elusive 'something' had begun a slow scratch, working at the surface of the back of Ryan's mind. A loose end, that was no more tangible than that, had started gnawing at him. They had missed something at Kirk's house. He was sure of it. What they had missed, or why it mattered eluded him but that changed nothing in his conviction that something had been passed over.

The code leading them to Devil's Kettle had been written in Jessy's duty book. He must have copied it over from the computer, that's where he had told Bob he had found it. That he had jotted it down made perfect sense but there was something about the procedural process of the whole situation that Ryan couldn't make add up. The code and the computer kept floating to the top of his mind but there was something else, he just couldn't get whatever that last piece was to solidify for him. So he and Bob were going back to Kirk's place while Shannon and Jacobs made their way into Brigand's Woods to the house at the end of Old Farmer's Road.

The evening air was full of sounds. The twilight symphony was beginning its swell. Soon all creatures would scurry for cover as the thunder rumbled ever closer. For a long while no one spoke. Then the air got heavier, the moment took on weight as the time for action grew near and the sense of anticipation deepened. It was time for the two parties to part their ways.

They said their goodbyes beneath the cover of bruised clouds.

In theory they would all be seeing each other again soon, but a theory was nothing until tested, and once tested, so many of them fail. They were all aware of the stakes but it was never as crystal clear as it was in that moment. A goodbye could be just that.

Everything that needed saying had been said with one exception.

Bob and Ryan stood up from the porch ready to make their way over to the dusty old Ford. Before they did though, Bob turned to Ryan.

"We should give it to them," he said.

Ryan looked at him for a long moment then nodded. He reached into his shirt, up by the collar, and pulled out the key. He lifted the string it was attached to from around his neck. Shannon stood and Jacobs stepped forward.

"What is this?" Jacobs asked unable to keep a hint of

excitement out of his voice.

"It's a key we found. Kirk Hanlon was pretty confident that it had belonged to Richard Devlin. If you find Eddie he might know what to do with it."

Etched along its shaft were the words: 'And to the locker...'

The look of awe did not fit his face as Jacobs reached up and wrapped his hand around the little chunk of silver.

Bob and Ryan walked to the pickup and got in. A second later the old engine roared to life and a second after that the steady hum it was producing dropped in pitch as Bob put the truck in gear.

Above them the thunder rolled.

13

Night, June 7th
The farmhouse at Old Farmer's Road

The cold steel pressed to the bridge of Eddie's nose expelled any rational thought. Forgotten truths such as his father's old nursery rhyme washed over him in waves then crashed and broke as if smashing on a rocky shore, never remaining full or whole. Just a continuous cycle of half-formed images rolling in and then dissipating, dashed before they could take shape.

The barrel of the gun that filled his field of vision did not afford him the luxury of focus. Rage only heightened the confusion that was being caused by these cascading memories. The unbridled hate he felt for the man before him was immense, consuming. "You killed my parents!" Eddie spat.

"I suppose it's just semantics but technically, for the record, *I* didn't kill them. What does the key open, Eddie?"

"Fuck you."

Sullivan lifted the barrel of the gun from Eddie's face, but with a quick snap of his wrist brought it back down on the bridge of his nose. There wasn't much force behind the blow but enough to cause Eddie's vision to blur and create a little light show on the back of his eyelids. The pain subsided after a second or two but the point was made.

"You killed them." He muttered.

"I just told you I didn't."

Pain exploded from Eddie's lower back, shooting up to his neck and dropping him to his knees. The blood soaked towel that had wrapped his forearm drifted to the floor.

Bellows had come from behind him, flanked him and planted a sucker punch in the area of his kidney. The pain was big and bold, flaring. He felt Bellows' breath, hot and rank against his ear.

"I did it. I killed your parents. Your mommy, she at least died with some decency. It was your daddy that cried and begged.

Eddie cracked.

A fiery anger split through the middle of his grief and confusion. He whipped his head to the side and sunk his teeth into Bellows' exposed cheek. Bellows yelped and began pounding Eddie's head hard with both of his fists, but not anticipating such a move from such an adversary, he had gotten too close. Now with Eddie's jaws latched onto the fleshy part of his cheek he didn't have a good angle with which to land a blow. Eddie sunk his teeth deeper, blood poured over, and into, his mouth. It was hot and gross but Eddie hardly noticed.

Sullivan pistol-whipped the back of his skull, and reflex caused him to release. He slumped to the floor. Bellows howled and kicked him, hard, in the gut. He gagged as his oxygen was displaced and Bellows' blood filled any void it had left. The realization of what had filled his mouth caused him to gag again. He spat hard onto the floor and tried to catch his breath.

Bellows kicked him again, this time physically lifting him into the air. He flipped and landed on his back, still gagging. He turned his head and expelled as much of the foul filth that was soiling his mouth as he could.

"That's enough." He heard Sullivan say. He turned his

head to look at Bellows. His vision was sliding in and out of focus but he watched as the hulking shape skulked off to the kitchen to dress its wound. It wasn't much but it felt like a win. With a great effort he rolled his head back the other way to look at Sullivan. He found him squatting next to him, getting down into his line of sight.

"Don't make me ask you again, Eddie."

"I'm not telling you anything until you tell me what happened to my parents." Eddie rasped.

"You're in no position to negotiate, you don't have any leverage."

"If you're just going to kill me anyway I don't need any leverage."

"There is a damn good chance you are dying tonight Eddie, but it doesn't have to be excruciatingly painful. If you tell me what I need to know I can make it nice and peaceful for you. If you choose to make me have Bellows force the issue, you can expect quite the opposite."

"You don't have the time to torture me."

"I have all the time in the world, Eddie. We're not going anywhere."

"You don't have the time that you think you do. Jacobs is coming."

"He doesn't know where you are."

While that was technically true, Eddie saw something in Sullivan's eyes shift. Could he count on the fact that Jacobs wouldn't find them? It had happened once before. Eddie opted to press the issue. "He found me on the boat."

Sullivan's eyes steeled but the set of his body was not exuding the confidence that it had a moment ago. "That was luck, that sort of thing doesn't hold."

"Are you sure enough about that to risk it?"

Sullivan said nothing for a moment. He glanced at his watch, attempting to do so with an air of nonchalance but Eddie could tell he was weighing the various scenarios. After another long moment he gave a small chuckle that did nothing to veil his aggravation and exasperation.

"Alright, Eddie, I'll tell you about your parents. It's not a long story and I can't say you'll be happy to have heard it once you do. They'll still be dead."

Eddie said nothing, and tried not to telegraph any emotion at achieving this little victory.

"It started with your grandfather. He made many enemies, one of which was the mother of my employer. Her name was Amelie. Your grandfather once stole a painting from her, and sealed in the backing of that painting were some very important documents.

"She used any and every asset at her disposal to find him and recover the painting.

"Through her marriage she was a very rich woman, but she was hardly a wife. Her husband treated her like property. She was not interested in being a well-cared for servant. Her husband and his father had destroyed her family, brought shame on her own father, and had forced his hand in the decision to sell his eldest daughter off into marriage. Amelie intended to have her vengeance.

"She found a man who had often sailed with your grandfather. For a hefty sum he agreed to put the two parties in contact. Pike was older at that point; your father was a grown man with a couple sons of his own.

"They brokered a deal in secret.

"Pike returned the painting as well as the damaging documents to Amelie; the only condition being that once she had destroyed her husband and taken control of his assets you and your brother would share an equal portion of a fifty percent share in the company. It would become effective on your thirtieth birthdays. Anxious to destroy her husband she agreed to the terms.

"It took just over six years for her to ruin Allan, abolish their prenuptial agreement and change his will. He came by a most unfortunate car accident soon after and she took control of what had become a huge and powerful corporation, Hawking Inc.

"It was now time for her to make good on her deal with

your grandfather. Some might say that Amelie was not a very forgiving woman, that she still held an insidious grudge against the man who had kept her from attaining these goals so much earlier. I think the truth is that while plotting the demise of her husband she fell in love with your father. It was his lack of reciprocation that ultimately fueled the drama we are living out today.

"After having her personal wants and needs denied for so long, being rebuffed by your father sent her into a quiet jealous rage. On the day the contracts were signed, Amelie took your parents out on her yacht. A yacht she had reported stolen a month earlier. They were intercepted by me and my men. Despite what Bellows here says he'd have been a little young for that sort of work at the time. One of my other men handled it quickly, a single gunshot to the head for each of them."

At that Eddie winced.

"Amelie had made only one mistake. At the same time that the yacht was on its way to the bottom of Lake Superior, Victor Leland's office was paid a visit by some of our men but lawyers are shifty conniving creatures. They are not to be trusted or underestimated, especially not a pirate's lawyer. My men went to the office, killed everyone there, and searched the premises for the contracts. But there was nothing. After the contracts were signed Victor Leland had never returned to the office. He had already disappeared along with you and your brother and the damning contracts that showed that you boys would eventually own half of the company."

He stopped talking and a thick silence filled the space previously occupied by his voice. Eddie's breathing had returned to a resemblance of a normal meter. He looked at Kirk Hanlon sitting on his parent's credenza, eyes wide. He had been privy to quite a little bit of storytelling this evening. Eddie tried to find his voice.

"If my parents were dead, and you'd already killed my brother, why not just kill me and forget about the contracts?"

"Don't think we didn't consider it, Eddie, but besides the fact that there would still be legal ramifications regarding the holdings of the corporation, if those contracts ever came to light you wouldn't have to be Sam Spade to figure that all of those deaths were connected. And the transfer of the shares wouldn't come into play until you boys turned thirty, and so now that it's your birthday, here we are." He stared Eddie down for a long moment. "And now it's your turn, start talking."

Eddie's body was achy, his head was throbbing and his mouth was salty from the residue of Bellows' blood. He was not ready to give up yet but the prospect of waiting out bouts of heinous torture in the hopes that Jacobs would magically appear was unappealing to his already wracked mind and body. He'd have to give them something and hope that an opening presented itself.

Eddie got to his feet, grabbed the towel he had dropped and rewrapped his arm. The bleeding had slowed, Bellows was skilled with his instrument and the cuts weren't very deep, painful but not devastating. Sullivan stood up with him and looked him in the eye. Behind him Bellows entered with a towel pressed to his cheek but Eddie stayed focused on Sullivan.

"My father told you that rhyme because he intended to have any information he held hidden away in his foot locker which he had always referred to as Davy Jones' locker. It's right here in the house."

"Don't bullshit me, Eddie. We've been over this house, extensively."

"Not well enough. Follow me." And with that he walked towards the kitchen, shouldering past Bellows and trying to walk tall as he did it. Quentin made no effort to get out of his path, in his own way telling Eddie that he wasn't through with him yet. Sullivan had Mason and the other guy that was in the house wait with Kirk and signaled for Bellows to follow him.

Eddie led them to the cellar stairs.

The cellar door was an old oak monstrosity, heavier than could ever have been necessary. With a not quite steady hand Eddie gave it a push and it swung open easily despite its size.

Eddie reached to his left and absently flipped the switch for the lights. Two hours ago he could barely remember this house and now his mind was recalling even the slightest detail without a modicum of effort. A couple of exposed sixty-watt bulbs popped on in the dingy darkness and Eddie began his descent into the gloom followed closely by Sullivan and Bellows.

The stairs creaked and groaned in ominous tones as the three men made their descent. The basement was split into two rooms. A doorway to the right at the bottom of the stairs opened into a large room filled with clutter, piles of stuff that had been dumped or moved down there at some point. Stored and then forgotten. Eddie longed for a chance to dig through some of the old ruin, wondering what other lost memories awaited him amongst the piles of junk, but he had come down here with a purpose.

He turned left.

This room was open from the stairway, separated only by the flimsy handrail along the steps. It had been a laundry room once but the appliances had been removed. Now all that remained was a stained utility sink. The area beneath the stairs was open as well and more bric-a-brac had been stored there. Eddie began moving stuff out of his way trying not to let his eyes linger too long on any items lest his focus waver.

"We've been through all of this junk, Eddie. You're wasting our time." Sullivan said from behind him, not even attempting to veil the exasperation in his voice. Eddie didn't bother to placate him with even a glance. He knew what he was doing.

After he had cleared a spot against the wall about four feet wide he stepped back out from under the stairs and looked around. Toward the back of the laundry area was a smaller room that really qualified as more of a closet but it housed some poorly built shelves that still managed to hold some tools and other odds and ends. Eddie walked back and rummaged around for a moment returning with an old wood-handled hammer.

Without a word he swung the hammer into the exposed, discolored section of drywall under the stairs.

He used the hammer to break up a couple spots then used his hands to clear out the sections where he had loosened the drywall. Every action sent small puffs of sheetrock dust into the air. He was inhaling a lot of it and it burned his throat but he didn't care. The sheet rock was attached to studs but the space between had been filled in with concrete blocks.

With a large portion cleared, Eddie stepped back out from under the stairs and straightened his back. He coughed a few times and then spat a wad of saliva, the consistency thick from dust and blood, onto the floor. He knelt back down next to one of the concrete blocks right where the wall met the floor. With his finger he poked at the mortar around the block and it crumbled out easily. He looked back at Sullivan and smiled.

Once he had cleared a little space around the entire block he pulled at it as best he could with the tips of his fingers. The fake block slid out with an ease he wouldn't have imagined possible after all the years.

The faux block was attached to the bottom end of a small locker, his father's own version of Davy Jones' locker. Eddie pulled up on the little slide and popped the latch. In a slow steady motion he opened the locker door. He could feel both Sullivan and Bellows leaning in behind him to see, all the anger and violence forgotten, at least for a moment, forgotten in the wonder of the chase.

The contents of Eddie's father's footlocker did not disappoint.

The miniature treasure chest inside was, simply put, gorgeous. The gold of the latches and hinges shined as though recently polished. The wood of the body looked well-oiled despite the fact that it had probably not been touched by human hands for going on twenty-some years. It was about nine inches long and six inches high. It fit perfectly in Eddie's hands as he grasped it and lifted it from the locker. With it in his hands he felt the power and potency of a family he'd never known flow through him. The revelation lasted no more than a second.

Sullivan pushed him aside and grabbed the chest from him. Eddie had been squatting and the shove made him sit down hard on his backside. The pain was sharp but the excitement of the find pushed all else into the background. He stared at his father's chest. Sullivan and Bellows were doing the same. The moment was all consuming.

Sullivan pulled out the key that just moments ago he had taken from Eddie's own little chest. Eddie wanted so badly to reach up and grab it. To take hold of what was his, but he knew now was not the time. Now he was worthless to these two and as soon as their momentary enthrallment with the box was through, he was probably going to die. He scooched backward on his butt putting a few more feet between him and the other two as well as putting himself a few feet closer to the stairs.

Sullivan slid the key home in the lock, meeting with little resistance.

It was at this very moment, watching his birthright being stolen from him that Eddie noticed something else odd about the little treasure chest. He almost did a double take in confirming that what he was seeing was true. He could not suppress the coming smile. It appeared as if pirates could go to great lengths to double cross their foes.

Sullivan turned Eddie's key in the lock and the small treasure chest popped open.

Bellows and Sullivan almost smacked heads trying to be the first to catch a glimpse of the contents of the miniature trove. They were like little boys. Eddie took the opportunity to slide another two feet closer to the foot of the stairs.

Sullivan reached in and removed a folded photograph.

Time teetered as if the whole world held its breath.

He unfolded the old photograph, looked down at it, and smiled.

"Well, I'll be damned it's a treasure map and it looks like our treasure was right under our noses from the very beginning."

It was in that instant that gunfire erupted from outside the house and without thinking twice Eddie made his break for the stairs.

His legs firing like pistons, Eddie shot up the stairs.

Bellows was not one to be caught off guard but his momentary preoccupation with the treasure chest slowed his reaction. He brought his gun up as Eddie attempted to race up the stairs. Eddie passed by not even a full foot from the muzzle of Bellows' Glock. Bellows had perhaps an eighth of a second that his gun was aimed at Eddie's head.

He pulled the trigger.

14

Night, June 7th
Kirk Hanlon's residence

Bob Gurley's dusty Ford slowed as it wheeled past Kirk Hanlon's darkened home and its occupants took in the state of the house. There was no way they would be walking up to the front door, leaving the truck out front for anyone to see. They would come in through the woods and the backyard but they wanted to know as much about what they might be walking into as possible. The house seemed to be empty, abandoned once the scene had been processed. They felt they could get in and out without alerting anyone to their presence.

The home across the street was set back, well off the road. Neither Bob nor Ryan could see Linda Burbach as she sat at her window. She had been involved in her own amateur stakeout since the interesting events had begun the day before.

All day yesterday she watched the police come and go

processing the crime scene. After all of the action had moved on she, ever vigilant, had remained at her post. Just in case. Just in case there was anything more to see.

She held her phone in her hand, ready to dial 911 at a moment's notice, and watched the truck that had slowed in front of the Hanlon residence now creep out of sight.

She turned her attention back to the house.

And she watched.

They drove a quarter mile past Kirk's house and turned east on County Road 82. They followed that for half a mile and then cut back into the woods behind his house on an old dirt road that didn't even warrant a name. When they thought they were in a good position to move through the woods to the yard, they stopped and got out of the truck.

Ryan had a flickering thought that there was a good chance this was where the guys in the utility company uniforms had parked the day before. He felt a mix of anger and revulsion propagating deep within him. He shook it off as best he could and they headed into the trees.

They broke into the clearing that was Kirk Hanlon's backyard and Ryan was struck by another odd feeling. Now it was of time turning back over on its self. He was remembering the way he had felt so exposed running across this same backyard just one day ago, trying so hard to convince himself that he would not find the Sheriff dead.

They reached the sliding patio door and Ryan gave it a tug. It slid easily on its track. Ryan and Bob shared a glance. As they crossed the threshold into the house, they both knew they were taking another pretty giant step. They were now trespassing on a crime scene. They might be able to rationalize being there but the fact that they had made no effort to clear it through the proper channels would hinder their excuses.

The house was dark. On another night the big glass doors may have allowed the kitchen to be bathed in a nice mellow glow from the moon. Tonight thick, heavy storm clouds had closed in on them and it was ominous and dark.

Both men stood still for a bit letting their eyes adjust to the gloom. A minute passed and despite the fact that visibility was just starting to increase, they knew they had to get a move on. Ryan started first and Bob followed behind him staying close. They skirted the small dining table and made their way out of the kitchen.

"You got your pen light?" Bob asked in a low tone almost impossible to hear. Ryan nodded but didn't make a sound. He pulled the mini Mag Light out of his pocket and handed it over to Bob. Bob gave the head a twist, turning it on. "If the study is clear we can go in but I don't want to step back into that room without knowing what I'm stepping into."

Again, Ryan nodded, nothing more.

Slow and steady they walked past the living room, and the window facing the street, and into the hall leading to the study.

From where she sat, deep in the dark, Linda thought she saw something, a glare perhaps, in the front window of Kirk Hanlon's house. She took a moment to be certain that it hadn't been just some trick of the light but was confident that what she had seen was accurate. On her phone she dialed nine and one and one, and pressed the call button.

The room was just as they had left it the day before. The blood on the carpet was dry but there were little markers next to what could only be partial footprints in the dried gore. Many of those prints would belong, most likely, to Bob and Ryan.

They stepped into the room and Bob played the light across the cluttered surfaces of the study. It was the same as it had been yesterday and yet just by the sheer force of the changes they had both undergone since then, the contents of the room had taken on new meaning.

"So really, what the hell are we looking for?" Bob asked.

Ryan said nothing but moved with a purpose. He

walked over to the desk careful not to kick over any of the little markers on the rug.

He looked long and hard at the computer monitor. Why had the thought of the code being on the computer gnawed at him so? He looked under the desk and saw the little green light still glowing, just as Jessy had one day ago. He shook the mouse and waited the eternity it took for the monitor to wake.

The monitor finally warmed up but was of little help. He could still see the original code, but only because he had previous knowledge of it. A bunch of other nonsense had been added to it. Neither of them had been there to watch Jessy mash the keyboard as he fell but that was why it now looked so random. It was no wonder that the BCA hadn't found or deciphered Kirk's code.

Still Ryan couldn't quite grasp what it was that had drawn him back here.

He drummed his fingers on the edge of the heavy wood desk.

As his fingers were tapping out their rhythm, with a sudden clarity that was so pure it was almost not to be trusted, Ryan remembered something that Kirk had said to him. They had been chatting outside in the parking lot of the station one afternoon. Kirk had mentioned he was doing some research on great lakes piracy. Ryan had made some quip about buried treasure, X marks the spot, and so forth. Kirk had told him that regardless of what he may have heard, when it came to real piracy, X never marked the spot. But that, apparently, was not exactly true.

Enlightenment dawned. It had been staring him in the face all along. He looked at the keyboard and his eyes registered what they already knew they would find.

X never marks the spot, Hanlon had said.

That little liar.

The X key was missing from the keyboard, but he knew where it was, he had seen it the last time he was in this room.

"Did you hear that?" Bob asked suddenly.

"What?" Ryan hadn't heard anything, his mind was elsewhere. He let his eyes drift to the left to a box of tissues sitting just to the side of the monitor.

Bob didn't reiterate but handed over the flashlight and made a quick break back towards the living room. Ryan paid him little mind.

Propped on top of the tissue box was the missing X key. With a hand that no longer felt like it belonged to him, Ryan reached up and pulled out a tissue. As it came out and the next one came up to replace it, a folded piece of paper floated out from between the sheets. He picked up the paper from where it had settled on the desk and unfolded it. It was a page from a book, a photo of a painting.

And again X marked the spot.

"Well I'll be damned." Ryan muttered aloud, but his awe was interrupted before it could even sink in.

"Ryan!"

Bob was hollering in a shouted whisper from the living room. Panic tinged his voice. "We've got trouble. Two state cruisers just rolled up!"

15

Night, June 7th
The farmhouse at Old Farmer's Road

They approached steady and silent.

Splitting without a word as the lighted windows of the farmhouse came into sight. They had not made a plan so to speak, but both knew what was to be done and what the other expected of them. Shannon's father employed them but there was little question as to who really ran the Security outfit at Loeffler. Shannon and Jacobs were a team with plenty of history and had seen plenty of action together.

They could potentially be outnumbered in the ballpark of four or five to one. It wouldn't be the first time they had faced such odds, and neither of them afforded it much worry.

Shannon broke from the cover of the woods right next to the garage that Bob had described to them in his tale and Jimmy had confirmed in his. She couldn't see Jacobs but knew he would come from her left, towards the front of the house. From her current position she could only see one man, stationed outside the front door. She was certain there would be at least a few other sentinels about. From her vantage point she could see the front door, the southeast corner of the house, and a large portion of the side yard. Deep in the shadows of the side yard she saw another guard.

She would wait for Jacobs. They had approached quietly but they wouldn't be making their move in the same fashion. Jacobs would remove the man at the door without any attempt at stealth then Shannon would clean up anything or anyone who surrendered their position at that point. A third person for the far side of the house would have been ideal but the situation was what it was.

She knelt in the shadow of the garage ready to take the one man she could see. She glanced to her left again but still saw no sign of Jacobs. She knew that she wouldn't. Jacobs wouldn't be seen until he wanted to be.

Shannon waited, anxious but not impatient.

She tuned into the sounds of the night around her. So full, so alive. It was orchestral and playing for its own self, nothing more. She let her ears fall into the groove, the rhythm of the song so to speak. The ability to do such a thing was atop the list of things that made her so good at what she did. It was not a skill that could be taught. Some had it, and some did not.

Jacobs never made a sound but Shannon heard the music of the night skip a beat and knew that they were underway. She was so in tune that the shot she squeezed off followed Jacobs' so closely that the two reports almost sounded like one. As soon as she fired, Shannon swept her eyes across the perimeter of the forest encompassing the house. Jacobs fired twice more. Their adversaries were in general trained well, but it only takes one mistake. Movement on her right gave up another man just inside the tree line. She squeezed the trigger again, dropping the guy. She still couldn't see Jacobs, but assuming that he had been able to track her shots as she had tracked his, they ought to be in pretty good shape. These guys had set up a standard triangular defense strategy. It only took her a second to locate a fourth guy, well to the back of the side yard.

She fired again.

She was crouched along the rear of the garage with a clear sightline of the house. The big roll-up garage door was on the opposite side facing out towards the road. The sidewall of the garage that housed a side door leading up the walk to the porch was around the corner and out of Shannon's sight to her left.

After taking the last man out, she stood and stepped out from the shadow of the garage toward the house. She heard a click to her left as the handle on the side door of the garage disengaged. She dropped back behind the rear wall a second before the shot rang out. The bullet whistled by, right where her head had been a moment before.

Someone had been posted inside the garage.

She waited in the settling stillness. She heard nothing but took no solace in the absence of audible clues. The moment that she realized the door had been opening, her entire sense had turned to survival. That lost moment was just enough to leave her unsure as to whether the door had only been cracked, or had opened all the way. Whoever had taken that shot at her could still be lying in wait within the confines of the garage. Or it was also possible they were now slowly, stealthily, stealing towards her along the adjacent wall.

She waited, still patient.

The symphony of the night began to tune up again. Insects, like instruments, coming in one at a time. She tried to separate the sounds, natural or human, but nothing defined itself as out of the ordinary.

In a half crouch she moved up to the edge of the wall again. She kept her head on a swivel trying to see both the corner she was heading for and the one she was leaving behind. Again she listened hard trying to discern anything discordant.

Nothing.

Slow, ever so slow, making as little sound as possible she pulled in a long, deep breath. She released it at an equally agonizing meter. She couldn't sit here all night. Weapon at the ready she swung around facing the long side of the garage.

Shannon registered the gun in her face at the same time she was registering the look on the man's face to which her own weapon was trained. They had gotten too close to each other and ended up gun to face in either case.

They both hesitated for a fraction of a second in their surprise. And in that moment of hesitation the man with his gun trained on Shannon felt the barrel of Jacobs' weapon come to rest on the back of his skull.

"Drop the gun." Jacobs said.

16

Night, June 7th
The farmhouse at Old Farmer's Road

Bellows' gun exploded and Eddie fell against the wall of the stairwell smacking his head. He saw stars. He had time to think about the fact that you still saw stars when you hit your head, even after you'd just been shot in said spot. Then he realized that despite the stars and despite being shot in the head, he had recovered his feet and was still running up the stairs.

Bellows' gun exploded again.

Eddie didn't feel the bullet impact and still his tired legs pumped, carrying him up the stairs.

Again the thunder of the gun filled the basement yet Eddie chugged on. He cleared the threshold of the cellar door onto the main floor. His trek up the stairs had felt like climbing a mountain face yet here he was, still standing.

He risked one look back.

The flimsy handrail that had been the only safeguard from toppling off the stairs on the way down was splintered in two spots and torn in half in another.

Every shot Bellows had taken, while intended for Eddie's head, had hit the handrail directly between the two. It slowed, or changed, the trajectory just enough. That thin piece of lumber had saved his life. He was awarded no time to pontificate on its intervention though as Sullivan scrambled into view at the foot of the stairs.

He slammed the cellar door closed, and ran.

Eddie made a hard left into the kitchen hoping to avoid the men in the living room. He raced through the kitchen pausing only for a moment to have a look into the living room before he dashed through the entryway and toward the stairs to the second level. He saw that he need not worry about Mason and the other guy as all of their attention was focused on whatever was going on outside. He caught Hanlon's eye as he raced by.

The poor guy was glued to his seat in terror.

Before he knew what he was doing, and against his better judgment, he veered away from the stairs and into the living room. Mason and his sidekick were at the windows, weapons drawn, scouting the battlefield outside. As quiet as could be, he summoned Hanlon to him.

He didn't wait to see what Hanlon would do.

He bolted back out of the living room. Hanlon was out of his chair and following. The two men at the window kept their attention out in the front yard. Through the living room and off to the left was a little mudroom that also led to the back door. They both ducked into the little room just as either Bellows or Sullivan reached the top of the stairs.

Neither could see from their vantage point but the magnitude of the screeching sound exploding from the direction of the cellar left little to the imagination. It sounded like whoever was leading the charge, Bellows or Sullivan, had ripped the cellar door right off its hinges. Eddie cringed at the sound and looked away. His gaze fell on the backdoor. He could see the patio out beyond it through the glass.

He could also see one of Sullivan's men out there, lying dead.

Eddie turned back to Hanlon. The look of terror hadn't left his eyes but he appeared to have regained some control of himself.

"What the hell is going on?" They heard Sullivan bark.

"Gunfire. They've taken out at least three of ours." It was Mason in the living room answering.

"Where are Eddie and Hanlon?" Sullivan again, this time his question was met with silence. Eddie shot Kirk a look and put a finger to his lips. This was no time to do something stupid.

"How many are out there?" Sullivan asked. His voice was level but Eddie could hear the anger underneath waiting for an opportunity to punch through.

"At least two, seems like more."

Eddie started getting nervous about the fact that he hadn't heard anything from the other sentry in the living room or Bellows. He turned and looked behind him, the mudroom that they currently occupied dumped off into a back hallway that led to the kitchen. Bellows had access to them from either the kitchen or the living room.

The silence filled every corner, every nook and cranny.

"Turn on the outside light." Sullivan said from what was an undeterminable distance away in the living room. The clack of the light switch seemed to reverberate through the quiet farmhouse. Kirk stepped in closer to Eddie, so close that they were practically hugging. The yard beyond the door next to which they stood remained darkened but they could see the spill of yellow light from the front yard.

"Sonuvabitch!" Someone shouted and then the silence was shattered by breaking glass and the repeated hammering of gunfire.

Despite the dead guy on the back patio Eddie decided enough was enough and that it was time to get the hell out of there. He steadied Kirk on his feet and stepped towards the door. Just as he was about to grab the door handle a shadow fell across the patio from the outside.

He pulled Kirk back with him and pressed them both against the wall to the left side of the door. The owner of that shadow was standing opposite them, outside, just out of their view. Eddie gauged the movement on the far side through the beveled glass of the door. The guy was inching along the wall towards them. He had come from deep in the backyard. He must have been staked out there.

Eddie felt Hanlon tugging at his sleeve.

The figure on the far side of the door had stopped. He was exactly opposite Eddie's position. Eddie's nerves drew taut.

Again the tug.

He turned to see Hanlon's terrified eyes swimming before him. Kirk was agitated, pointing towards the kitchen through the small hall. Eddie was assaulted by another spectral shadow closing in on him. It was less a shadow though, as it was a blocking of all light from that direction. Like an eclipse.

Bellows.

To think would be to die, so Eddie released himself to action. He reached out and rapped on the window of the door. He got the exact response he wanted. A gunshot ripped through the glass. He hesitated half a second to be sure the guy outside wouldn't keep shooting but not giving him enough time to pull back. Then he reached out through the shattered glass, grabbed the hand holding the gun which was still aimed at the window, and pulled it through. The arm attached to it, reticent to relinquish its property, came with it. Letting instinct have full reign over the situation, he twisted hard on the gunman's wrist. He willed without words Hanlon to stay out of the way.

Turning back towards the entryway to the kitchen wrenching on the gunman's wrist, he saw Bellows appear and at the same time heard a distinct pop from the wrist still grasping the gun. In a split moment that passed too quickly to be quantified, Eddie realized he'd broken the man's wrist. The slight sound of the fracturing bone was enough to alert Bellows though and he halted his trajectory into the mudroom.

Eddie pressed the gunman's now limp finger to the trigger and a bullet tore from the muzzle towards the entryway to the kitchen.

But it was empty.

Bellows had reversed his direction as quick as he had come and disappeared from Eddie's line of sight.

The man with the broken wrist and his arm sticking through the haggard, glass teeth of the shattered window cursed a blue streak. His hand, despite the wrecked wrist, was still clenched on the grip of the pistol.

In a single fluid motion Eddie yanked the guy forward by his arm. His head smashed into the remaining part of the door and his body went limp. Eddie saw a couple flashes of white as a few liberated teeth pinged off the patio.

Silence, again, descended.

Eddie removed the pistol from the gunman's grip as, unconscious, the man slid to the ground on the other side of the door. Both Eddie and Kirk cringed at the tinkling sound of glass falling as his arm slid back to his side of the wall.

The new fallen silence was supreme.

Eddie strained to hear any hint of movement but nothing came. Without a word of warning, in an act that was either sheer bravery or sheer stupidity, Hanlon stepped toward the living room and stuck his head around the corner. He pulled back fast, like a turtle in trouble then turned to Eddie and shook his head.

There was no one there.

Had they high-tailed it? Eddie couldn't really believe it. He wished he could muster the same courage, or stupidity, that Hanlon had a second ago, and have a peek into the kitchen. He couldn't though. Bellows might be there, and where Bellows was, so death would follow.

The absence of sound was crushing.

17

Ryan launched himself out of Kirk's study.

He was carrying the torn-out book page that he had found in the tissue box, but all he really needed had already been committed to memory.

Hanlon had discovered the location of Plundering Pike's treasure. He couldn't believe Kirk had been able to keep it to himself. It would have to have been the biggest discovery of his career. Ryan fought down his own excitement.

"What the hell's goin' on out there, Bob?"

"Two cruisers just pulled up, someone knows we're here. Out the back, now!"

Bob was already heading for the patio door. Ryan started to follow but had to hazard a step over to the picture window to have a glance outside. He didn't move the drape but peeked into the small space open between the shade and the jamb. A State Trooper was crossing the yard towards the front door. His gun was drawn, but not leveled. His investigative nature piqued but not on high alert yet.

He heard the sliding glass door slip open nice and quiet as Bob made his exit. He hustlted after him but as he entered the kitchen he stopped short. Bob had made it half way across the backyard but through a window in the kitchen that faced the side yard Ryan saw another Trooper making his way around towards the back of the house. He held himself still as a post as to not draw the attention of the Trooper by movement in the window. Once the Trooper was past the window though, there would only be seconds before he'd clear the wall to the backyard and see Bob's back racing for the woods.

There was no time to think, only to react. His reactionary trigger would have to fire true. The Trooper was at the edge of the window and then out of his line of sight. He grabbed a ceramic cookie jar off the counter-top right next to him, whirled around, and threw it back towards the front of the house. He had a clear line of sight to the front window. The cookie jar traversed the space and hit the window hard. Not hard enough to break the window but hard enough to shatter the jar. As the ceramic pieces fell to the floor he heard a yell from the other side of the window.

"Shit! There *is* someone in there."

Ryan had dropped out of sight below the counter but could see the shadow of the Trooper at the side kitchen window reverse direction and head back towards the front of the house to provide back-up. Ryan broke for the open sliding door as soon as the shadow passed. Bob had already made the tree line. Ryan was half way there. Then he was three quarters of the way there, and still no further alarm had been raised.

He had reached the edge of the woods when the stillness was broken by another shout. "They went out the back!" It came from inside the house. The Troopers must have seen the sliding glass door sitting open. He was confident that he now had the cover of the trees but redoubled the effort of driving his pumping legs. Had he the time to think he may have ruminated on the fact that he was now being chased through the very woods through which he had chased real criminals yesterday. But thought would have to be relegated to a later date.

The longest minutes of his life finally expired and he broke into the clearing where the truck was parked. Bob was already in the driver's seat and had thrown the passenger door open for Ryan. He ran right up into the cab without slowing. The engine was already humming and Bob cranked the wheel and crushed the gas as soon as Ryan had crossed the threshold.

The truck hurled around back towards the main road. Gravity did its work and pulled the passenger door, slamming it shut so hard behind Ryan that he let out a little squeal.

As they reached the road and were about to turn, in what little throw there was from the taillights, they saw the two State Troopers emerge from the trees. Bob made a hard right and again laid his foot on the gas as heavy as he could, hoping the make of the truck and the license plate would be indistinguishable at that distance.

The Troopers would have to hoof it back to the house and their cruisers. Through the woods as the crow flies from Kirk's house it was a straight shot to their position and only took a couple of minutes. Going by the road to the same spot was a winding trip and would take longer. By the time the Troopers reached their cars and took up pursuit, Bob and Ryan would have at least three or four minutes on them. The downside was the old Ford was shaking itself apart as Bob pushed the speedometer to seventy, he had a feeling the Troopers' cruisers would probably be moving somewhat faster.

"How much time we got, Bob?"

Bob checked the speedometer again; he wasn't going to get it much past seventy. Then he checked the rearview mirror, nothing yet, he didn't expect there to be, yet. "Four, maybe five minutes, and that's counting on them having to take it slow because of the roads."

"You keep whipping this bucket of bolts. About three miles up we can ditch this road. I used to hunt in this stretch of woods every now and again. Hank Marshik has a chunk of land out here and there's a small access road that runs through it off this highway. We can cut across to County 12 and sneak out to your place."

"If we can get to my place we can drop the truck and take Norma's car." He trailed off for a moment. "Not that I know where the hell we might go anyway."

In all the excitement Ryan hadn't had time to tell him about what he'd found in the tissue box. He looked over to Bob. The dashboard illuminated his tired grin.

"I know where we need to go, and you are not going to believe it."

A weighty silence filled the car.

Ryan didn't elaborate at the moment and instead turned his attention to the window. His focus was now directed into the night looking for the access road. After a moment he pointed out the turn onto Hank Marshik's land. It was perfect, very inconspicuous. Bob made a hard right turn. In the distance behind them they could see no cars, but the cloud cover at the horizon was just beginning to pulse, blue and red.

18

Time slowed as the yard was bathed in the soft yellow light of the outdoor floods.

The distance between heartbeats became infinite and for Jacobs it made this easy. Shannon broke for the house so quickly that it was almost as if she knew the light was coming. She didn't, but there was not a second of hesitation behind her action. The man with Jacobs' gun pointed at the back of his head reacted naturally.

He turned towards the source of the light.

It was natural. Natural and predictable and it was a sure sign of a lack of focus. Jacobs, never one to lack focus or become predictable, wasted none of the advantage spotted to him. He stepped in close behind the man and in a simultaneous fluid motion he used his free hand to pull his opponents gun arm down while bringing his own weapon up. He snapped his neck forward, head-butting the guy right at the base of his neck. The moment of disorientation would be all he needed.

Using the man as cover, Jacobs turned to the house and let loose, firing at any window within his line of sight.

Shannon was firing as well, never breaking stride as she raced for the cover provided by the front of the porch. Bob Gurley would have recognized the corner by the stairs where Shannon took cover. Jacobs' weapon clicked, audible but quiet after all of the gunfire. The lapse in the pounding of gunshots lasted no more than a second before those in the house began their retaliation.

Jacobs had dragged the disoriented man to the nearest corner of the garage. The knock to the back of the head had left the guy woozy but still standing and he stumbled along. When the inevitable click of dry fire came Jacobs was partially protected around the corner, he used the man's body to complete his coverage. A second later his human shield began a little dance as bullets smacked his flesh and drove him backward pinning him to Jacobs. If there were more than two or three shooters in the farmhouse he would not get a sufficient chance to break for better cover.

As if to accentuate this fact, a bullet grazed him and another smacked into the wooden siding at the corner of the garage right beside his head. The one that grazed him had nicked his left calf. It wouldn't qualify as a hit and was in a meaty part of his body, but the pain was still searing, fiery and hot. He checked it as best he could from his position. Not much blood, it was little more than a scratch. Had it been another three inches higher and a little to the left though, it would've blown out his knee.

Shannon had squeezed against the corner of the porch and the stairs. From her vantage point she could see back down into the yard where Jacobs was. The gunfire was coming from above her position and she watched the bullets tear into the man he was using as cover out by the garage. She slithered around in front of the stairs, like the sheriff all those years ago. In the house the men were firing from the sidelights on either side of the door. Down in front of the stairs she was out of their sight and, she gauged, out of the line of fire. She was centered between them. She could pop straight up to take her shots but accuracy would be essential. If she missed either of them she wouldn't have time to get herself clear and Jacobs hadn't yet had time to reload.

She stood and she fired.

The newfound silence had dropped like a stone and now action was inevitable.

Eddie steeled himself.

Crouched on the floor of the mudroom with Kirk, heart hammering, Eddie Watson accepted Edward Pike III. He was here, in his childhood home, and he was cowering like a child. Action *was* inevitable and now Eddie prepared himself to rise to its harrowing challenge.

The lack of moonlight made the blood on the shattered window stand out black.

Never taking his eyes off of the entryway to the kitchen, Eddie stepped past Kirk towards the living room. As he passed, he whispered to Kirk putting his mouth so close to the other man's ear that it would have been a comical embrace had the situation been different. As silent as possible he whispered.

"Watch the entry to the kitchen, if you see so much as a shadow, squeeze my shoulder but don't say a word."

Eddie drew his head back far enough to see Kirk nod then he stepped to the arch leading to the living room. He took a deep breath, made a ten count to himself and took a quick peek around the corner. From his position he couldn't see the whole living room, part of it was cut off from his line of sight, but he could see enough. Kirk had not intended to tell him that no one was there but rather that no one in there was still among the living. He could see both men, Mason and the other, on opposite sides of the front door slouched before the windows. The floor around both men was a mosaic of blood and glass.

He looked back to Kirk and the portal to the kitchen beyond.

Nothing moved.

On wobbly legs Eddie made a tentative step into the living room. Kirk moved with him, still resting one hand on Eddie's shoulder, the whole of his attention cast to covering their flank.

Eddie listened.

The fact that there was now no audible sound from the kitchen did not surprise him. He did not expect either Sullivan or Bellows to make themselves an easy mark, but every second they remained concealed added physical weight to the tension he was already teetering on the edge of controlling.

Eddie had turned back towards the kitchen and so he didn't see the handle of the front door turn. It slipped open a crack as it disengaged from the lock. The thudding sound as it was kicked all the way open caused an echo to pass through the house and drew his attention as time slowed. Eddie cranked his head in that direction but his neck had taken on a plodding motor control that was usually reserved for the realm of dreams.

The door flew open.

The hinges screeched as it swung inward. Eddie dropped to one knee and brought his weapon up. Mentally ready to take the shot.

If either of them had lost their cool, one of them would have been dead. Neither of them did. Eddie in his neat, well trained, shooters crouch was looking at his former neighbor in an almost mirror image of himself.

Shannon cracked a smile.

Eddie followed suite.

Jacobs appeared, gun trained over Shannon's shoulder.

Without breaking his crouch Eddie signaled over his shoulder to the kitchen. Jacobs acknowledged him, made eye contact with Shannon as he passed, then they both moved past Eddie across the living room taking up posts on either side of the doorway to the kitchen.

They moved in.

From the silence that followed Eddie judged that Bellows and Sullivan had at some point vacated the kitchen. At that very moment his suspicions were confirmed as he heard an engine roar to life down by the garage. He raced to the door just in time to see the taillights flash on then disappear behind the garage and out of sight. Jacobs ran back out of the kitchen.

"Who was that?"

"I'm pretty sure it was Bellows and Sullivan." Eddie replied. "They found some sort of a map…"

Jacobs looked to him then ran down the porch steps

and out into the yard. "Shit. By the time we get to the cars they'll be long gone. Any idea what was on the map?" he asked as he returned to the house. Shannon had rejoined them in the living room as well.

Eddie shook his head. "I didn't get a good look at it."

"Damn." Shannon muttered. Both she and Jacobs drifted off into heavy thought for a moment.

"Sullivan mentioned something about it being right under their noses from the beginning," Eddie said. He was met with silence as everyone considered what that vague phrase might mean. But then Eddie was distracted by something else. Something he had noticed right before the shooting started but then it had slipped his mind. "The map they found was in a little treasure chest downstairs. I noticed something odd about it. Let's go have a look at it."

"First we'd better make sure we're actually alone."

Jacobs and Shannon searched the upstairs and found no one. While they cleared the upstairs, Eddie found a glass of water for Kirk. He was still not speaking and he had started shaking, as though his body was just catching up to the terror his mind was still trying to process. Shannon and Jacobs returned just as Eddie was attempting to hand the glass over to Kirk. He couldn't quite seem to get a grip on it and so Eddie just set it on the end-table next to him.

Shannon stepped over to them. "I'll stay with him. You guys go see what you can find out about that chest."

The two of them descended the steps to the cellar. What was left of the handrail leaned this way and that. Eddie thought maybe he could understand how Kirk had just kind of locked up. The temptation to do the same welled up in him as he recalled his last trek up these steps and how sure he had been that he had taken a bullet in the head. Without good ventilation, the room was still hot with the smell of spent gunfire.

Once they reached the floor, Eddie stepped past Jacobs and went to his father's little treasure chest. It was lying on the floor where Sullivan had dropped it, already having what he thought he'd come for. Eddie turned it over and saw what he had hoped to find. His key was still sticking out of the lock and he pulled it free.

"They wanted this key all along. It opened the chest which is where they found the map, but do you see this?" He pointed to the ornate metal weaving that ran all the way around the bottom edges of the chest. Near both corners there were little holes that were almost camouflaged by the metal artwork. He slid his key into one of the holes. "My key has the first part of my father's rhyme etched into it. Sullivan went on and on about a key my brother had. I think that together they would open a secret chamber or something. I don't know if we can break it open but whatever is in there, it's got to be important."

"We don't need to break it, Eddie," Jacobs said pulling out the key that Ryan Tomlinson had given to him.

"Richard's key?"

Jacobs nodded and slid the key into the other slot. He looked at Eddie whose face was full of anticipation. With a nod of his head they both turned the keys in unison.

Much like Eddie's box that had secreted his key, the bottom of the little chest popped open and away from its body. Inside was an aged looking piece of parchment. Eddie lifted the paper out of the box, unfolding it slowly with cautious precision. His excitement was nearly boiling over. What would this new little treasure bring?

He spread it out and had a look.

The anxious smile on his face faltered then fell away.

"What is it?" Jacobs asked.

"I don't know. A phrase of some sort... It looks like it's written in a foreign language."

"What?"

Eddie held the piece of parchment up so Jacobs could see it. It read:

Rosa dei venti corsi.

Jacobs could only shrug. Then Shannon was yelling

down at them from upstairs.

"Guys, I think you should get up here."

Eddie grabbed the piece of parchment and they raced up the stairs. They came into the living room to find Shannon kneeling next to Kirk. He had calmed himself enough to be able to hold his glass of water on his own with just a slight trace of the previous shakes. Shannon looked to the two of them then back to Kirk.

"Go on. Tell them what you told me."

He ran his tongue out over his lips and somehow brought the tremor in his hands all the way back under control.

"I know where the treasure is," he said his voice shaky. "It's in the fog-signal house at Split Rock Lighthouse."

"How do you know that?" Jacobs asked, his tone not harsh but definitely pointed.

"It was marked clear as day in the Angel at the Rock. When the painting was stolen from the lighthouse Pike's son doctored it to denote where the treasure was hidden."

Kirk's voice strengthened as he spoke and rose in pitch at the end of his last sentence. The immediate excitement in the room was appreciable. Jacobs and Shannon seemed to be on the balls of their feet leaning into Kirk, but Eddie was still distant. He was staring at the little piece of parchment in his hand.

"But what does this mean then?" he asked extending the paper out towards Kirk. Kirk took it and looked at it but then shook his head.

"I have no idea."

"It must be important," Eddie said. "To have been hidden like it was."

"It might be, Eddie," Jacobs said. "But right now our business entails whatever might be waiting at Split Rock."

19

Ryan stood in Bob's driveway leaning against Norma's Ford Escape. The pickup had already been stowed in the garage and Bob had gone inside to talk to Norma. Not to tell her what they were up to of course, but just to check in. He came back out, took a look back at the house, and satisfied with what he saw pulled out the pack of smokes he had purchased-

When was that?

It felt like years ago but upon doing the math it had only been the night before last. It had been a hell of a couple of days. He lit one and leaned against the car filling his lungs with the foul poison and enjoying every second of it.

They had made it a quarter mile or so onto Hank Marshik's land before Bob had killed the headlights. The clouded night sky had reflected the dull red and blue pulse of the State Trooper's flashers as their cruisers approached the little turn off and then, thankfully, receded in the other direction. Bob and Ryan had continued on, easing along without the aid of headlights for about another ten minutes. They'd only come another mile or so in that time but they were hesitant to turn the lights back on until they were sure they had lost the Troopers. Once they felt it was safe, Bob flipped the lights back on and gunned up and down back roads until they reached his place. Both men had been anxious to put the pickup to bed for the night, knowing that the entire area would soon be crawling with more Troopers and possibly multiple other agencies as well.

Bob finished his smoke, dropped it on the driveway and crushed the embers with his foot.

"You just gonna leave that butt for Norma to find?" Ryan asked. Bob was relieved to hear the hint of a smile in his voice.

"You mind your own business and I'll mind mine alright? Now let's go see if we can't find ourselves some of this so-called treasure." But before he did anything else he bent down and picked up the pinched filter and carried it to the garbage can at the side of the garage. Ryan laughed as he climbed into the passenger side of Norma's Escape.

"Norma drives this thing, huh?" Ryan asked the smile still present in his voice.

"She hates it, but I told her she can't live in godforsaken northern Minnesota without having four-wheel drive."

"You really rule your roost, don't ya?" Now the smile wasn't just in his voice but lighting up his face. He knew of course the only thing Bob ruled around that house were the things she allowed him to. In town he was the sheriff but at home he was always a deputy.

"You best keep an eye on your mouth as she seems to be running away from you," Bob retorted and was only slightly surprised to find that he was smiling a fat, broad smile himself.

They were like little boys heading off to hunt for buried treasure.

Only they weren't little boys, not anymore, and they had no idea what sort of 'treasure' it was they were hunting. Bob dropped the vehicle into reverse and almost peeled out, whipping into the street. They might have to check themselves. The thrill was beginning to trickle towards outweighing the risks.

They opted to drive through town. In Norma's car they would be safe from attracting any unnecessary attention and they wanted to get a feel for their town. The vibe they sensed was scared and quiet. It was nearing eleven and the whole town felt shut down and closed up. Not that Castle Danger would usually be a scene of hustle and bustle at eleven p.m. but it was more than that. It didn't feel slow, and quiet. It felt locked down.

They rolled past the city municipal building and the station, slowing to check it out. There were a few State Police

Cruisers parked out front. They could both imagine Gale Sebathany and the others in there, hopefully only temporarily, dealing with life after the two of them. Maybe tomorrow some things would have changed and they could go back to their old lives, or maybe tomorrow their old lives would be forever out of their reach.

Those sorts of thoughts were enough to dull their moods at least a bit. They hooked up with Highway 61 and headed north towards Split Rock.

20

Late in the Night, June 7th
Split Rock Lighthouse

Sullivan and Bellows came by boat, the same as Bellows and his men had a few short days ago. They carried no cargo, none of the literal dead weight they had transported on the previous trip, only the photo they had removed from the little chest at the farmhouse. The lighthouse appeared in the distance striking out against the dark night sky. It was lit by floodlights, a remnant left over from the crime scene.

For the first time Sullivan allowed himself to consider the implications of what they hoped to find up there. He had been a young man the day Eddie's parents died. Up and coming. He had spent much of his adult life chasing down the contracts that gave Eddie half the rights to the company owned by his employer. He had grown older, and Hawking had grown fat, and along with the company he had, himself, become very, very, rich. Working for the Allan's he had amassed more money than he could ever spend. He wondered, in vague terms, what sort of money that would've meant for Eddie.

At times over the years he had been called an evil man. At a point he had stopped needing the money, but he still needed the work. Did that make him evil? If so then he supposed the answer was yes. He wondered if he could retire once this business that had consumed his life was put to rest. He couldn't quite imagine how that would work for him.

Next to him, Bellows was silent. His body was rigid, taut but not tight. Neither of them knew exactly what to expect upon arrival. Just yesterday this place had become a crime scene and by their own hands. They would have to approach with caution.

Bellows brought the small craft in quietly, sliding onto the shore with a deft ease. He killed the engine. They climbed out and began the trek up towards the lighthouse through the trees. They climbed the sloping hill in silence. Sullivan's heart was picking up its pace as he tried to keep stride with Bellows who maneuvered the dark forest floor without a sound. Sullivan was no stranger to some adverse conditions but they were most definitely in the realm of Quentin Bellows here. He was in his element, going to work. Bellows slowed and stopped, raising a hand for Sullivan to do the same. For a moment they just stood, silent and waiting.

Then in the distance, from the direction of the highway, came the rumble of an engine.

Bellows cocked his head to listen and Sullivan, despite the smothering dark, got a decent look at his cheek. The one Eddie had torn up with his teeth. It wasn't a pretty sight. It was a good thing Bellows wasn't one to put too much stock in his looks. He would bear a rough scar at the very least. The car, to which this particular engine belonged, was slowing. That was alright, anyone who watched the news knew what had happened at the lighthouse and they would slow to have themselves a look-see, but this one continued to slow. The droning hum continued to drop then the engine cut.

They waited just a moment, still and quiet as the night around them. Bellows looked to Sullivan, his eyes focused, not the slightest trace of panic.

"We'd better pick up our pace, we may have visitors sooner than we would've liked."

He turned and they both took up a trot heading in the direction of the now visible pool of light thrown by the floods in the distance.

As they approached Split Rock, Ryan felt his stomach tie up in knots. He looked over to Bob and, from the twisted up grimace on his face, he could assume the feeling was mutual.

Yesterday they had sat here and looked at those two dead boys. Only two days ago Richard Devlin had still been a thing of the past.

Two days ago Jessy had still been alive.

That thought hung, visceral and real, in the car between them. They shared an uncomfortable glance. It was as if his ghost had just ethereally appeared between them. Bob's eyes took on a shine and he turned to look out at the darkened night, the darkened trees, and somewhere out there, the black hole of the lake. Ryan piped up before his emotion could get the better of him.

"How should we go in, Bob?"

"We'll stop up here in about a half mile. We'll leave Norma's truck off on the side of the road. I'll mark it as abandoned, date it, and hopefully that will keep any passing Troopers from paying any real attention to it at least until we're finished here. We'll leave it where the Gitchi Gami State Trail runs right along the highway up here. We can catch the trail and walk the last stretch up to the lighthouse."

He slowed Norma's Escape and pulled onto the soft shoulder. He killed the headlights and let the darkness settle in.

"Well...I guess this is it," Bob said as he reached up and turned the dome-light from 'door' to 'off'. They opened their respective doors and exited the vehicle into the night as quiet as possible. They drew their weapons and stood on the edge of the highway both eyeing the thick, shaded forest around them. Something treacherous was waiting out there, deep in the lingering darkness.

And still, into the woods they went with a quiet caution, in pursuit of the treasure of Plundering Pike.

21

The black void that was the lake would have been complete had it not been for the beacon calling from Split Rock. It was not the lighthouse that was lit, warding ships off her rocky wharf but the cold, white sodium arc floodlights marking the spot where the bodies of two boys had been dropped just days ago.

The water cut smoothly around the bow of the light, high-powered Conquest. Eddie marveled at the powers of acquisition held by Shannon and Jacobs. Without a word or call, they drove directly to the marina, walked to the boat and started it. Loeffler obviously had some resources. Whatever the company's particular area of expertise may be, their reach was undeniable.

Eddie turned his thoughts to the past and the lake across which they cut their swath. He tried to imagine his father out here on these very waters, facing Sullivan. Knowing he was going to die but also knowing he had taken steps to ensure that the family legacy remained in the family. Tears that would not fall stung the corners of his eyes as equal parts grief and rage welled up from the pit of his stomach. He couldn't remember her but the thought of his mother at the hands of those men stirred new emotions in the already convoluted melting pot of Eddie's psyche.

Jacobs throttled back as the glow of the floods off Split Rock grew large.

Eddie stood, sensing a change in the air, the weight of a long-charted course of action hurtling toward them. He moved forward to the bow of the boat joining Shannon and Jacobs. The three of them back together again, just like the morning at the cabin. Could it be possible that it was just this morning? Kirk was back in that same cabin now, riding out the proverbial storm as a real one rumbled ever closer. His position was enviable.

The Conquest's engine was smooth and quiet but the closer they got to their destination the louder it seemed. Jacobs slowed even further, throttling it back to a nearly inaudible purr. The growing waves lapped at the fiberglass hull and the manufactured electric light hung in the distance like a small moon.

They were aiming to come in a good hundred yards or so south of the lighthouse where the trees were thicker and would aid in their climb to the apex of the cliff on which the lighthouse stood. They were about twenty-five yards from the shore when they saw the small boat marooned on the shore. Jacobs angled their own craft in just up the shoreline from it. The presence of the other boat left little doubt that Sullivan and Bellows had made the same deductions as to the whereabouts of the so-called booty.

They had just stepped foot upon the shore when from further up, behind the lighthouse, multiple gunshots cracked the quiet stillness of the night.

As they worked their way through the tangle of trees toward the light, Sullivan fell a few paces behind Bellows. They were closing in on the grounds of the lighthouse and the other buildings housed there. The range of the crime scene lights bloomed out, widening with every footfall. They still had the cover of the trees but it was thinning. A small road ran along their left in front of a row of small buildings that had once been the lighthouse keeper's residence and were now part of the tour of the grounds.

They stepped into the clearing in front of the lighthouse. The lighthouse stood on their right and across a large platform, on their left, was the low, squat building that housed the fog-signal. Sullivan reached into his pocket and touched the picture of the painting that he had retrieved from the footlocker at the farmhouse. The photo was of the Angel at the Rock, the painting depicting the Angelina shipwrecked below Split Rock Lighthouse. He had been out here many times while this debacle was still in the planning stages. He had pored over photos, mapping out every last detail of the plan. He knew the second he looked at the picture of the painting what was wrong.

On the roof of the fog-signal house in the painting there was a weather vane showing the points of the compass. The actual building had no such feature. The kicker though was the angle that was represented in the painting. It caused the shape of the weather vane to look like an X. Sullivan smirked, then tucked the picture back into his pocket and turned his attention to Bellows.

Bellows made a panoramic sweep of the grounds. He gave a nod to Sullivan; they were still alone so far. They moved to the foot of the stairs that led up to the platform between the entrance to the lighthouse and the fog-signal house. They were well lit as this was the precise spot where Bellows had left the bodies. They made haste and hit the stairs at a healthy clip.

They had just reached the top when a gunshot cut the quiet and debris kicked up from the concrete of the stair to the right of Bellows foot.

"Go." He yelled to Sullivan and turned and began to fire without the slightest hesitation.

Ryan Tomlinson fired as soon as he saw the two men on the stairs and then he hesitated, just for a moment, but it was too long. It was all the time Bellows needed to wheel and unleash a hail of gunfire towards Ryan's position in the trees.

He stood as tight in line with the tree in front of him as he could, it being his only cover. The tree howled as bark was torn away and bullets poured deep into its many rings. The barrage lasted a lifetime to Ryan, crack and thud, crack and thud, the sounds ripping open the night. Then at last the sound of dry fire.

The empty click rang through the suddenly still air.

Ryan brought his weapon up prepping to fire but was usurped. A second after Bellows dry fired, another shot rang out from Ryan's left. Looking up he realized Bob had drifted off from his own position. Now it was Bob firing from his relative cover fifty or so feet away. The first shot tore into Bellows' shoulder. The second went wide. Despite the new hole in his shoulder, the few seconds that passed was all the time it took Bellows to reload. He unleashed again, this time in Bob's direction. Sullivan had already disappeared around the corner, behind the fog-signal house. Ryan came around the tree to take a shot while Bellows attention was focused elsewhere.

His focus did not remain elsewhere for long.

Bellows swung his weapon across his field of vision before Ryan was set to take his shot and he had to dive back behind the tree as the side opposite him was peppered again. The gunfire rang out loud and brutish for a few more seconds then the eerie quiet fell again. Ryan counted to three and tried to force himself to look out from behind the trunk of the tree. No luck. He counted to five and this time was able to stick his head out.

The platform between the towering lighthouse and the fog-signal building was empty.

He turned to see Bob making his way back towards him, gun trained on the stairs and platform the entire time. Dire situation and all, he couldn't help thinking that the Castle County Sheriff's Department had sure come a long way over the last couple of days. Bob reached him and hunkered down behind the closest tree.

"Did you count two of them?" Ryan asked.

"Yep, looks as if they both went into the building with the fog sirens."

Both men took a few long, measured breaths.

"Let's go find those sons of bitches." Ryan said standing upright but keeping his eyes on the vacant platform the whole time.

Bob stood up as well, but with a little less speed and agility than did his counter-part. Ryan put out his hand and helped him, but it was a warning that they'd do well to heed. They may be out here hunting some kind of treasure, but they were no longer boys. Making caution a priority they stepped out of the trees and into the lighted clearing that stood between them and the stairs.

The immediacy of the silence after so much noise and violence was unnerving. The grass around their feet wavered in the slightest of breezes. With a slow steady pace, guns at the ready, they made their way across the clearing and started up the steps.

Reaching the top they turned to the left facing the building with the fog sirens. Putting the monstrous brick tower of the lighthouse to their backs and, giving themselves a wide berth, they moved around to the front of the little building. The short ramp running up to the entrance was empty and the door stood open. The handle and the lock had been blown away. Beyond the threshold the darkness gaped.

Jacobs was standing beside the boat where they had come ashore. When the gunplay began he turned and looked up at the lighthouse then back to Eddie. "You still have the weapon you took from the farmhouse?" Eddie nodded. "Good. Stay here and stay ready." Then he was gone darting between trees and racing up the hill towards the lighthouse. Shannon lingered for just a moment.

"You'll be alright here?" she asked, anxious to be on her way.

Eddie nodded once with perhaps the slightest hint of reluctance but she didn't notice. She was already gone as well, grabbing trees and hauling herself up the hill like Jacobs had just seconds before. Moments later they both had disappeared into the woods and the night.

Eddie, left alone, looked down at his forearm. He had ceased to register the pain, and now the crude symbol of the Plundering Pike was beginning to clot. Apropos, he supposed, that he now bore the family crest, the sole surviving heir of Plundering Pike.

He removed his gaze from his newfound body art and turned it up to the lighthouse atop the cliff. The gunfire had ceased for the moment and he stared through the quiet night at the silhouette of the darkened beacon. It was thrown into relief by the flood lights behind it.

Gunfire erupted again.

A second later he saw two huddled forms tumble around the pathway that ran behind the lighthouse tower and take cover. He could not tell from where he stood the identity of those shadowy shapes, but he didn't think Shannon or Jacobs could have made it up to that point yet. So he was left anxious and without answers. He let his hand slip to the handle of the gun in his belt.

He was debating abandoning his post and ignoring Jacobs orders when he felt a small vibration from his pocket. It was his phone. He had left it in the car back at the Devil's Kettle so it hadn't been taken from him along with the 9mm. No contact information was displayed, just a number. No one other than Jacobs had ever used the phone to contact him. He was clueless as to who else would even have the number. With a slow hand he pressed the button to accept the call and made a cautious hello.

At first he was greeted only by rough static. After a moment he was able to make out a voice but it was cutting in and out. "Hello?" he said. The sound cut in and out for a second then came through.

"Eddie, its Kirk. Jacobs gave me this number." He said in an explosive exhalation. He was agitated about something. "I've been working on the phrase on the parchment. I was wrong about the fog-signal building. That's not where it's hidden."

"Whoa, slow down. What do you mean?"

"The phrase is in Italian, translated it means: rose of the wind's course. At first that made sense. Sometimes a compass is referred to as the 'rose of the winds' so I thought that it was affirmation about the weather vane on the signal house. But the longer I sat here and thought about it, it wasn't adding up. Like you said, why go to all the trouble of the two keys just to re-affirm the clue that was already in the painting?"

"Okay…" Eddie was trying to listen but was also trying to pay attention to what was happening up at the lighthouse. A cacophony of weapons being discharged had just cut the night air again. There was some sort of commotion going on with the shadowy figures behind the lighthouse as well but their position remained unchanged. "So what do you think now?" he asked trying to keep some focus on what Kirk had to say.

"I did some research and I think in this situation 'corsi' is supposed to mean Corsican, not 'course'. Rose of the Corsican Winds." He was still talking a mile a minute but not getting to the point quick enough for Eddie.

"So what does that mean?"

"The Corsican wind is called Libeccio which is the corresponding wind for the southwest compass point. In the lantern room of the lighthouse there is a giant ornate compass painted on the wall behind the Fresnel lens, I think that's what they meant by The Rose of the Winds, not the weathervane on the fog siren, you've got to get up to the lighthouse and check to the southwest of…"

"Hello? Kirk?"

There was nothing. The call had dropped but Eddie had the pertinent information. As if to punctuate the necessity of action another volley of gunshots pierced the quiet. Eddie dropped the phone into his pocket, checked his weapon, and ran for the hill leading to Split Rock.

The dark was absolute.

Sullivan played his little flashlight around the interior and was overwhelmed by disgust.

The building was empty.

The walls were painted with images and information about the old equipment and apparatus that once made the fog signal functional. The old gasoline-powered air compressors that had run the sirens were painted on one wall, on another were the diesel engines that later replaced them. On each of these walls there were informational placards but otherwise the place was empty. His blood boiled, Pike had done it again.

"Shit! There's nothing."

"What?" Bellows said his voice quiet but agitated.

Sullivan didn't answer. He wanted to scream, the anger peaking, but then he noticed something. One of the walls had a very light background painted on it. It was so faint that it was almost indistinguishable but as Sullivan looked closer the background came into focus. The indistinct image was of the fog-signal and lighthouse again. It would have seemed normal to visitors, a slight image of the main attraction of the historical sight they were here to see, but again the fog-signal house had an added piece adorning the top.

"Light." Bellows said in a harsh whisper from next to him and Sullivan extinguished the flashlight.

The dark overtook them and they listened to the small but distinct sounds of their adversaries approaching around the side of the building. Sullivan drew his weapon but knew it was just precautionary. He'd let Bellows handle things for as long as possible.

The sheriff and his deputy came round into view through the door. Sullivan did not hear the slight twitch of pressure Bellows applied to the trigger, but the thunder of the gun was deafening in the small room.

Both he and Bellows stepped clear of the door as the fire was returned. Seconds after the return volley began, Bellows started firing again as well. Still firing, Bellows exited the building.

Moments later the shooting stopped.

Sullivan was sure Bellows would've expected him to follow but he had to have another look at the image painted on the wall. He clicked the light back on as another barrage of gunfire began from outside, but he stayed focused. He'd reunite with Bellows or he wouldn't. They were in the end-game and his business was here.

He returned his attention to the lightly painted background. Again a weathervane had been added to the top of the signal house but it was different than the one that had been painted into the Angel at the Rock. This one included an

255

ornamental pointer on top of the weathervane that, if it were real, would move with the wind and point out the direction it was blowing. Instead of the traditional rooster, this one was adorned by a wooden ship and the bowsprit, the spar extending out from the bow of the ship where the figurehead was attached, was pointing straight and true towards the image of the lantern room in the lighthouse across from it.

Ryan and Bob moved slow and cautious up the ramp to the blackened portal leading into the fog-signal house. Their weapons were trained on the darkened doorway as they approached. No sound emanated from the interior abyss. All was calm. It was anyway, until they were just steps away from the threshold.

A muzzle flash and ensuing crack boomed from inside the small building. Bob stumbled backward. Ryan did the same but went down. Bob looked to Ryan crumpled on the ground and was horrified to see a crimson stain spreading out, dyeing his shirt. They had stumbled down the ramp out of the direct line of fire for the moment. Bob unleashed a hail of bullets at the doorway with his gun hand and grabbed Ryan by the scruff of his shirt collar and tried to haul him up with the other. With a yelp of pain Ryan managed his feet. The assault began again from the signal house. They stumbled to relative cover behind the lighthouse tower. They hunkered down and Bob tried to take stock, Ryan had not taken another hit but his partner was not well.

He was huffing and holding his gut, his hands were turning red as his own blood slipped out and over them.

"Hang on buddy. Can you hang on for me?" Bob asked just shy of begging. Ryan nodded. It would have to do for now. Bob slid a few feet down the base of the tower and tried to get a visual on the signal house.

Jacobs and Shannon broke into the glare of the floodlights just as Bellows appeared at the foot of the stairs coming down from the platform. Bellows launched a hail of bullets in their direction but they easily stepped back into the protection of the trees. His shots were not well directed, he was just covering himself as he ran across the small road that ran in front of the row of houses that comprised the lighthouse keeper's residence. They held their fire as he cleared the far corner behind one of the little houses. Jacobs turned and fired two single shots up into the air. The floodlights shattered and the former pool of light fell to dark.

Shannon and Jacobs shared a glance and then stepped out onto the road. The lighthouse keeper's residence was comprised of three small two-story houses all in a row to their left. Bellows had disappeared behind the furthest one from them. They moved down the little road with their weapons trained on the third house. Shannon kept her eyes on the windows while Jacobs watched the area between houses. There was no sign of Bellows so he was either behind the far house or had managed to enter it.

They were nearing the middle house when Shannon whirled at another expulsion of pain that was vocalized from up on their right, up by the lighthouse. It had sounded like Ryan. They communicated without a word and Shannon broke off in that direction. Jacobs stopped, keeping his focus and his weapon trained on the houses, watching for any movement until Shannon had reached the top of the stairs behind him. From the corner of his eye he saw her reach the platform. She cleared her immediate vicinity then moved out of view behind the lighthouse.

Slow but with a heightened sense of awareness Jacobs moved into the shadows between the middle house and the one behind which Bellows had disappeared.

Shannon made sure no one else was on the platform and then crossed behind the lighthouse tower on the side nearest the lake. She came around the corner and found Bob and Ryan huddled there. Bob had torn Ryan's shirt and was using it to apply pressure to his belly. Ryan was lying against him, inanimate.

"What happened?"

"They were in the other building. They shot Ryan as we approached. At least one of them made a break for it."

"We saw him. Jacobs is tracking him. Is there anyone still in the building." Bob only shrugged. "Okay, is he alright?" She asked indicating Ryan.

"I don't know. His breathing is steady but he's losing blood and now he's passed out."

"Stay here. I'm going to check the signal house."

He nodded and she stood and moved back out onto the platform. She opted to forgo the ramp that led right to the door of the signal house and instead skirted the building following the wall. The elevation of the ramp put the doorway about hip-high on her. From that position she could see the whole room except for whatever was on the opposite side of the wall from her. The room was empty as far as she could see. She slowed her breathing and prepped to go. In a quick fluid movement she rolled onto the ramp under the railing and trained her gun on the portion of the room she previously couldn't see.

The one room building was empty.

She stood and entered, spinning quickly back to the entrance to be sure she wasn't flanked. Nothing moved. Silently lightning tore across the sky and moments later thunder cracked through the quiet as the storm continued to close in. She made a quick tour of the small room. There was one window on the wall opposite the door. As she passed it she could see the row of houses where she had left Jacobs. She watched for a second. There was no sign of either Jacobs or Bellows. She was about to move on when motion in the front window of one of the houses caught her eye. Someone was inside. Seconds later she was back out of the building and bounding down the stairs towards the row house where she had seen the movement.

The rumble of the thunder was closer now. It would mask Jacobs' approach to the house but it would also cover any movement by Bellows. He came around the rear corner of the house and cleared the immediate area. Bellows was nowhere to be seen. The lightning flashed and the thunder rolled behind it, the storm was very close now. He made a quick assessment of his surroundings.

A black-ish goo in the grass behind the house caught his eye.

Blood.

He followed a few small drops that led towards the rear entrance of the little residence. Just outside the door the trail was thicker. Bellows must have stood at the door for a moment unable to contain the blood he was spilling. Jacobs examined the jamb and saw that the wood at the lock was split. Bellows had busted it. He had to have timed his strike with the thunder or Jacobs would have heard it. With his weapon trained before him Jacobs pushed the door open.

Eddie came out of the woods with the lake on his right and the lighthouse dead ahead. He had stopped before crossing out of the tree line to try to discern who it was huddling at the base and saw it was the Sheriff and Ryan. He'd never met them but Jacobs and Shannon had told him about them, and who they were.

This was not the moment for introductions though. He had other business. He clambered up to the path that ran around the lighthouse but went the opposite way avoiding a meeting with the two men on the far side. He came around on to the platform. Other than the sheriff and the deputy he had seen no one.

Thunder and lightning ignited the air as Eddie smashed the lock and entered the lighthouse proper without hesitation. The first drops of rain began to fall.

Sullivan was about to break from the signal house for the lighthouse when more gunfire from Bellows informed him that yet another party had joined them here in the fray. He exited the small building but instead of heading right, down to the main platform, he went left to the far side of the signal house. The walkway ended at the edge of the building. There was a railing there and then a small drop off to a rocky outcropping four feet or so below. Sullivan slid under the railing and down onto the outcropping. A few moments later he heard Shannon move down the far side of the building above him and then enter. There were no windows on this side of the building so he knew he wouldn't have to worry about her seeing him out here.

He raised his head up high enough to get a visual. He couldn't see the sheriff but he could see the foot of the wounded deputy behind the lighthouse. He was about to drop out of sight and wait to see what Shannon would do after leaving the fog-signal house when Eddie came into view. Sullivan watched him break the lock and enter the lighthouse with a purpose. Somehow it seemed Eddie had come by the same information that Sullivan had discovered painted on that wall. The truth of Pike's plunder resided in the lantern room of the lighthouse.

Jacobs crossed the threshold into the lighthouse keeper's residence as the rain began in a slight drizzle. He kept his tread light. Bellows would not miss much. The blood outside the door indicated he was injured but Jacobs would not make the mistake of allowing that to cause him to underestimate the man. Inside there was no further blood trail so Jacobs would have to track him by other means.

Everything about the house was small. It had been restored for museum purposes to echo days gone by. Every article of furniture was an antique. He moved steady through the small kitchen. He could not hear Bellows at all. Having no clues to pinpoint his target was causing a slow itch at the base of his neck. It was a warning sign. He was facing a worthy adversary and he was unsure as to who held the upper hand.

Coming through the kitchen into the living room the silence was supreme. His eyes roved, scouring every inch of the room. It was a small table-top mirror that alerted him to his folly.

In the reflection he saw Bellows.

Behind him, back near the front door.

The weapon in Bellows hand was not aimed but was coming up to fire. Time slowed. Jacobs was fast, probably as fast as Bellows but the millisecond of advantage that Bellows held would be enough. Instinct had caused Jacobs to whirl and bring up his own weapon, but again, it wouldn't be in time. Forever he rotated, watching as Bellows' gun closed in on position to fire.

And then, sudden salvation.

The window beside the front door shattered inward. It was straight-away behind Bellows and in this delayed reality Jacobs saw him give the slightest flinch. Bellows flinched and then a large portion of his head disintegrated as the bullet impacted.

Bellows wavered then crumpled to the floor in front of him.

Jacobs stepped to the window and saw Shannon standing out in the yard with her gun still trained on the window. At that the sky opened up and the rain began to fall in earnest, pouring down. A second later, behind Shannon, he watched Sullivan race from behind the signal house and disappear into the lighthouse.

Eddie stepped off the spiral staircase into the lantern room at the top the lighthouse. The rain was spattering in light bursts on the giant windowed wall that faced the lake. The thunder rolled and the lightning crashed sending dazzling prisms of sparkling light off the giant Fresnel lens dominating the center of the room. The rain escalated to a downpour and began pounding the windows. The lightning was flashing at regular intervals, throwing the light in all directions, refracting in a manic display.

Eddie turned and faced the wall behind the lens, the wall opposite the windows.

On the wall was an almost floor to ceiling painted

image of an ornate compass.

The Rose of the Winds

What was it Kirk had said? Libbecio, look to the southwest. Eddie did so but saw nothing other than the painted brick of the wall. He followed the line of the compass off to the southwest and still there was nothing. His frustration mounted but then he did notice something. There were marks etched into the brick where the wall met the floor.

Between claps of thunder he heard the echoing footfalls of someone entering onto the spiral staircase below him. He tore his gaze away from the wall and risked a look out into the vestibule. Down below he saw Sullivan, head down, pumping his legs, ascending the stairs. Wildly, he looked around him. There was nowhere to hide. It was a big room with nothing in it but the giant lens dominating the center of the room. He ran to the far side of the lens, opposite the stairs. It was no good.

There was no cover.

Sullivan had almost reached the lantern room.

In a second he would crest the top of the stairs and Eddie was just standing there.

Much like at Itasca, Eddie remembered the gun in his hand.

This time though it wasn't heavy, he leveled it with ease. A calm fell over him and he waited.

Sullivan raced to the top of the stairs and into the room without pause. Eddie didn't hesitate, he fired. The bullet hit Sullivan in the chest and stopped him short. He wavered for a moment and then dropped his gun. Eddie fired again but his own weapon jammed. Again he did not hesitate. He dropped the gun and ran at Sullivan. Sullivan was dazed, slowly raising his hand to the new hole bored into his chest. Eddie hit him with both hands right under the rib cage and pushed up. They both left the lantern room behind and flew precariously onto the stairwell.

His upward push had lifted Sullivan just enough, the back of his legs caught the railing but the rest of him was up and over and carried him off into the open shaft of the tower.

Eddie's momentum carried him straight across the stairs and he hit the railing chest high, knocking the wind out of him.

Breathless, Eddie watched Sullivan fall.

He saw Jacobs and Shannon run into the lighthouse and onto the spiral staircase only to come up short a second later when Sullivan hit the floor behind them with a sickening thud. Jacobs went to the body and checked it but Eddie already knew from the awkward tilt of his head that he was dead.

Jacobs yelled up to Eddie but his ears were thudding in time with his heartbeat as he labored to take a breath. Jacobs and Shannon raced up the rest of the stairs and by the time they got there Eddie was managing some intake of air. He had slid down to a sitting position on the stairs and they helped him to his feet.

They helped him back into the lantern room and he slumped against the wall. He indicated the scratches where it met the floor.

"What is it?" Eddie asked.

"It looks like Roman Numerals," Jacobs said behind him. Eddie nodded. "Do you know what it means?" Jacobs asked. This time Eddie shook his head.

"Hey!" The call came from down below them.

They all turned towards the shout which came from Bob downstairs. He had moved Ryan out of the rain into the entryway of the lighthouse. They ran down the stairs. Eddie made it down on his own but not without some serious effort, his breath slowly returning. Bob, still cradling Ryan, dropped his phone next to him and looked up at them.

"The ambulance is on the way. What did you find?"

"Looks like Roman numerals etched on the wall." Jacobs said.

"Roman numerals?" A voice croaked. They all turned to Ryan who had found the power to speak. They nodded. Bob managed a smile. "Kirk..." Ryan trailed off and coughed. A weak groan followed, coughing was obviously causing him pain. He would need attention and very soon. He managed to go on though. "Hanlon...he had Roman numerals written on the maps…in his study."

Eddie, Shannon, and Jacobs all looked to each other but Shannon spoke. "We should get back to the cabin and get Kirk."

"And if you're going, you should go now, if you're here when the state boys get here you'll be tied up answering questions all night." Bob said.

"You can cover for us?" Jacobs asked.

"I'll have some explaining to do I imagine, but I'll think of something."

"If you can buy us time to get to Kirk and he can tell us what those Roman numerals mean," Shannon said "We'll have the Allan's nailed. You'll have the full arsenal of Loeffler's support behind you."

Bob gave a quick nod. "Then get the hell out of here."

22

And the dawn broke.

Out in the world people woke up and went about their lives. Babies cried and were fed. Chores were tended to. All across the North Shore life continued, normal and mundane.

In their little rented cabin the morning came like mornings do after a night of hard drinking. Slowly, like waking up and knowing you went too far the night before but had somehow dodged the more crippling effects of the hangover and instead were left with a little fuzz on the brain and an insatiable desire for greasy food.

The collective conscious of the group pulled them back from the realm of sleep at about nine fifteen in the morning. Eddie, who hadn't believed his adrenaline would ever allow him to sleep again after the amazing revelations of the day before, slept the hardest and the longest.

On the day he would always remember as the first day of the rest of his life, eventually Jacobs had to wake him.

8 hours ago –

The headlights of the car splashed across the cabin as they pulled in. Eddie knew Kirk was alone in the cabin and he recalled the anxious way he felt the day he was alone in there, awaiting Jacobs' return. He wasn't anxious now, but couldn't really put a finger on how he felt. His adrenaline was still pumping but his body was weary. Sullivan was dead and he had yet another piece of this seemingly endless puzzle. But if resolution did not present itself soon he wasn't sure he would be able to take much more. Jacobs put the car in park then he and Shannon got out and approached the cabin nice and slow. Eddie followed behind.

Jacobs mounted the few steps to the porch and knocked on the door. "Kirk, it's us." He called out. There was no answer at first and a slight tension began to mount. He knocked and called out again, and still there was no response. He was about to pound the door a third time and substantially harder when they saw the shade move to the left of the door. Jacobs and Shannon had their weapons out in a blink of an eye.

At last they heard Kirks small voice from inside the cabin.

"I'm here, it's me. I just needed to make sure it was you."

Jacobs opened the door, gun still trained ahead of him as he entered. It was obvious the cabin was clear, Kirk had just been anxious, and they were all actually able to relax.

The momentary fear Kirk had felt was replaced by excitement and after a few seconds of silence he spoke again. "What did you find?" he asked on a breathless puff of air.

"We're not exactly sure. We're hoping that you can tell us." It was Jacobs that spoke but Shannon stepped forward and handed him a piece of paper. Written on it were the numerals they had found etched into the brick at the base of the wall in the lantern room of the lighthouse.

XLVII.CCLXIX
-XCI.CCLXXXII

The smile that lit Kirk Hanlon's face told them everything they needed to know. There was no question that he understood what it was supposed to mean.

"How did you know to ask me?"

"Ryan Tomlinson saw similar numerals on maps in your house," Shannon said. "What is it?"

"It's longitude and latitude"

"Are you sure?" Shannon asked.

Kirk nodded. "Pike liked to use Roman numerals to code his position if he was sending it to someone. And the best part is," he paused. "I'm somewhat familiar with these coordinates. It can't be far from here. The position noted here is not far off from where Grand Marais sits. It has got to be just a little south of here on highway 61."

Now –

And so once Eddie had been roused, they headed south. Kirk, after a fair bit of begging, was allowed to join them. He would be present when they finally found whatever resided at the end of Pike's little treasure hunt.

Towns drifted by. They drove through Silver Bay and on towards Beaver Bay. It was on the outskirts of this little town with the silly name that Kirk sat up and told Jacobs to pull off on the left.

The car rolled to a stop on a gravel parking lot. The sun was hot but not yet pounding.

An antique shop of sorts sat before them. Rows of tables filled with trinkets, treasures, and junk filled the space between the parking area and the building itself. Sitting there like a fleet of ships, it beckoned them.

Eddie was already out of the car and striding toward the

building. He was filled with a feeling that was equal parts confusion and predestination. Jacobs and Shannon fell into stride behind him. Still at the ready in case the action was not all in the past quite yet.

Eddie pushed open the door. The welcome bell jangled, echoing in the comfortable dank of the room. Like the tables outside, the interior was lined with a labyrinth of shelves, piled full of more of the same from outside. Some fine antiques, and some antiquated trash. The only open space in the whole place was right down the middle when you first walked in. It ran from the front door to an old wooden desk that served as the check out.

Eddie walked halfway between the two.

An older gentleman, somewhere on the back-end of his eighties, sat behind the desk reading a newspaper. At the sound of the bell he dropped the paper the slightest of degrees to eye his patrons, ready to pull it back up quickly if they didn't look promising for a sale.

When he saw Eddie he stopped and for a moment he just stared. Then with a deliberate effort he folded the paper he'd been reading and set it aside. He turned and reached back for his cane and, with a healthy modicum of effort, he stood.

"Young man," he said. "I've sat behind this desk for many years selling this junk, and all the while I've been waitin' for you. And now, just like that, you're here." Eddie was at an utter loss. The old guy stepped out from behind his desk. He was no longer looking at Eddie but giving his full concentration to his feet. "Well, I can say you took yer sweet time in comin'." He continued as he shuffled past a still befuddled Eddie. "I'd a retired three years ago if I hadn't had to sit here and wait for you, Edward."

No one spoke

The old guy extended his hand towards Eddie. "Brian Anders," he said. Kirk's gasp from behind them was audible. Eddie reached out and shook the calloused hand but couldn't make his mouth move. "No need to introduce yourself, Eddie. I know who you are, known your family a long time." The old man looked at him for a long moment. "You've got the look of your father and your father's father." For a moment he seemed lost in his own reverie. Then he shook it off and returned his gaze to Eddie. "I guess you'll be wanting that which you came for. A bit of treasure?" he said with a wink.

"Yes, sir." Eddie managed.

Brian Anders moved past him into the sea of shelves and trinkets.

Despite his cane and the obvious effort it took him to keep his feet, he managed to navigate the shelves and clutter with a deft ease. He traveled a short maze of shelving units and came to a stack of paintings leaning in one of the corners. They were all big monstrosities, in overindulgent wooden frames. One by one he flipped through them and leaned them against the shelves opposite where they sat. When they'd all been moved, with a laborious effort he opened a plastic bin they'd been leaning against. There were more paintings in the bin, he flipped through them as well until he found, and selected, the one he was looking for.

It was a bad oil painting of an eagle perched in a tree beneath an abundance of blue sky.

"Carry that back to my desk for me would ya?" he asked Eddie. "A small price to pay for the spoils you'll soon receive." He favored them with another wink.

Eddie carried the painting to the desk. Jacobs and Shannon cleared the aisle for the old man to make his way, following Eddie. Once back at the desk, he grabbed a pocket knife from one of the drawers. He wiggled the blade into the small space at the mitered corner of the frame then popped it up splitting the frame and the seam, making it easy to pull the remaining sides off. The frame pulled free but the brown paper backing remained intact attached to the canvas. The canvas was stretched over a small interior frame and stapled over the top of the backing. "You mind giving my old hands a help and pull those staples out of the canvas?" he asked handing the knife over to Jacobs and indicating the staples that held the canvas to the inner wooden frame.

Jacobs did as he was asked and as the painting came loose they all realized it had been stretched over another canvas underneath.

It slipped away revealing the Angel at the Rock, complete with the addition of the weather vane. All heads came together as they leaned close to see the exposed painting beneath, even Brian Anders who had been present at the original unveiling of the painting commissioned by Eddie's grandfather, leaned in closer.

"Been a long time since I've seen her up close," Anders said. "Set her face down on my desk there if ya would." He put his hand out asking for his knife back. The painting was face down on his desk with the paper backing exposed. With the knife he made a long diagonal slit in the paper backing. He closed the knife with an intense effort and laid it on the desk. "Here we go," he said with a fiendish smile.

The man slid his wrinkled calloused hand into the slit in the crinkled brown paper and fished around. A moment later he brought out a manila envelope. The backing tore further revealing the backside of the canvas. There was visible writing penned upon it.

He held the packet out, at first no one went for it. After a moment it was Shannon that took possession of the enclosed documents.

She pulled out a thick wad of papers folded in half. She spread them out and skimmed them. Shannon smiled and handed the papers over to Eddie, but she nodded to Jacobs.

Contracts. Eddie looked them over.

Once, then twice, then a third time, still not quite believing that which his eyes swore to be true.

His father's signature.

His birthright.

His father had brokered a deal for the controlling shares of one the most successful companies in the country. Then knowing he would not live long enough to see the fruition of his labor he had concocted a treasure hunt for his sons.

"Is this actually legal?" Eddie asked, his voice only the ghost of a whisper.

"It's all legal and all binding, son. That is assuming you've reached the age of thirty, which it seems you have. Happy birthday by the way," the old man said, his voice soft. A solemn quiet lingered. Specks of dust danced lazy circles in the bits of morning sun that managed to creep through all the clutter in the front window.

"So what does this mean?" Eddie asked.

"It means you now own a very large percentage of Hawking Inc." Shannon said. "Loeffler has lawyers standing by to process the paperwork for you. Victor Leland should have handled the execution of the contracts, and I'm terribly sorry for your loss and his untimely passing, but it will only strengthen the case against Amelie and her son. Between these contracts and what is on the back of that painting," she pointed to the Angel at the Rock, "we should be able to put the Allan family behind bars for quite a long time, which will in turn make you the majority shareholder of Hawking."

Eddie stared at the sheets of paper, struggling with the magnitude of the words. The old man with his crooked smile still in place, in turn stared at Eddie. Kirk stared down at Pike's handwriting that was teasing him from the backside of the Angel at the Rock.

Time stretched, drew out infinite. Behind the Beaver bay antique store Mother Superior went about her business unaware that another twisting tale of her mighty shores was coming to a close.

The sun rose higher in the sky, the day became full.

June 8th was going to be a scorcher.

June 9th

Bob Gurley stepped out onto his front porch, the morning paper tucked beneath his arm and a cup of coffee in hand. The screen door swung shut behind him. He set the coffee on the little porch table and looked at the trees swaying in the breeze across the highway. He listened to the rustle of leaves that he would watch fall come autumn. He stretched and then took up his position in his wicker chair.

He unfolded the newspaper and had a look. The front page was dominated by the arrests of Amelie Allan and her son, D.B. Allan III. There were photos of the son being removed from the family estate in handcuffs, the mother being rolled out in a wheel chair behind him. Bob skimmed the story but he knew more than any reporter so it was cursory at best. He flipped to the continuation of the story and there at last, was a picture of Eddie. In the background he could make out Shannon and Jacobs. He smiled. Eddie looked happy, as Bob supposed a suddenly very rich man would.

There was no mention of him, or Ryan, or Kirk. That was just fine by him. As details emerged and the dots were connected their names would likely begin to show up and often. Vindication on Devlin was probable in light of the newfound facts, but that would come in time and Bob was happy to wait.

Ryan had come out of surgery with a very good prognosis. The bullet had come out clean and had managed to avoid major arteries and organs. He would be back to work again in the not so distant future.

For Bob that would be another story.

The investigations regarding what happened in Kirk's home and the second time around at Split Rock were ongoing but the facts were there. He and Ryan would be cleared to return to duty but Bob thought those days may be behind him.

He had taken part in an amazing and, if he hadn't been there to see it himself, an unbelievable story. His body was achy but beyond a little lingering soreness he felt pleasant and relaxed. He pulled the pack of cigarettes he had purchased the other day out of his pocket.

He crushed them and tossed them into the wastebasket beside the table.

Another chapter closed.

He then waited for his wife to join him. In a few minutes she would come out and sit down in her chair. They would enjoy their coffee together. A cup of coffee and the first of many mornings in what would be a well earned retirement.

The breeze rustled the leaves as it blew through the trees, and Bob Gurley smiled.

September 2017
Nordeast Minneapolis

Thank you

       I would first like to thank my family: Katy, Joey and Vivian. Your love and support made this book possible. A special thank you to my mother-in-law Mary Pat Elsen who read and edited many versions of this book and always provided her honest and constructive feedback. I would also like to give a special thanks to Jean Moelter who helped in so many ways to see this project to fruition. I'd like to thank my dad, Elliott Hays, for being such a big part of the process and constructing the original 'first edition' of this book, and of course my mom, Chery Day, as well as Wendy Hays and John Day for their never-ending support. To Dennis Curley, Julie Williams, and Abby Pesquidox for their invaluable insights along the way. Dan Marshall and Ryan North for helping with cover art and construction. Erik Herrlin, Mike Soule, Erik Schindler, Robyn Hart, Bev and Steve Palmquist, Zach Hays, Timmy Hays, the Pesquidox boys: Boris, Xavier, and Andre. And of course you who have this book in your hand today, thank you for taking the time to go on a small adventure with me. I hope we meet again soon, on the edge of another wood, where together we can peek into the growing gloom and see what mischief may be afoot there in the dark.

Made in the USA
Columbia, SC
27 April 2019